PASS

A brutal attack by Apache raiders shattered everything Abigail Briscoe believed in—destroying the last shred of her compassion for the Indian tribes of the open frontier. And now, to rescue her kidnapped sister, Abby must put her trust in a handsome Comanche warrior whose rage she fears—and whose piercing ebony glare fills her with apprehension . . . and unwanted desire.

COMANCHE RAIN

Hardened by loss and the white man's cruelty, Nokona is determined to resist the golden-haired beauty whom Destiny has placed by his side. But their shared pain and dangerous purpose must ultimately bridge the gaping chasm of hatred that separates their worlds—as soul-searing need, relentless and powerful, conspires to unite their hearts forever in love.

**The breathtaking
COMANCHE Indian Romances
by GENELL DELLIN:
COMANCHE WIND
*COMANCHE FLAME***

The COMANCHE Trilogy by
Genell Dellin
from Avon Books

COMANCHE WIND
COMANCHE FLAME
COMANCE RAIN

The CHEROKEE Trilogy

CHEROKEE DAWN
CHEROKEE NIGHTS
CHEROKEE SUNDOWN

If You've Enjoyed This Book,
Be Sure to Read These Other
AVON ROMANTIC TREASURES

LORD OF SCOUNDRELS *by Loretta Chase*
MY LORD CONQUEROR *by Samantha James*
ONCE UPON A KISS *by Tanya Anne Crosby*
A STRANGER'S KISS *by Shelly Thacker*
TO LOVE A DARK LORD *by Anne Stuart*

Coming Soon

PROMISE ME *by Kathleen Harrington*

GENELL DELLIN

COMANCHE RAIN

An Avon Romantic Treasure

AVON BOOKS ◆ NEW YORK

COMANCHE RAIN is an original publication of Avon Books. This work has never before appeared in book form. This work is a novel. Any similarity to actual persons or events is purely coincidental.

AVON BOOKS
A division of
The Hearst Corporation
1350 Avenue of the Americas
New York, New York 10019

Copyright © 1995 by Genell Smith Dellin
Inside cover author photo by Loy's Photography
Published by arrangement with the author
Library of Congress Catalog Card Number: 94-96358
ISBN: 0-380-77525-5

First Avon Books Printing: April 1995

AVON TRADEMARK REG. U.S. PAT. OFF. AND IN OTHER COUNTRIES, MARCA REGISTRADA, HECHO EN U.S.A.

Printed in the U.S.A.

RA 10 9 8 7 6 5 4 3 2 1

For Renée Roszel,
friend for all the years

1

The red feather slashed through the pale brown of the dried grass, shining, the color of blood. Abby shut her eyes but she still saw it, a bright wound on the featureless plains.

Somehow, the sight made a shiver ripple over her.

That was *silly*!

She made herself look at it again. The feather was rising now, lifting on the wind, starting to dance along beside the wagon as if welcoming them into the Indian country.

"A harbinger of spring," Mama commented.

She turned around from her place beside Papa to point it out to Abby.

"Now, *there's* a pretty for Baby Sister." She raised her voice over the creaking of the turning wheels. "Reckon she'll see it before it blows away?"

1

A shriek of delight from seven-year-old Hannah answered the question.

She darted across the track of the slow-moving wagon to follow the floating feather, her blond curls flying. Goose bumps broke out on Abby's arms. She leaned out of the jump seat, reaching toward the child on the ground.

No! No, Hannah, leave it be!

But she bit her tongue. To say such a thing would be sillier yet. Hannah'd had little enough amusement on this long, hard journey—why shouldn't she chase and capture a pretty prize?

"If she hadn't got down from here when she did," Papa said, "I do believe she'd have bounced this wagon box completely to pieces."

"She's all stirred up about getting to Fort Sill tomorrow and meeting the Comanche children," Abby said.

"Well, she's bringing enough plunder to give them for gifts," Papa said. "She showed me what all's in that treasure box of hers."

Mama laughed. "That's where she'll put that feather, too. Hannah's the most enthusiastic missionary in the family."

"Would you look at her now!" Abby said.

Hannah, golden hair bouncing, was running farther and farther ahead through the tall grass, skipping and jumping, waving

the vermilion feather as high in the air as her plump little arm could reach.

"She's so full of life she's about to burst," Abby said, laughing.

Mama turned completely around and patted her hand.

"Someday you'll have one of your own just like her."

Abby felt the familiar flush rise to her cheeks as she shook her head.

"No," she said, lightly, trying to turn the subject of her spinsterhood away, "not just like her. She's too beautiful for someone plain like me to have."

"You're pretty, too!" Mama argued as she always did. "And, Abigail, you ought to marry. You're a natural mother!"

"I'm twenty-seven," Abby said. "I'm an old maid, but still I'd only marry for love. And love has never come to me. No, Hannah's the closest thing to a daughter I'll ever have."

When they looked again, Hannah had disappeared over the gradual rise the horses were climbing.

Abby touched her father's shoulder.

"Baby Sister's gone on ahead to the reservation to civilize the Indians, Papa," she teased, loving to watch his kind smile. "By the time we get there she'll have already preached all your sermons."

He gave his low rumbling laugh. "Yes, and she'll have taught the men to plow."

"And the women to cook with flour," Mama said.

All three of them were laughing out loud at the mental images of Hannah in the mission field when the wagon creaked onto the crest of the low, rolling hill, dropped over it, and rounded a bend.

The horses stopped.

Abby stared, frozen in shock.

Painted Indians barred the way.

Naked Indians, bristling with weapons of war.

Mounted on ponies that stood immovable, as if they had grown from the ground.

The lead warrior, his face and chest striped with zigzags of yellow and black, white feathers standing stiff in his hair, sat still as death.

Abby's marrow congealed.

Hannah lay across his lap.

She twisted toward her family, half lifted her head.

"*Ab-by . . .*" she cried, piteously.

The Indian slammed his knee into her head as he lifted his lance and aimed it at Papa.

"My husband, would you please pause in our journey when we reach the creek up ahead?"

Tope's sweetly spoken request for a stop, her third one of the morning, set Nokona's teeth on edge.

4

But he fixed his gaze on the far distance and answered her calmly.

"Why not push on until we eat?" he asked, and urged his horse into a longer trot, hoping that the rest of their small band, following close behind him, would do the same.

Evidently, all fifteen of them would have to push and drag his wife if they ever were to reach New Mexico.

"We need to bathe this feverish baby," Tope answered. "Must you rush him away from his home country so fast that you kill him?"

Nokona's quick temper flared.

"He'll die if I *don't*," he snapped. "Or live as a captive on the reservation. All of us will. Getting to Sky and Rafael's *rancho* before our supplies run out is all that'll save us."

Tope sighed. "Maybe we'll find a buffalo herd on the way," she said, in her sad voice.

Hot, familiar frustration roiled in his gut. What did she expect him to *do*? Work a miracle?

"The buffalo are gone, Wife," he said, bluntly. "You'll have to learn to eat beef. *If* you are so fortunate as to arrive at El Rancho del Cielo while you can still eat."

She didn't answer. He knew, without looking to see, that her eyes had filled with

tears. For these past few moons, she had cried all the time.

By the Sun Father, why couldn't she understand that they had no choice? None of them wanted to leave Comancheria, give up the old way of life and go to live on the charity of relatives. He, himself, wanted it least of all.

In spite of his reluctance, though, last fall he would have persuaded his father to join him and lead this pitiful little band then to Sky's home. But Tope's begging and pleading had held him back until it was almost too late. This last Big Cold had come and sapped the last of their strength.

And *still*, after all their suffering and searching, she wouldn't support him in his desperate decision!

He threw her a furious, sideways glance.

Immediately, his anger vanished beneath a wave of pity.

She rode her gaunt mare holding a child called Little Otter in her arms. Stick-thin, trembling arms. She had been carrying the boy all morning.

No wonder she kept wanting to stop and rest.

"That *baby* has six summers. He is old enough to ride a pony of his own," Nokona said.

She looked at him with huge, glittering eyes.

"He's too sick."

6

Little Otter didn't look sick. Or feverish. He only looked exhausted and hungry like the rest of them.

But Tope would never believe that.

"Let someone else hold him for a while," Nokona said. "My mother would be happy to do it."

He turned in his saddle to look back at his followers, searching for Fire Flower's red hair, even now only lightly streaked with silver.

Trying to find another sight to fill his eyes to replace the one of Tope's sorrowful face, he gazed down into the child's.

She was pretending, no doubt, that this orphaned boy was hers. For all the ten winters and summers that they had been married, she had looked for, longed for a baby. They both had. But no baby had come.

Many of the band, most of them, in fact—men and wise, old women—had urged him to take a second wife, to have children with her, and even Tope had said that it was not right for him, their young chief, to be childless. She would share his children, she said.

But he had never even considered such a thing. He wanted children, yes, as much as any man could, but he didn't want any other wife. Despite her flaws, Tope was his heart, had been his heart since that long-ago day when he had first seen her tiny, delicate figure running out from her village, her hand shading her eyes so she could see who he was, riding into the Kotosteka country with her recently found distant relative, Rafael de Montoya.

Now that young, curious, cheerful Tope was gone and in her body lived a woman grown sad and scared. Somehow, she both clung to and mourned their old way of life. That obsession and the boy, Little Otter, claimed her complete attention. She only noticed Nokona when she asked him to do the impossible.

"His skin is hotter than ever," she said.

"He's only tired and hungry!"

She answered with a reproachful sigh. Then she rode silently.

Cursing under his breath, Nokona stood in his stirrups to scan the bare-limbed line of trees ahead that showed where the creek ran in its bed. He saw no movement, nothing at all that could signal danger.

"All *right*," he said, tightly, sitting back into the saddle.

Then his temper slipped free.

"You listen to me, Tope," he said, harshly, slashing at her with his voice and his eyes. "We'll not stop again after this. That boy isn't sick—you're only delaying us, behaving as the most disloyal of wives, pulling back against the decision that Windrider and I have made!"

He glared at her furiously, then sent his horse shooting out ahead of hers. He lifted

8

one hand high and signaled a stop, gesturing toward the trees.

The voices of the sparse band behind him rose in anticipation. Without looking back, he knew that everyone followed him toward the little grove. Its trees had no leaves yet but the air was warm already.

Thank the All-Father. Spring was coming, at last.

He slowed to a trot and rode through the scattered cottonwood trees, looking sharply everywhere—into the clear, chattering creek, up into the whispering branches, across the plains to the rolling horizon. Nothing. No one.

Yet a cool feeling touched him, made him want to shiver, like a strange shadow thrown by the sun.

But he hadn't heard an owl call. He hadn't seen a coyote cross their trail.

He set his jaw. Tope's constant fears were making a warrior into a coward.

He rode back toward the trail and signaled for them to come.

Everyone except Nokona dismounted and two of the almost-grown boys took the horses down to water. Tope stretched Little Otter out on the winter grass while she went for water to bathe him. Some of the children played along the creek, picking up rocks and skipping them, splashing into the coolness of the water, retreating from it, squealing.

9

The children of their band. They seemed so few now, compared to even one winter ago. That was when High Wolf had decided that the buffalo would never come back and that they must follow the other Comanche onto the reservation. Most of Windrider's people had gone with him and with his wife, Bright Moon, who had followed him without a murmur of regret. Her devotion to her husband was legend.

But he knew Tope was devoted to him, too. She was simply caught up in sadness.

"My Chief! May I take your horse to water?"

The eager, young voice startled Nokona. He looked down into the bony face of Yellow Bear, one of the three adolescent warriors left in the band.

He clicked his tongue. *Warrior.* The boy was too thin and weak to fight. At least, on Sky and Rafael's *rancho*, he would have plenty to eat.

Nokona stood in his stirrups, stepped down.

"Thank you, my son."

Yellow Bear led the stallion away and Nokona turned to look for Windrider and Eagle Tail Feather, meaning to talk with them about the best route to take when they came nearer to Fort Sill. They could *not* take a chance of being discovered by the soldiers.

But something made him turn his face toward the northern horizon.

The word *soldier* suddenly jumped out of his mind and turned into a body. There, over the rising, rolling low hills of the prairie, through the tall grass brown and pale with the weak sunshine of winter, came a man riding. A soldier, dressed in blue, mounted on a solid bay, typical of the horses of the United States Cavalry.

The soldier was a day and a half's ride away, but no doubt he was stationed at Fort Sill.

He would be on the lookout for the few small bands of the *Nermernuh* who had not come into the reservation with the others.

And he had seen this one.

Instinctively, Nokona half turned to reach for the rifle or the bow on his saddle, then he remembered that the horse was at the creek.

It was just as well, he realized, immediately. Somewhere nearby, the man probably had companions. There were still too many Apache roaming in this direction and too many hostile Kiowa for any soldier to ride far from the fort alone.

Yes. This soldier had, perhaps, more companions than Nokona did, and all of his would be men, well-armed men.

The man came on at a good, brisk clip, riding straight for them, clearly unworried.

Probably because he could see the women and children.

Nokona's mind raced. Somehow, he must get rid of him with only words for a weapon.

"Ho!" the soldier shouted. "Hello the camp!"

He rode down the hill and into the middle of them as if he claimed to own the creek.

"I need to see your pass!" he yelled, as if every one of the Comanche was deaf. "Your pass!"

He pretended to reach into his pocket, pull something out, and unfold a sheet of imaginary paper.

"Your pass! Does anyone here speak English?"

Nokona stepped forward, but the soldier didn't hold his horse still to talk to him. Instead, he rode in among everyone, sending mothers scrambling to protect their children and bringing Windrider, Eagle Tail Feather, and the few young warriors up from the bank of the creek.

"Stay where you are!" the soldier shrieked, and pulled his sidearm from its holster. "Don't swarm on me, now!"

Nokona walked toward him anyway, trying to damp the fury and fear making his gorge rise, fighting them so he could think. If the soldier was asking for their pass, he must think they were residents of the reservation. If he continued to believe that, he might go away and leave them alone.

"This is a short excursion," Nokona said, in his most authoritative voice. "For that, we do not need permission."

The soldier, almost to the creek bank by now, turned to see who had spoken. He waved his pistol in a great, sweeping arc and slid it back into his holster.

"Well!" he boomed, as he rode back up the slight incline and out of the trees. "That's more like it! At least you've got somebody here who can talk!"

He stopped his mount, leaned on his saddle's pommel, and frowned at Nokona across the heads of the people, now frozen in place.

To his right, on the ground not far from his horse's feet, Tope calmly knelt and began to bathe Little Otter.

She gave Nokona a quick, trusting glance. He would take care of them, the look said. She knew that, and she was not worried.

Her face held no trace of resentment for the sharp way he had just spoken to her.

Love, pure love, for her suddenly rose in him. For an instant, it eased his awful turmoil.

The soldier's voice boomed at him again.

"You need a pass, Chief," he said, firmly. "Anytime you people ride as much as two days from the fort, you have to have a pass or a military escort."

"We are less than two days from the fort," Nokona said, trying hard for an easy, conversational tone.

"If you can fly, yeah," the cavalryman growled.

"This is just a little hunting trip," Nokona said. "We wanted to get out and see if there are buffalo since the winter. We'll return to the fort in one sun."

But the soldier wasn't listening. Suddenly, he was looking all around him, through the trees to the horses at the creek—laden with weapons—and the pack animals burdened with everything Windrider's band possessed.

"Hey!" he blurted, glaring at Nokona. His eyes had narrowed to slits. "*You* ain't reservation Indians! You . . . why, you're one of the holdout bands!"

He whirled his horse and laid spurs to it as he reached for something hanging from his belt. A whistle. He blew it once, twice, as the horse charged forward.

Nokona's blood leapt.

By the Sun Father! He would ride right over Little Otter!

Tope scrambled to her feet, instinctively trying to protect the boy, turning to face the danger coming at them.

Nokona got one glimpse of her frightened face before the cavalry mount

14

rammed into her with its shoulder. It knocked her down, she fell hard, backward, onto and across Little Otter.

The horse, trying by instinct to avoid stepping on a human being, slowed and gave a little crow-hopping jump. As he recovered and leapt forward beneath the sharp spurs, the big bay's right hind foot, clad in its iron shoe, struck Tope's head with a sound like a melon bursting.

She didn't move. She would never move again.

The whole world went black, then red.

A raw, screaming howl came out of nowhere, the enraged bellowing of a wounded bear. Nokona was already running, already knowing that he would launch his body through the air at the cavalryman before he realized that the shrieking was ripping its way from his own throat.

A ghastly cry filled the air, filled the world.

Abby looked up from the ground, from the tracks of the Indian horses she'd been following since the sun came up. The cry's awful pain stripped naked every nerve in her body.

Hannah?

No. Somehow she knew that no child could make such a sound.

But *someone* was, just up ahead.

15

Her aching limbs went even weaker with dread, but she kicked both heels into Chester's fat sides to urge him up the next low, rolling hill. No matter who it was, she had to see.

She had to look, and keep looking everywhere for Hannah, no matter what. If she ever slowed down or if she stopped, the horrible whirlwind of panic and sorrow and hatred and fear roaring around inside her would pick her up and carry her right off the edge of the earth.

Chester reached the top of the rise.

Abby's raw eyes consumed the valley below in one wide stare. Her heart stopped. It *was* them!

Yes! The Indians were there. She had caught up with them at last!

Her vision blurred, then, and the whole sight swam in front of her. God was helping her, and now she would get her sister back!

She ripped her hand, sticky with blood, from Chester's mane and wiped away her tears as she sent him jouncing faster and faster down the little hill.

Hannah. She had to see Hannah.

But what she saw was a rider on a galloping horse and an Indian with feathers in his hair running alongside. A footrunner keeping up with a horse!

She stared. The Indian was tall and broad-shouldered, with long legs that flowed like a mountain lion's in the wind. Never had she seen anyone who could run that fast.

Then, with a cold, shaking shock, she realized that the rider was a white man.

In a blue uniform.

A soldier!

Oh, thank You, God, for sending a miracle! That soldier was sent to rescue Hannah.

And that savage was after him.

He was going to get him, too. The Indian had a superhuman speed. Of course! It was the speed of the very Devil himself.

She had to stop him.

Abby kicked Chester as hard as she could, and he broke into his lumbering gallop. The Indian was reaching up with both arms, grabbing at the soldier, trying to pull him from the saddle.

"No!" Abby screamed, urging Chester to go faster. "Leave him alone!"

The soldier reached for the gun at his hip.

He almost got it free of the holster.

But the savage was too fast and too strong.

He caught the soldier's arm, snatched a handful of his shirt, dragged him from the running horse, and threw him to earth with no more effort than if he'd been a sack of meal.

"Don't hurt him!" Abby screamed, sending the words out of her dry throat with the last scrap of strength that was in her.

She hit Chester with the end of the lines.

He thundered toward the two men, moving faster.

But the Indian didn't even look up.

He dropped onto his victim, straddled him, held the writhing soldier between his knees.

The heavy muscles in his thighs flexed beneath his shining, coppery skin.

A knife flashed in his heathen hand.

"No-o-o!" Abby yelled as Chester carried her closer. "No, no, no, *no!*"

But the ruthless barbarian brought the blade slashing down. The soldier let out one high-pitched, pathetic wail. His blood welled up and flowed out of him, turned the brown grass to a gleaming red.

As red as Hannah's feather.

Screaming without words now, Abby pushed the big workhorse on. She dropped the lines and reached into her skirt pocket for the picket pin she had snatched from beneath the wagon seat, the only weapon she could find when the attack began.

She would drive it through that red savage's black heart. For the soldier.

For Mama and Papa.

For Hannah.

She grasped it in both hands and lifted it high.

The Indian sprang to his feet and whirled

to see her, all in one graceful movement as though he was dancing in a dream.

His eyes flashed wild and hot, straight into hers.

His face, dark and hard as the iron in her hands, held a look so fierce that it stopped her heart.

But he was not the one who had taken Hannah.

Four feathers stood straight up in a cluster at the crown of his head. One black and three blue. None red. None white.

They floated back and forth in front of her, then she saw Hannah, flitting through the spring sunshine waving them, two in each of her small hands.

Hannah vanished.

Abby's arms dropped and her weapon was gone. The horse rushed on.

Abby's legs went loose. She pitched to the ground at the savage's feet.

2

The keening cries lifted higher, sweeping upward in a wild wave of sound, then dropping to low, desolate moans that died away. But only for a moment.

They started up again, sent a shaking chill chasing through Abby.

Chasing her out of comfortable, dark oblivion into the light.

Her eyes opened to bright blue sky.

But the voices that had wakened her remained dark and gloomy. They grew stronger.

She turned her head to see whose they were.

Immediately, her body went stiff with fear.

Indians.

The Indians who had taken Hannah.

They were across a little creek-filled gully from her, halfway up the side of a hill, wailing and crying while they gathered rocks

21

and carried them upward in a slow-moving wave of people. Women and men and children.

Abby's breath caught.

Hannah? Was Hannah among the children?

Her aching eyes darted from one to another. All the little heads were dark, all the clothes were brown and tan, made of skins.

There was no white dress, no tumble of blond curls.

Hannah was not there.

But she saw the savage who had killed the soldier.

The sight of him froze the air in her lungs.

He carried a huge, flat rock and he led all the others, yet he never looked back, as they climbed behind him. His naked shoulders, ax-handle broad, bulged with the weight of the stone, yet he carried it easily, while his long, well-strung legs took the hillside with the stride of a conqueror.

She tried to look away from him but she could not.

He was the most powerful man she had ever seen.

Every motion he made stirred the claws of the terror lurking in her stomach, in her mind.

He had killed the soldier in the blink of an eye. He could do the same to her.

Perhaps he, or the one with the black-

and-yellow zigzags across his face, had already done the same to Hannah.

Frantic, now, she pulled her gaze free of him and searched her surroundings.

This wasn't the same place where she had first caught up with them, where he had killed the soldier.

This wasn't that same place! There had been trees along that creek and no hills.

Her fear deepened into a panic. The low, rocky hills swirled around her. They had traveled; they had brought her with them here to wherever this was while she was unconscious.

Now she was their captive, too.

But they were paying her no attention. The one who had killed the soldier was leading all the rest up the side of the hill, his hard-muscled body moving with the sure, sinuous grace of a wild animal.

He was looking up.

Abby lifted her gaze to follow his.

In a scooped-out place in the hillside was a blanket-wrapped bundle, tied with ropes. When he had climbed up to it, he stopped and stood there for a long time. Behind him, the women wailed louder.

He knelt and carefully placed the large stone he held onto the bundle, then he straightened to his full, commanding height and stepped to one side. His grim profile cut its shape from the blue of the sky.

It held her. His face gleamed in the sun,

so hard, so chiseled, skin into bone, that it looked carved from stone.

He stared off into the far distance, not moving.

One by one, the other Indians came forward and put the rocks they carried onto the bundle also, piling them up, stacking them on top of each other. Soon, before Abby could quite realize what they were doing, the rope-wrapped package had disappeared.

Several women began digging up dirt and pouring it in among the stones. Their eerie, ululating cries grew steadily louder. Others, men, women, and children, turned away and walked slowly back down the hill toward the creek.

Toward Abby.

She struggled to get up, her mind screaming to run.

But pains shot through her body from every direction and collided in her head. They threw her down again, flat, forcing her to lie entirely still as she prayed for the sickening exhaustion to leave her.

The sky swayed back and forth. Her eyes squeezed closed.

"Don't try to move just yet," a voice said. "You can rest a little bit longer."

The voice had spoken in English. Or had it?

All the horror that she'd been through must have destroyed her hearing.

24

Or her mind.

Abby splayed her scraped hands out on each side, palms down onto something furry, striving to get some balance.

"I'm going to put some salve on your hands and bathe the blood from your face," the voice went on. "You just lie still, now."

It *was* English. With a lilt to it, like ... like that of the Irish.

It was a woman's voice, and she didn't sound cruel or mean.

Abby opened her eyes.

A red-haired woman knelt over her, touched her arm with gentle fingers.

"What awful thing has happened to you, my dear?"

She had splendid, deep green eyes, which looked sadly at Abby. They showed signs of recent tears.

Her red hair was shot with a bit of silver, but it was massively thick. And curly.

The woman was beautiful, even though she was probably in her late forties.

"Don't try to sit up yet," she said. "You're hurt."

Yet, her skin was tan and her loose dress was made of beaded buckskin. She wore a beaded clasp in her hair.

"Do you *live* with these Indians?"

Abby could barely force the words from the cracked desert that was her throat.

The woman smiled.

"Yes, indeed," she said. "Now let me have your poor hands."

Abby pulled her hands free from the fur. They brought bits of it with them, stuck to her fingers and her palms. The woman made a clicking sound of pity.

Abby's eyes closed again. Moving any muscle in her whole body made her head hurt so mightily that she thought she could not stand it.

"How did I get here?" she muttered. "Did *he* touch me?"

"Did who touch you?" the woman said.

She began to dab water on Abby's hands. It felt cool and good, but it stung mightily, too.

"The cruel one. The one who killed the soldier. I pitched off my horse right at his feet. Did *he* bring me here?"

"No. It was two of the women who scooped you up when we ran."

"Ran?"

"From the other soldiers. That one had two friends who galloped in, shooting. If our warriors hadn't behaved like they were fifty strong instead of five, they would've caught us—our horses are in poor condition."

Abby tried to take all that in through the thundering pain.

Disappointment poured through her. Two more soldiers. If only they could have saved her!

And Hannah.

"What's your name, dear?" the woman asked.

"Abby."

"Abby, I'm Jennie," she said, and began spreading something on Abby's hands that stopped their hurting, something that felt smooth and wonderful.

"Jennie ..." Abby breathed. "Thank you."

She forced her eyes open in spite of her great weakness.

"Where's Hannah?" she croaked. "The little, blond girl the savages took last night?"

"Little girl?"

Jennie looked puzzled. And sad. She was so sad. Tears had left tracks down her cheeks.

Abby's heart doubled its beat.

"Surely she isn't dead! The horrid warrior with the black-and-yellow zigzags of paint across his face is the one who took her," she blurted.

She dragged herself up onto one elbow.

"Do you know where he is? You're white, you must help us! She's my little sister, my baby. Why, I've practically raised her!"

Jennie looked at Abby and shook her head.

"There's no little blond girl in this camp."

27

"Yes, there *is*! I followed the tracks of the savages that took her and they led straight to this bunch of Indians!"

"But this bunch of Indians didn't steal a child," Jennie said, gently.

Her calm, sure tone and her steady, honest gaze sapped the strength from Abby's arms. She fell down again, flat on her back.

But she couldn't give up.

"They *did*," she insisted. "Yesterday. Maybe they hid her from you."

Jennie put her hand behind Abby's head and lifted it to meet a gourdful of water she held in the other. Abby took a sip, then another.

The liquid felt marvelous to her dry throat.

It stung her parched lips, but she drank, then drank again.

"Do you know where you were when . . . you started following the tracks?" Jennie asked.

"Fairly near to Fort Sill."

"What happened, Abby?"

Abby's mind wouldn't tell her. Her numb tongue refused to recount the horror.

"I have to find my little sister," it said, and her voice shook awfully. "Jennie, you have to help me."

"I will if I can. I promise you that."

Something about the kindness in her tone made words come spilling off Abby's tongue.

28

"I rode all night long," she said. "I nearly fell off a thousand times because I'm used to a buggy, not to riding horseback. I clung to Chester's mane all night, forever, while he trotted through the dark."

She sat up again, very slowly, so that she could see Jennie better, she needed the kindness in her face.

"It was just by the grace of God that I was able to catch Chester," she said. "Those savages stole all of the other horses—Chester's partner, the spare team, and Papa's saddle horse."

"You were very brave and determined," Jennie said.

"I saw the tracks when daylight came," Abby went on. "And I knew that I had their trail. I knew then I was going to find Hannah and save her."

"Was your family going West to settle in California?" Jennie asked, quickly, almost as if her words were meant as a distraction.

She began to wash Abby's face.

"My family was going to Fort Sill to live on the Comanche Reservation," Abby said, her tone rising higher with each word she bit out, "to be missionaries. To give our lives to teaching the Comanches about God and how to farm and cook and read and write!"

"Ah! The very first missionaries to come to the *Nermernuh*!"

"If that means Comanches, yes," Abby

snapped, her hysteria rising with the throbbing pain in her head. "And *they*, in return for our kindness, attacked us savagely without warning, nearly killed me, burned our wagon, and took my sister captive."

"Ahh," Jennie breathed. "What about your parents?"

Her parents. Abby's memory slammed shut.

Her mind went totally blank.

She gave no answer. She couldn't.

Jennie waited, listening, but she didn't press for one.

After a moment she spoke again.

"Oh, Abby," she said, with a little catch in her voice, "I'm so sorry you had to go through such a terrible experience."

"What I've gone through is nothing compared to my little sister! She's only seven years old and all the rest of the family between me and her are boys and she's been everybody's pet all her life!"

She scrambled to sit up. She was shivering.

"*What* could that horrid, painted savage have done with her? Think! Jennie, you can learn where she is!"

But Jennie shook her head sadly. Her green eyes met Abby's with the look of a solemn promise that she was telling her the truth.

"Whoever took your little sister, it wasn't

this group of Indians—Windrider's band of Comanches," she said. "It wasn't any Comanches. It must've been the Apache—probably young warriors, out to prove themselves and get revenge on the whites."

Abby knew she wasn't lying. Yet she could *not* admit that her terrible, bone-shaking night of riding through the dark hadn't brought her to Hannah.

"I followed the tracks of *this* bunch," she said, stubbornly. "And I got here just in time to see that ruthless barbarian with the blue feathers in his hair drag a white man off his horse and kill him in cold blood!"

The horrible memory made her voice screech wildly upward. She tried, shaking all over, to get to her feet. She couldn't.

Jennie tried to steady her where she knelt.

"Now, now," she soothed. "In the night, perhaps you lost the raiders' tracks and picked up ours."

"Is it true?" Abby cried. "*Can* it be true that Hannah isn't here?"

"She isn't here."

"Then where *is* she?"

Jennie put both arms around Abby and hugged her, hard.

"Maybe we'll hear or see something," she said. "When we can, we'll make inquiries. Sometimes we cross paths with some Apache—they're our enemies, but we have contact at times."

Abby tried to assimilate that.

"In just a few minutes," Jennie said, "we must be riding again. Let me wash that wound on your head and get you into some different clothes."

She wet a fresh cloth and touched it to Abby's throbbing head, then to the backs of her hands, washing them gently, carefully, one finger at a time. The cool water eased the burns on Abby's skin, but the pieces of her heart still blistered in flames.

They lessened a little bit, though, as Jennie spread more of the soothing salve on every hurt she had cleansed. Abby took a long, deep breath, her first in a lifetime, it seemed.

A friend.

Out here on these endless plains, after a night alone in Hell itself, she had found a friend.

"We're wasting time here! What are you doing?"

The deep, angry voice whipped them like a lash. They both jumped.

Abby clutched at Jennie with her burned, torn hands, holding to her in a vise grip in spite of the pain. She had to be sure of her before she looked up.

When she did, her blood congealed.

He stood there, within an arm's reach, the Indian who had run the soldier down and killed him.

He spoke English, too!

How? How could that ever be?

The sun glared behind him, she couldn't see his face. But she didn't want to.

Her stomach roiled, as it had done a thousand times since the attack. She wanted to get up, to run, to streak as far away from him as she could, but his very presence paralyzed her.

Her knees bored through the soft robe.

"I'm getting Abby ready to ride," Jennie answered.

Only then did Abby remember that he had asked a question.

Poor Jennie, she thought. As a captive, she had to give a patient, respectful reply in spite of the overbearing way he challenged her.

"This is Abby," she said, gently pulling her hands from Abby's frightened grasp to make a gesture between them. "Abby, this is Nokona."

But he spoke harshly again, without acknowledging the introduction.

"Who is she?"

Jennie turned her face from him, held back Abby's hair with one hand and, with the other, dabbed the cool salve once again to the terrible, swelling knot just above her right temple.

"She's the daughter of a missionary family traveling to Fort Sill," she said. "The Apache attacked them."

"Why would they be going to Fort Sill?"

33

"To live on the reservation. To teach The People how to live the white way and the white religion."

"What?"

Abby glanced up into the shadow of his face. Dark or not, she glimpsed a new, fiery hatred spark in his eyes.

"You have come to my people to teach us your *religion*?"

His low voice vibrated with an incredulous scorn strong enough to scorch her skin.

She tried to sit up straighter, to square her shoulders to throw it off. She tried to glare right back at him.

But her head roared with fear.

"Her family was attacked and her sister was stolen," Jennie said, again speaking softly into the fierceness of his anger, "probably by some Apache."

"Then the Apache have done a good thing!" he cried. "That's one less missionary to intrude on us!"

He lanced Abby with his burning gaze. She could feel its heat even though she couldn't lift her chin to meet his eyes.

"Your people have planned the death of my people by deliberately setting out to kill all the buffalo."

He folded his huge-muscled arms across his chest.

His tone dropped then, to a cold calm as deliberate as death.

"You have taken the land where we've roamed, you've decreed that we must live inside of houses and scratch open the face of Mother Earth for food. *That* is unforgivable."

He came a step closer.

"But *this* is the ultimate insult! Now you intruders have become so incredibly arrogant as to meddle in the sacred spiritual lives of strangers!"

He stood staring at her, contemptuously raking his eyes over every part of her, as if she had two heads or five arms or only one eye in the middle of her forehead.

Then he turned to Jennie.

"You surely aren't planning to bring her with us?"

"Of course," she said, calmly. "What else would she do?"

"Who knows? She will be a burden."

"No-ko-na!" she protested, patiently.

Abby thought crazily that the beautiful, lilting word should not be the name of this savage man.

But it was.

Nothing in the whole world was as it should be. Not anymore.

The earth was spinning wildly upside down.

"Nokona," Jennie said, "without us, she'll not survive for two suns."

"If she had stayed in her own home, she would have survived."

His withering tone said that Abby was already as good as dead and he could have cared less.

"But she didn't," Jennie said, reasonably.

She finished packing up her medicines and began pulling Abby to her feet. "She is here and she is with us. We must take her to New Mexico."

"No!" he said, and a new rushing of his rage pulled his voice paper-thin. "No. I will not have it. She will not ride with this band."

His agate eyes flicked back to Abby.

"Let her starve," he said. "Let our wild animal brothers eat her. Let her die of thirst."

He turned away.

"Leave her here."

3

"Who *is* that cruel savage anyway?" Abby cried, as soon as he'd gone out of earshot. "As soon as I find a friend out here in this godforsaken wilderness, he takes you away!"

She slapped her sore hands against her thighs again and again, in spite of the stinging pain.

"He killed that soldier and he wants to kill me," she wailed. "He *will* kill me by leaving me here to starve!"

"You're going with me," Jennie said, soothingly. "You won't starve. No one's taking me away from you."

She caught Abby's hands and held them still.

"Don't listen to Nokona—he doesn't know what he's saying."

Abby stared into her sad, green eyes.

"You're the one who doesn't know what

you're saying, Jennie. If you disobey him, he'll kill you, too!"

"No, he won't."

"He *will*! Didn't you hear him? He gave you an order to leave me here and he's a ruthless barbarian. Think about it, Jennie."

"I understand these people better than you do, Abby," she said, and let go of Abby's hands to pat her on the shoulder. "That was Nokona's wife we just buried. His grief is making him crazy."

Abby stared at her. Jennie must be wrong. Such a heartless being as Nokona *couldn't* be crazy with grief. *He* couldn't feel grief.

She swung her gaze to the hillside covered with rocks.

"That was a . . . burial? But there was no coffin, nothing that looked like one! Oh . . . that bundle, tied with a rope—"

"The *Nermernuh* custom is to bury the dead in a sitting position, facing the rising sun. We folded Tope's arms around her knees and wrapped her in the blanket."

Jennie gasped and laid a finger across her lips.

"I shouldn't have spoken her name," she said. "Don't repeat it."

"Why not?"

"To save the family from fresh grief. To avoid attracting her spirit. The Comanche don't return to a burial site for the same reasons."

38

Abby nodded.

"I won't say it." Then she blurted, "Are these Indians really that considerate of each other's feelings? It's hard to believe."

Jennie patted Abby's arm.

"They're human beings, you know."

Then she stood and slipped her bags of water and medicines onto her shoulder.

Abby got to her feet, too, struggling to stay with her friend.

Gently, Jennie took Abby's elbow and tugged her forward.

"Come on and change into different clothes, now," she said. "Those you're wearing reek of fire and blood—you don't want to smell that all the way to New Mexico."

But Abby couldn't take a step.

"I can't put you in such danger!" she cried. "He'll kill you, too, Jennie, if you disobey him! You'll have to leave me here."

"I can't leave you; you're my new friend, you said so yourself. Come, now, we must ride."

An idea hit Abby like a tree falling. It almost wiped out the pain in her head.

"Oh, Jennie!" she cried, then she lowered her voice so no one else could hear. "We *are* friends," she said, speaking rapidly, aware that some of the Indian children were coming nearer to them, "and we're both white. We're both captives of these savages. Instead of waiting for that awful Nokona to kill us, let's escape, Jennie!"

She turned her back to the children and finished speaking in a whisper.

"We can escape together!"

Jennie's tear-stained eyes lit with a sudden smile. She gave a small, surprised chuckle.

"We'll talk about escape when you're feeling better," she said, and put her arm around Abby's waist to turn her around. "You're not *yourself* right now, either, any more than Nokona is. And you're barely able to stand up—we'll be lucky if you can ride."

"But he'll kill us both if I go with you!" Abby cried, the panic starting to roil inside her again. "You heard him!"

"No, no! I'll save us," Jennie soothed, urging Abby along beside her as she headed for the blurred shapes of the horses, tethered in some trees.

Abby let herself be pulled along.

"He has no heart," she warned. "I saw him kill that soldier without mercy and you're as white as he was. As white as I am."

"Oh, not quite," Jennie said, with another little chuckle.

She held her hand out beside one of Abby's.

"My skin has darkened a good deal," she

40

said. "It's been a long time since it was as pale as yours."

"Because you've been a captive for a long time?"

Jennie chuckled again.

"Because I've been with The People for a *long* time," she said.

"And they haven't killed you."

"No," Jennie said, walking a bit faster, urging Abby along, as they moved among the sad, staring faces of the members of the band, "they haven't killed me and no one is going to kill you. You can rest easy about that."

"Jennie, you're very brave," Abby said. "*Very* brave."

"So are you," Jennie said. "Didn't you ride through the dark all night long, in a country you didn't know, searching for your sister?"

Abby tried to think about that, but the awful terror she had felt came back.

"I suppose," she whispered.

The horror brought beads of sweat to stand on her upper lip and tears to swim in her eyes. First the Apaches, and then Nokona's murderous attack.

Nokona was a dangerous man.

But she had no choice except to disregard him and take her chances.

In no way was she strong enough to get back onto Chester and ride to Fort Sill alone, even if she knew where it was.

If she did that, how would she get food and keep warm at night? She'd never even built an open fire. At home she'd made fires in the stoves, on the wagon trip Papa had built the campfires.

Plus, these people, if Nokona didn't kill her first, might come across the Indians who had Hannah and help get her back. The soldiers would have no idea how to do that and Jennie had promised that these Indians would help.

Jennie urged her, wordlessly, to move a bit faster.

They entered the shade of the trees.

"We haven't much time," Jennie said, leading Abby straight to a red-colored horse. "You must change and then I'll put you on my mare and we'll see if you're able to ride."

Abby looked over her shoulder.

"Jennie," she said, slowly, her voice shaking with fear. "Where's Nokona right now?"

"He's probably already gone," Jennie said, as she opened a large, painted bag that was tied to a high-backed saddle. "He usually rides ahead as our scout."

She pulled out some fringed pieces of buckskin that resembled what she was wearing and nodded to a spot behind the horse.

"Come back into the trees and I'll help you change," she said.

Abby numbly went with her and stood like a statue while Jennie unbuttoned her dress. However, when she pulled it down off her shoulders, panic came over Abby like last night's dark.

She snatched the edges of the front and tried to pull it on again.

"It's my dress," she said, barely able to breathe. "I can't take it off. Mama made it for me. This shade of blue is her favorite color—she calls it periwinkle."

"You'll feel much better in something clean," Jennie said. "I'll give you something to eat and drink while we ride and you'll feel like a new person."

"I have to keep my own clothes," Abby cried, and her voice started sliding up again, although she tried to control it. "Everything else is gone. I have to keep this dress!"

"You *will* keep it," Jennie said, gently. "I promise you."

She stroked Abby's shoulder, tried to loosen her hold on the cloth without hurting her burned fingers.

"Next time we camp beside a creek," she said, "probably tomorrow night, we'll wash your dress. Then, the next day, you can wear it again."

Abby couldn't turn loose.

"Why don't we wash it tonight?"

"Tonight we'll be riding long after dark, trying to put as much distance as we can between us and the soldiers and Fort Sill. That was one of their soldiers that Nokona killed."

Abby considered that. Tried to make her head stop hurting so her brain could work.

"We could slip through these trees and the two of us ride back *toward* Fort Sill," she said. "Since you have food and water. Do you know how to build a fire?"

She peered through the trees to find Chester.

"Yes, I can build a fire!" Jennie said, her kind tone becoming sharper. "Now, mind me, Abby. I know what I'm doing."

She sounded exactly like Mama when she decided to take someone firmly in hand.

"We'll take good care of your dress," she said. "You can wear it again soon. Now, let me have it and you get into these clothes and these moccasins—your things all smell terrible and they'll keep your mind on the tragedy!"

So Abby let her take her dress and her petticoats that wouldn't fit under the buckskin skirt, her shoes, and even her chemise and her corset because when Jennie said it again, she realized that they all *did* smell like the fires of Hell itself. And it had been Hell.

She might stop trembling inside if she didn't relive it all every time she took a breath.

So she stripped down and shakily got into Jennie's clothes, which felt soft and light, swinging loose against her skin. They made her feel like a stranger to herself, like a shocking, shameless woman wearing nothing at all.

The moccasins were a bit short—she was a taller woman than Jennie—but they molded to her feet and to the ground beneath them. The long fringes on the blouse tickled her arms as Jennie led her to the horse that bore the painted saddlebags.

Suddenly the terrible need for something familiar swept through her again.

"I'll ride Chester," she said, as Jennie began to help her mount. "He's my papa's favorite."

Jennie made a little sound of pity deep in her throat.

"Your horse has been carrying you all night and all day—why not let him rest until tomorrow? This is my own gentle mare and she'll take good care of you."

So Abby gave up, and, with a little help, climbed into the tall saddle and arranged the buckskin skirt to cover her legs.

"I'll get a horse for myself and I'll be right back to ride beside you. Stay right here."

The mare took a step forward, Abby lurched in the saddle, but its high pommel and cantle held her upright. She grabbed the front of it anyway.

"I'll stay," she muttered, and tried to smile down at Jennie in return for her comfort.

All around her, the savages were mounting their horses, tying things to saddles, preparing for the trail. Two of the women were casting curious glances from her to Jennie, chattering back and forth in their own tongue.

The only word Abby understood was "Nokona."

His tyrannical voice rang in her ears again. *Leave her here. Let her starve.*

Her scorched hands froze into fists, one on the saddle, the other around the braided horsehair rein. How could she, or Jennie either, ever think they could get away with this?

The instant he saw Abby on the trail, Nokona would probably drag *her* off the horse and kill *her* with his knife, exactly as he had done to the soldier. Jennie wouldn't be able to save her.

She held on tighter and twisted to try to see Jennie, who had gone off among the other horses. She was darting toward Abby at a little trot, leading one that had no saddle.

Jennie threw herself onto the barebacked horse and everyone began moving, as if at some invisible signal, out of the trees and down along the rocky creek. No one looked back at the place where they had buried

Nokona's wife, but the wailing broke out again from time to time.

Once, Abby dared to glance quickly over the riders ahead of and behind her, but there was no tall, broad-shouldered warrior with feathers in his hair. He must have gone on ahead, as Jennie said.

But scouts always came back. He would see Abby when they stopped for the night.

Her mind, her whole self, fled from that vision.

But her fear for Hannah was stronger; it beat in her heart.

She must risk her own life to try to cross paths with the Apache and Hannah. Abby clung to that hope, used it as a torch to hold back the snarling wolf of terror that threatened to devour her.

Riding with these Comanches was her only chance to find her sister. She must remember that.

Her strong, practical side, her usual self, began to recover a little bit. She ate some pemmican Jennie gave her and drank some water. She dozed in her saddle in the early spring sun.

She was better off with these people than she would be alone.

Except for Nokona.

He didn't reappear, though, while they rode all the rest of that day and long into the night. When they finally stopped to stretch out on the ground for what seemed

47

to be only a few minutes, she was too tired to chew the jerky Jennie gave her and too numb to fear Nokona.

Almost.

"Is he coming into camp?" she whispered, as Jennie laid out a bed for Abby beside her own.

"Maybe for a few minutes to tell Windrider what the way is like ahead."

She nodded toward the edge of the camp as if Abby could see the man she was talking about, but the night was black. Her voice held great affection when she spoke his name.

"Is Windrider the one we rode up for you to talk to a time or two?"

"Yes. He'll keep guard for us tonight while Nokona will stay alone on the plains with his sorrow."

She stroked Abby's hair.

"But even if Nokona slept here, he wouldn't hurt you. He won't hurt you, Abby. Truly, he won't."

Abby didn't believe it. But finally, she made a sound of assent and stretched out on her blankets so as not to mistrust Jennie, her friend.

The next day, the wild land, and the hard, rough ride seemed to go on forever. Every muscle, every bone in Abby's body was sore, her head throbbed, and her legs and buttocks were raw from riding so far so fast the day before. Her burned hands felt better, though. Jennie's salve had worked wonders.

Another good thing was that there was no sign of Nokona—Jennie said he had, indeed, come and gone in the night. They wouldn't see him again all day.

But another worry took that one's place.

"What if we're going *away* from Hannah instead of in the same direction?" she burst out, turning to Jennie, who was riding beside her.

Jennie's green eyes were sad again this morning, even though her tears had all been spent. They grew a shade sadder as they fixed on Abby.

"We don't know," she said, softly. "There's no *way* of knowing where your sister is, but most likely they took her West."

Abby glanced over her shoulder at the morning sun. If the Apache had done what was most likely, this was the right way.

Pray God this was the right way.

"Jennie, she was screaming my name, begging me to save her," she burst out, the awful words pushing against each other to leap off her tongue. "But I couldn't get out from under the wagon fast enough and they rode off, carried her off into the dark."

Her voice caught on a sob. "Hannah's always been afraid of the dark."

"Did they not see you?" Jennie asked. "I'm surprised you escaped them."

Abby leaned closer to her as their horses moved at a steady trot.

"This place you doctored with the salve is where one of them hit me."

As she pulled back her hair, the knot on her temple throbbed even harder.

She touched it.

"I fell, hard, pitched right underneath the wagon. I guess they thought I was dead."

"That was a terrific blow."

"Yes. Hannah's screams woke me up. I came to looking up at the wagon box with everything above me on fire."

Then, suddenly, Abby couldn't talk anymore. They rode without speaking for a little distance, the subdued voices of others in the band calling out from time to time and the thumping of hooves and the creaking of saddles filling their silence.

"Sometimes," Jennie said, "captives end up in Santa Fe to be sold or traded. That's fairly near where we're going."

Sold? Traded?

A shock ran through Abby. Right after it came the fear again, stronger this time, running in her veins in the place of her blood.

Then her common sense whispered through the terror.

Probably being sold or traded would be

better for Hannah than staying where she was now.

Agony squeezed her heart, twisted it.

She had to find Hannah without delay!

But how? How could Jennie, a captive, a woman, persuade the hardened warriors who led this band to make inquiries about a white child whom they hated?

And how could Jennie, a captive, a woman, get away with defying direct commands from a ruthless savage like Nokona?

Abby's empty heart sank into the ground.

She shouldn't have come with them. She should have let Nokona leave her way back there and tried to find Fort Sill on her own.

He would come back and kill her and then she and Hannah both would be dead.

They rode all morning and well into the afternoon with no sight of him. But then, when the sun was halfway down the western sky and Abby judged it was about three o'clock and that her aching body could not ride a moment more, a murmur of relief ran through the whole group.

A rider was approaching them, visible in the far distance.

Apprehension ran over her skin like a serpent's slither.

She sat up straight and threw a quick glance at Jennie, who was still faithfully riding beside her. Jennie, too, was watching.

Soon, too soon, before Abby could compose her breathing and slow her pounding heart, he was close enough to recognize.

Nokona.

He slowed as he reached the front of the band, turned, and rode for a moment or two beside Windrider.

Then, without warning, Nokona pulled his horse out into a wide arc and rode down the outside of the whole band until he came to Jennie. His quick, hard eyes flicked from her to Abby in a deadly look that shriveled her heart.

Jennie spoke first. To Nokona. With a sweet, tranquil look on her face.

"I knew when you had time to think about it, you'd want me to bring her."

Astounded, Abby stared at her. What in the world was Jennie talking about? How could she possibly say such a thing?

Sweat broke out on her palms.

Nokona had been completely explicit, totally adamant about not bringing Abby with his band!

His black gaze rested on Jennie.

She met the look straight on, held it.

Nokona's hard, straight lips parted to speak, but he closed them again. To Abby's consternation, they lifted at the corners, then, in the ghost of a smile and he shook his head, all the while looking at Jennie.

Almost in a fond way.

Icy cold fingertips walked up Abby's spine.

"Always taking care of me, aren't you?" he said, shaking his head again, now really smiling. "I should've known."

He shrugged his broad shoulders, making their muscles flex like knotted ropes beneath his coppery skin.

"Thanks," he said, and reached out to brush Jennie's cheek with the tips of his fingers.

In a truly possessive way.

Then he whirled his horse and rode off, back to the head of the line, stood in his stirrups and shouted something in Comanche while he pointed to a faint grove of trees that had just popped into view on the horizon.

Jennie looked at Abby.

"I'll be back in just a minute," she said.

She put her heels to her horse and rode ahead to talk to a woman on a black-and-white spotted horse.

Abby's bones dissolved and her whole body went light, as if she were floating in space. She had nothing to hold on to and nothing held her down, she was connected to nothing on the face of the earth.

She didn't have a friend, after all.

4

For an endless moment, Abby couldn't breathe.

She *was* alone in this awful land of savages, just as she had been through that endless, hellish night before last. A white woman she trusted to be her friend and keep her alive, to protect her from Nokona's wrath, was only a heartless hoax, a mirage like she had read sometimes appeared on these plains.

But she couldn't be deluded anymore. Now she saw the truth.

She could trust no one.

A pure panic, as strong as the fear that she'd been fighting from the moment the wagon had rounded the bend into the faces of the painted Indians, poured into her veins. It whipped up her pulse and scrambled her brain, bombarded it with one question after another.

What was it between Nokona and Jennie? What did they plan to do to her?

I knew you'd want me to bring her.

For what?

Did Jennie mean it when she said Nokona wouldn't actually hurt Abby?

When the next few minutes, which seemed like years, finally passed and the whole band reached the grove of trees Nokona had pointed out, she threw herself from the horse to the ground as fast as her stiff, sore body would move. She had to get away somewhere and try to think.

Dear Lord in Heaven, she had to try to figure out her true situation.

The consuming fear tried to rise again, but she fought it down. She'd never been one to panic. She was known for her level head.

She had to think.

Why would Nokona want Jennie to bring her along?

And why, if she meant to betray Abby, would she say such a thing to him in English, with Abby sitting right there?

None of it, not one single thing, made the slightest bit of sense.

With one hand on the horse's haunch she steadied her shaky legs while she untied the bag hanging from the back of her saddle.

"Abby!"

56

A quick glance showed Jennie dismounting close by. *Too* close for a traitor.

"I ... I'm going to wash my things," Abby called to her, jerking the garments from the bag and hugging them all to her. "Are we stopped for the night?"

"Yes. We're stopping early because we all need rest," Jennie said. "You'll have plenty of time, you needn't hurry. Wait a moment and I'll give you some cactus soap."

Abby waited, although her whole body was screaming to run to the river, to get away from Jennie and all the fringed, beaded, buckskinned savages milling around her. She needed to get out of the heathen clothes she wore and be decently dressed again in her underwear and her dress. Maybe that would give her back some of her old strength.

"Wet your clothes and these pieces of root," Jennie said, "then rub them together ..."

"All right, I will. Thank you."

Abby grabbed the small bundle of soap roots from Jennie's hand, turned, and ran through the trees toward the water. Her legs felt stiff and sore and she staggered a little, but she kept going without looking back.

Her mind raced madly as she threw herself onto her knees on the creek bank and thrust her dirty clothes into the cold water.

The icy water stung her hands, but she ignored that and fumbled in the little skin bundle for a bit of root to rub against the blood and smoke stains.

She couldn't grab Chester and run away, she thought, while she soused her things wildly up and down in the creek. She had to stay with these people.

She had to. Because she didn't have enough skills to survive on her own and they were the only people for many, many miles who knew how to make inquiries about Hannah.

A terrible thought, colder than the water in the creek, fell into her frantic brain.

What if Jennie had only promised to help look for Hannah to cajole Abby to come with them peacefully?

But that made no sense.

They could have trussed her up into a bundle like the woman they'd buried and tied her onto a horse. What difference did it make whether she came peacefully or screaming like a banshee?

Abby drew several long, deep breaths and looked back at the memory of Jennie's reaction to the story of Hannah. Once again she could see the sad, green eyes, watch the expressions on the beautiful face.

She had been sincere. Her sympathy and her horror and her kindness had been real. Every instinct in Abby told her that.

Yet—*something* was a lie. Nokona had

meant it when he commanded Jennie to leave Abby behind to starve. All her instincts and what little of her usual common sense she could muster screamed the truth of that.

If he hadn't, he'd have to be the greatest actor on earth. And why would anyone playact a scene like that?

She pounded at her garments as if the answers to her questions would come out with the stains. The smells that rose from them, of blood and of fire, made her eyes sting with tears and her brain churn.

A slight breeze moved the limbs above her head.

And carried Nokona's voice to her ears.

She froze, her hands submerged in the chill water. Dear Lord! She had caused him to come looking for her just by thinking about him!

The low, rich sound of his voice came again. From closer. Behind her, in the trees.

Through a terrible effort of will she managed to pull her clothes out and lay them on the bank. Then she tore herself free of the solid earth, turned, and ran into the sheltering brush.

He had sounded to be back toward the camping place and the horse herd. She'd creep in that direction and try to see him before he saw her.

The trees were barely budding now, but they grew thick in places, and growing along the river there was some tall cane or rushes, too, that had survived the winter. The tan of her buckskins would blend with all of that.

She watched the ground as she went and stepped on the cushioning dead leaves, tried to avoid small sticks that might snap. After she'd gone a few yards, she heard him again.

Her breath stopped. He was there. Very close to her.

She slipped behind the largest tree trunk and waited, listening to him say one word, then, in a moment, another remark or two, none of which she understood. If he was with Jennie, if they were plotting about Abby, they weren't speaking English.

And he wasn't bothering to whisper.

She made herself lift her arms and part the tangled branches, forced her dry eyes to look.

Quickly, she closed and then opened them again.

Surely she'd been mistaken. Surely what she thought she had seen couldn't be real.

But it was.

Nokona was playing mumblety-peg with a small boy!

Mumblety-peg or some game of theirs that was similar.

First one of them would throw a knife at a spot on the ground, then the other would do it.

They gestured and talked a good deal.

Her mind could hardly take in what her eyes were seeing.

Nokona! Nokona, the ruthless killer, was playing with a child, *talking* to a child!

Then he took the boy's arm, slid his huge hand down to cover the tiny one, and lifted it into the air, aiming the shining knife. Nokona said something else, then pulled the child's hand back with his and sent the knife flying at its target.

This wasn't a game, Abby realized. Both were serious, concentrating fiercely. Nokona was teaching the boy how to handle the knife as a weapon.

He snatched his own from its sheath, whirled, faster than thought, and threw it at the trunk of one of the trees. It hit the hard wood with a thud, went in, and stood quivering there.

The little boy exclaimed, then ran to recover it.

Nokona took it when the child brought it back, then, speaking rapidly to him, returned it.

Again, he took the small hand in his, lifted and lowered it to show the heft of the weapon.

He was offering to let his pupil try his larger knife, demonstrating how to hold it.

Then he stood aside. The child, who, Abby realized, was not more than five or six, got a grip on it and whirled around.

But it flew from his hand too soon, sending the blade flying straight at Nokona instead of at the tree trunk. The boy cried out in dismay.

The knife cut Nokona's upper thigh. In that instant the sunlight caught the crimson glitter of blood. Then the blade fell to earth.

The little boy cried out again, obviously apologizing as he ran toward his teacher.

Nokona took a step toward him.

"Oh, dear Lord!" Abby whispered. "Run, child, run!"

Now he would kill the boy right in front of her eyes, just as he'd killed the soldier!

She had to hide her face, she had to turn away.

But she couldn't.

However, Nokona merely bent over, picked up the weapon, and handed it back to the child. He shook his head and made a sign that the accident was nothing, then gave a brief command and a gesture which appeared to mean, "Try again."

The child obeyed.

While the little boy's back was turned, Nokona reached down, tore loose a handful of the dried winter grass, and stuffed it beneath his breechclout. To stop the bleeding, no doubt.

Abby stared.

This *was* Nokona. Wasn't it?

There was no mistaking the feathers in

his hair, the muscular breadth of his shoulders, the hard power of his profile. Nor the low authority of his voice.

Yet he was somebody else. A different Nokona, sensitive to the feelings of a child.

She watched, unable to look away, until the lesson was over. Nokona encouraged the boy to throw both knives again and again, giving him pointers until he hit his target four times in a row. Then they sheathed their knives and Nokona dropped a huge hand onto the child's shoulder as they walked away, back toward the horses and the camp.

Abby stayed there, clinging to the tree, watching the spot where they'd disappeared into the tall cane. Vaguely, beyond that place, she could glimpse the horse herd, going to water downstream from where she was, and the slow movements back and forth as the women made camp.

Would Nokona take out his hurt on someone there since he hadn't punished the boy?

Finally, she got up, went back to the creek, and finished her washing, her throbbing head dizzier than ever from the mystery she'd observed. The man was a barbarian enigma.

And he held her fate in his huge hands.

Her own hands trembled so that she jerked her corset across a sharp rock and tore a three-cornered hole in it. She dropped it onto the bank and picked up her dress to rinse it.

Nokona, unpredictable, scared her worse than Jennie, traitorous. Would he pretend to be nice to her, too, sometime, and then, when she least expected it, turn and drive a knife into her heart?

She couldn't trust him and she couldn't trust Jennie.

Never, even when she ate or slept, could she let down her guard. Not for an instant.

The thought brought a deep, sucking weariness.

She slapped her seat down onto the muddy bank and, heedless of the cold mud and of the water running through her moccasins, buried her face in her wet dress.

Why was she continuing? Why didn't she just throw herself into the river and drown?

The words reverberated back and forth inside her head. Why didn't she?

Because you were not raised to be a quitter.

The answer came in Mama's voice so clearly that Abby opened her eyes into the soft color of her periwinkle blue cotton dress. Mama had made it for her.

And she *wasn't* a quitter.

She always did what was necessary. Abigail Briscoe never indulged in immoderate emotions. Instead, she did whatever needed to be done, whatever was her duty.

Right now, it was her duty to survive and to save Hannah.

Letting the dress fall, Abby raised her head and stared at the toes of her moccasins sticking up out of the lazy waters of the creek. She was strong. People said she was smart and she was capable. Didn't people from all over Robertson County come to her for help with everything from doctoring their animals and sewing their clothes to writing their letters?

Hadn't she collected money and books and started the first library the county had ever had?

Hadn't she taken Hannah over as a tiny baby while Mama recovered her strength, then raised her and taught school, too, while Mama brought up the boys and cooked and ran the whole house?

She pushed up to stand on her feet on the slippery bank.

Most certainly she had. And she wasn't going to let any painted Apache warriors steal that child away from her, not while she had breath in her body.

She was sick to the bone of having things happen to her and her being helpless. She needed to take some kind of control, to *make* something happen.

To *do* something.

And she was sick to death of being scared all the time!

She knelt and began to rinse out her clothes, determinedly pushing her fear to

65

the back of her mind so she could think. Jennie was a white woman.

That meant, no matter how long she'd been a captive of the Comanches, that sometime, somewhere, she'd had some moral training and some Christian teachings. She would appeal to her on those grounds, to beg her to at least talk about Abby's immediate future, to tell her the truth about what that remark about Nokona wanting her to bring Abby along had meant.

Yes. Talking to Jennie would be the first step.

After that, she would think of what she should do next. From now on, she would do *something*, just as she always had—she was through with being nothing but a victim.

She took her clothes into the middle of the grove and spread them onto the lower limbs of the trees to dry. If she could figure out the key to Nokona, she might save both herself and Hannah.

Maybe he was cruel to adults and kind to children.

Or cruel to whites and kind to Indians. But he wasn't cruel to Jennie. Instead, he was in league with her.

She puzzled over that as she moved through the trees toward the camp. Having a plan made her whole body feel stronger and her fear feel weaker as she left the little grove of trees and started toward the fire that the band had built downstream. Already, the fragrance of some kind of stew cooking was wafting on the evening air.

Abby's mouth watered. Yes. She had to stay with these people and do her best to deal with whatever happened until they could help her find Hannah. If she were alone, she would have no food and no fire.

She walked slower through the whispering winter grass. Soon, within the next day or two, it would be March. Nearly spring.

And during the springtime, she would find Hannah.

She lifted her face toward the west, toward the sun beginning to slip down in the sky. Hannah was out there somewhere.

The creek and the trees were nothing but a narrow brown ribbon curving through the pale tan expanse of the plains. Endless plains. Their rolling grass covered the earth all the way to the horizon.

That was another reason she had to stay with these people. Without them, she'd be lost. She would survive Nokona and Jennie and she would survive the journey to their destination near Santa Fe. If they hadn't met any Apache to make inquiries about Hannah by then, she would go there and do it herself.

Santa Fe was a town. Somebody there would speak English.

Perhaps Hannah herself would be there, being traded or sold, and she could draw

money from the bank and buy her herself!
Or find a lawman to rescue her!

Dreaming on about seeing her sister
again, Abby moved on deeper into the last
curving stretch of trees, picking her way,
watching the glow of the campfire grow
larger.

"*Tsaa*," a voice said.

It sounded from right in front of her. She
stopped still.

A huge tree with low-sweeping branches
grew a short distance away from the others,
farther from the camp than from the creek.
Beneath it, almost hidden in the thick, tall
grass, she saw two people on the ground.

Jennie! That red hair was unmistakable.

Sudden, sharp curiosity drew Abby a
step closer.

And Nokona!

He lay prone on his back, one knee bent,
the other long, powerful leg stretched out
straight. His arms were up, hands crossed
beneath his head, his eyes were closed.

Another murmured word drifted out to
Abby. In his voice, this time.

Jennie murmured something back.

Suddenly, Abby felt a burning heat suf-
fuse her face.

Jennie knelt beside Nokona, at his bare
hip. His breechclout was turned back, lying
on his flat stomach!

Abby couldn't see whether he wore any-

thing else over his private parts, but ...
still! Jennie was a woman! A white woman!

While she watched, Jennie closed her
containers of medicine, which she must
have been using on the knife wound he'd
taken, and then, tenderly, she leaned over
his long body and stroked his forehead.

Abby's heart stopped. What in the *world*?

He opened his eyes. His lips moved, but
Abby couldn't hear his words.

Then, as Abby's eyelids glued themselves
open in astonishment, Jennie kissed him!

She got up onto her knees, put her hands
on his huge shoulders, leaned forward, and
kissed him on the cheek.

Then, in the most gentle, comforting way,
she laid her face against his, cradling his
cheek, stroking his hair.

Abby stood as if struck by lightning.

Dear Lord in Heaven, give her strength!

And the sense God gave a wooden goose!

Of course!

How could she have forgotten all the
horror stories, whispered to her behind the
hands of Papa's parishioners from the minute he had announced his call to the Indian mission field? Horror stories about
Indian warriors ravaging the body of every
white woman they could get their evil
hands on.

Terrible tales of rampaging sexual hunger and ruthless cruelties.

So why hadn't she realized that, since

Jennie was a captive, she was also a sexual slave? Probably because she was too innocent.

And because those hysterical recountings had seemed so preposterous that they couldn't be true.

But they could be. They probably were.

Her own eyes were telling her so.

She felt like a Peeping Tom, but she couldn't look anywhere else.

She couldn't move.

Her mind raced in a thousand directions. Jennie seemed quite a lot older than Nokona.

But, of course, that would make no difference in this kind of a situation! Jennie was white. That was all an Indian warrior would care about—imposing his will on a white woman.

Yet—why was Jennie touching him so lovingly? Perhaps she had no choice.

Of *course* she had no choice!

And neither did Abby.

The thought fell into her mind and through her paralyzed body like a shooting star.

This answered the question that had been plaguing her ever since Jennie had made that remark to him.

This was the reason that, once he thought about it, Nokona would have wanted Jennie to bring Abby along.

Abby's dizziness assailed her full force

70

and she clutched at a tree trunk to steady her body while her mind flew in circles.

Many Comanche men had more than one wife. She had learned that in the first days of studies about the tribe. That was one heathen practice that Papa had vowed to stamp out.

Nokona was one of those men. He had Jennie and he had had the one who had died. Tope.

Abby would be her replacement.

5

Abby turned and fled toward the camp like a child flying to its mother. At the edge of the trees, though, where she could clearly see the women moving back and forth from the cookfires to the skin bags of food and water, fringes swinging from their sleeves and skirts, she stopped.

Hugging the trunk of a huge hackberry tree, she stared at them. There was no haven here.

Nokona was important in this band, she'd known that from the very beginning by the way he acted and the way the others treated him. Abby was nothing but another white captive. Nokona would have his way with her.

Unless she ran away.

Her sore hands pressed harder against the rough bark of the tree as she leaned around it to search out the horse herd, grazing between the tree-lined creek on the

73

far side of the open area and the fires of the camp. Chester was there, his gleaming black withers rising high above the smaller horses and Indian ponies.

But, fast as the idea had hit her, her common sense drove it away. If she ran out onto the endless plains alone, she really *would* be helpless, a total victim of whatever might happen to her.

And starvation certainly would come. She couldn't build a fire, much less kill something to cook over it.

The smell of the stew drifted into her nostrils again and her stomach growled demandingly, in spite of everything. She had to stay with these savages. She had to.

Act like a lady, Mama always said. *Act like a lady and you'll be treated like one.*

Nokona was a savage, so that might not be true with him, but he did speak English. Maybe she could bribe him.

Yes. That's what she would do.

If Nokona tried to take her into his bed, she'd offer to give him money instead!

Relief flooded through her. As soon as they got to Santa Fe, she could draw money from back home through a bank. Surely Santa Fe had the telegraph.

Clinging to that thought, she let go of the tree and moved toward the cookfires. She walked into camp, Jennie's bag of cactus soap swinging from her hand, and went to Jennie's things, put it into the painted bag.

74

When she straightened up and turned around, two women dipping the stew into wooden bowls beckoned—one of them held out a portion to her. The other hurriedly thrust a horn spoon into it and they both smiled at her.

Abby accepted, sat down, and dipped into it.

The warm liquid soothed her throat and flowed into her empty stomach with a wonderful comfort. It tasted like beef stew. Quickly, she took another bite.

"Delicious!" she proclaimed, smiling and gesturing to make herself understood.

The cooks' sad eyes brightened and they smiled back. They got bowls for themselves, then, and joined her, introducing themselves with names that sounded like Mota and Wanaru. With sign language, they tried to include her in their sporadic, murmured conversation. Occasionally, one of them got up to serve someone else.

Abby ate one bite after another, surprised that her appetite could be so hearty. The meat in the soup was tough—it had been dried or something—but its flavor was good and so were the roots and corn that had been added.

It gave her strength to think some more.

She could still talk to Jennie—in fact, that might be even more helpful now that she already knew what that remark to Nokona had meant.

I know you brought me along to replace No-kona's other wife in his bed. What will happen to me if I refuse him?

Did you mean what you said about making inquiries for Hannah, about helping me find her?

Her fingers let go of the handle of the spoon and she dropped it into the empty bowl. That was the most important question. Could Jennie be trusted at all?

She threw up her head and looked in the direction of Jennie and Nokona's tryst, but they still were too involved with each other to be coming into camp.

"Tuku!"

Abby turned to find a child at her elbow, holding out an empty bowl to Mota. Smiling, even though she moved wearily as she got to her feet, the Comanche woman took the bowl and went to the pot of stew to refill it.

Just as Abby made a move to get up and ask for another serving, too, she realized what she had been seeing. The second helpings had all gone to children. None of the adults had come back for more.

Wanaru's and Mota's own bowls as they sat down with her had been no more than half-full.

None of the bowls had been more than three-quarters full. Rations were scarce.

A strange feeling came over her.

At home, on the prosperous farm, there

had never been a shortage of food. All her life she'd known food in abundance.

And here were these people, a family like hers, barely existing.

Her heart twisted. They might be heathen polygamists, but they were sacrificing food for themselves to give it to their children.

She took an empty bowl that one of the adults brought back to the fire and stacked it in her own to wash. Wanaru and Mota were tired and still hungry, as she was. She would help them with their chores.

They accepted her gestured offer and showed her what to do. Before they'd finished, Jennie and Nokona returned to camp. Wanaru divided the last of the stew between them.

Abby avoided them. Even when Nokona had eaten and gone to sit with the men at one of the other fires, she stayed busy and away from Jennie, responding only briefly to her remarks. She could barely make herself speak to her yet.

The sand she was using to clean the cookpot ground itself into her fingertips. When could she *make* herself go talk to Jennie?

But someone called to Jennie, then, a high, piping child's voice, and she left the fire.

Abby's heart constricted as she watched her go.

Traitor. Could she believe anything she said?

The least she could have done was to warn Abby from the very beginning about what lay ahead.

Then the sun sank completely, fast, and the quick dark of early spring fell thick around them. The worst question of all stuck a knife into Abby's heart.

What if Nokona came to her bed in the middle of the night?

Abby woke from her fitful doze before sunrise, thankful that it was morning, light enough to see, and Nokona hadn't bothered her. Surely he wouldn't do so now.

She lay still and peered through slitted eyes to see where he had placed his bedroll, but sleeping lumps of bodies wrapped in blankets were scattered everywhere and she couldn't tell one from the other. Except to know that Jennie was beside her.

It would be a fateful day. Today she would *make* herself talk to tricky Jennie.

Abby slipped out of her bedroll. She would put on her own clothes right now. Then she'd be strong enough to do that.

At the edge of the trees, she stood on tiptoe and looked around, a little disoriented at first, but then she saw the big hackberry and started in the right direction. The trees and bushes loomed like specters in the gray light, the breeze blew cool. She shivered.

But she didn't slow down. She plunged past budding limbs that snatched at the fringes on her sleeves and briars that tore at her skin. She would be ready for whatever came today, she would be her old, capable self. She would survive so she could save Hannah.

When she found her things, she ripped off the buckskins and put them on, even though they were still damp. It felt strange, at first, to have the corset stiff around her and the layers of underthings and dress hanging about her legs. The cloth and the stays held the cold from the night air and made her shake, the tightness of the fit shortened her breath.

But she felt a little bit like herself again. She lifted her hands to smooth the high collar around her neck.

Mama made this dress for her. Dearest Mama.

She washed her face in the cold creek, then removed her three remaining hairpins and plunged her head in to wash her hair. It still smelled of the fire, too, and she wanted all that memory gone. No more would she be a victim.

She was Abigail Briscoe, of the Robertson County Briscoes, and she was a thoroughly capable person. Somehow, God helping her, she could get through these next few days with her virtue intact.

Once her sister was safe, once she had family with her again, everything would be all right.

But she shivered some more, anyway. The sunlight was bursting over the creek and the prairie beyond it, filling her eyes with hugeness. She closed them against it.

Once her sister was safe, everything would be all right.

She repeated that litany over and over again to herself as she pinned her hair into its usual knot at her nape and headed back toward the camp that was beginning to wake and stir. Today she'd try to ride along with Mota and Wanaru in addition to Jennie and ask them all about what might be expected of her.

Jennie could translate, and, with the use of signs, maybe Abby could tell by the other women's faces whether she could be trusted. After all, she and Mota and Wanaru had communicated last night with surprising success.

She drew in a long, deep breath of the fresh morning air and tried to relax as she made her way through the brush. She didn't have to worry about Nokona until camp tonight. During the day he always rode ahead to scout the way.

Jennie called to her as soon as she came near the campsite.

"Here's a bag of jerky to tie to your saddle. Rations are so short we need to cover a lot of distance today—we aren't cooking any breakfast."

Nokona was nowhere in sight. Abby walked up to Jennie, took the provisions, and gave her back the clothes she'd provided.

"Thanks for letting me wear these."

"You're welcome."

Jennie pointed to a pile of gear near Abby's bed. She, apparently, had rolled up the blankets and tied them.

"I found that extra saddle for you and a different horse for today. One of the boys will bring it up in a minute."

Abby closed her hand, hard, around the bag of jerky and looked into Jennie's green eyes. Apparently sincere, honest eyes.

Resentful words pushed to the tip of her tongue.

Don't try to control every detail of my existence—I'll take care of myself.

Why haven't you told me I'm here to replace Tope?

How can you be Nokona's woman and still be so calm and unconcerned?

But she didn't say it. Somehow, speaking of such things might make them happen to her sooner.

"I'd like Mota and Wanaru to ride with us today," she said. "They're being very kind to me."

"Of course," Jennie said, smiling. "But I don't know how much talking we'll do. To-day'll be some hard, fast riding."

Abby whirled away from the treachery of that kind, caring smile, picked up her skirts, and ran for the horse herd. Forget whatever horse Jennie had picked for her. She would ride Chester today.

In her own clothes, mounted on her own horse, she'd feel much better. Besides, Jennie was trying to preside over her as the number one wife. Well, she, Abigail Briscoe, was not number two wife yet!

Several people were ahead of her, moving among the horses to choose their mounts for the day. Abby fixed her gaze on Chester's looming, black withers and dashed into the herd.

"Chester!" she called, remembering, even in her agitated state, to keep her voice low so as not to spook all the horses. "Come here, boy!"

She whistled. Chester threw up his head and whickered back.

Some of the other horses whinnied, too, and began milling around, but Chester never moved. True to his gentle nature, he stood still, waiting for her.

But a small, spotted pony darted directly at her, ears back and teeth bared. Then, in a heartbeat, it was past her, snapping at her over its shoulder and kicking with both hind feet.

Abby screamed and threw up both hands in a useless defense as she cringed backward. Her shoulders bumped into warm horseflesh that leapt away; the other horses around her jumped and snorted.

She recovered and ran on toward Chester.

A man called out some Comanche word in a low, angry voice and another man answered.

She didn't turn to look. She rushed through the herd toward her own horse, keeping a close eye out for more flying hooves.

Chester stood, a wisp of grass hanging from the corner of his mouth, waiting for her.

"I'm going to ride you today," she cried, and threw both arms around his neck just because he was her own. "I've been missing you, Big Chester!"

She let go of him and put her hand beneath his chin to lead him into camp to be saddled.

The next instant the breath whooshed out of her lungs. The ground dropped from beneath her feet and she dangled in the air, screaming.

She was caught, somebody had her!

Her blood stopped flowing.

Nokona.

She knew it, from some primitive instinct deep within.

No. No! She would not be grabbed up and carried off to be ravished without fighting back.

"Let go of me, you savage!" she yelled, gasping with every word to drag air back into her chest.

Even if he won, which he would, even if it made him kill her, she would get a few licks in before the end.

Twisting and kicking, she struck backward with her elbows and fists, trying with all her might to break his hold.

"Be still and be quiet," he ordered, in a low growl in her ear. "You'll end up stampeding this herd."

"Oh," she shouted, as loudly as she could with him squeezing her in two, "so horses are more important to you than women! Put me down or I'll send them all running to kingdom come as soon as I can get enough breath to yell."

She landed an elbow in his hard midsection. It jarred her all the way to her clenched teeth; it felt like hitting a rock.

He gave a little grunt, more of surprise than pain. But his grip didn't loosen in the slightest.

She hit him again.

"Did you expect no resistance?" she taunted, then groaned as he caught her arm and forced it flat to her side.

"I'll resist you!" she cried. "I'd *kill* myself but I have to stay alive for my sister's sake."

She kicked harder and hit backward with her free fist, but she missed him.

He dropped her feet to the ground, turning her somehow in his hands so that she faced him, but not loosening his hold.

"Kill yourself? *What* are you talking about?"

"I'm telling you that I'm not Jennie!"

"*Jennie*?" he repeated, incredulously.

He shook her slightly.

"What, in the name of the Sun Father, does that mean?"

She glared up at him, anger pumping through her veins so hot that it drove out her fear. He loomed so close that his muscular chest, crossed by a rope looped over his shoulder, nearly touched her heaving breasts.

Abby tried to step back, but he held her where she was.

"It means I saw you with her when she was tending your wound and kissing your cheek!" she said, defiantly.

He might hold her there but he couldn't do that and stop her mouth at the same time.

"It means I know she's your woman because she's a white captive! It means I know that she brought me along to replace your other wife!"

With every declaration she made, a light flared in his eyes. But the expression on his face didn't change.

He simply stared down at her with his

85

unrelenting hands holding her caught in his trap.

She pushed and clawed at his forearms to try to free herself, but they didn't give. His muscles were not even flexed, he wasn't even trying, but she didn't have a prayer against their raw power.

She lashed out again with her voice.

"It means I *won't* be your concubine!"

His narrowed eyes stayed steady on hers. But something in them changed.

And something inside her, in the very core of her, contracted.

He smiled.

"You would if I wanted you to."

The drawl of the words was a slow, seductive caress.

It stopped her breath.

Behind her, Chester shifted away, snuffled into the grass.

Nokona's long fingers tightened, burned their shape through her clothes.

Her blood blazed, leapt like a natural hot spring in her veins.

"No. I wouldn't."

His smile broadened, lit the chiseled angles of his face.

Her heart began thudding like a wild thing against the cage of her ribs.

"Then how do you plan to pay your way to New Mexico?"

The familiar flush of heat flooded up her neck and into her cheeks.

"I'll do my part of the work! I'll earn my keep!"

His dark eyes moved over her face.

"You blush," he said. "So you are too shy to earn your keep?"

She felt herself blush harder, wished to step back, away from him, to twist out of his grasp and turn her face away.

But a great lassitude pervaded her limbs.

"I am too *proud* to earn my keep!"

His crooked smile grew broader, he shook his head.

"Don't speak too soon. You're not tough enough to earn your way by working."

That stiffened her back, sent an anger coursing through her veins stronger than the strange languor. No one, *no one* ever questioned Abby's competence.

Nor her courage. And now she was no longer afraid of him. Not since he'd smiled.

"*You* don't know how strong I am!" she cried. "I can do anything I set my mind to!"

She stepped back.

He let his hands fall.

She was free.

Except for the pull of his hot, dark eyes.

"I'll show you!" she declared. "I'll do as much of the work as anyone in this band, you included. And when we reach Santa Fe, if you think I owe you anything, I'll draw money through a bank and pay you."

"Ah!" he said, and still his deep look

held her. "But I have no use for money, Shy Woman."

The sudden nickname sounded like an endearment, spoken in his lazy drawl, in his low, melodious voice, with his eyes like ebony fire in the weathered copper of his face.

It sent a trembling thrill along her skin as if he had touched her with his hand.

And then he did.

He reached out and traced a line of fire down the side of her neck with one fingertip.

Abby's heart stopped beating.

Again. She wanted him to do that again.

No. He must not.

Dear God in Heaven, what was the matter with her? She was losing her mind.

And her morality.

And every shred of her common sense.

Turn around. Turn around and climb onto Chester. Ride away. Ride away from this man.

As if he saw that desperate urge run through her head, he put his hands around her waist once more. They fitted so easily, so exactly, they seemed to belong there.

As effortlessly as breathing, he picked her up and swung her up and onto the broad back of the draft horse.

"Go," he said, dismissing her in that same careless way. "Go now and get your packs. We must ride hard while Father Sun shines."

He turned and slipped into the herd of milling horses.

Abby watched as he flipped the rope over his head and threw it, flowing, into the air, making it float over the heads of the other horses to catch his own.

He pulled back on the rope and drew the big stallion to him as easily as he had picked her up and set her onto Chester. The muscles across his back and shoulders swelled beneath his smooth copper skin.

Her palms ached to run over them.

She lifted her hand and pressed her neck with her fingertips, at the place where she could still feel the fire of his touch.

Dear God in Heaven, what was she doing?

She ripped her head around to keep from looking at him anymore, clapped her legs to the Belgian's sides, and pulled on his mane.

"Go," she said, as Nokona had done to her. "Go now."

Her voice sounded strange to her ears, hollow. Hollow as she felt inside, hollow as an empty gourd.

She had been wrong in what she'd thought before.

She *did* still live in fear of Nokona.

But now she feared her own self more.

6

After she'd gathered the meager packs that Jennie had given her, Abby ran Chester over to a spot between Mota and Wanaru so that she wouldn't have to ride beside Jennie—she simply wasn't sane enough to try to talk to her right now. Abby nodded and smiled, signed greetings to Mota and Wanaru, barely knowing what she was doing, while the caravan formed in the clearing where they had camped.

The weird, hollow feeling was giving way to a hurricane of strange emotions that threatened to sweep her right off the horse's wide back and out onto the vastness of the plains. Anger, at Nokona and at herself. Wonder, at the way her body had responded to his touch—confusion, absolute disbelief—at the power of her desire for him to touch her again.

Fear that she was losing her mind.

He was a savage red Indian. How, *how* could she crave his hands on her?

She wove her fingers into Chester's mane and hung on as the band moved out, boys pushing the horse herd up close behind them, everyone lifting into a long trot before the leaders had barely stretched out the line. Jennie waved and smiled at her, then rode her fast red horse up beside a pony carrying two small boys. One of them climbed off and onto Jennie's mount with her without either horse slowing down.

Abby saw that he was the little boy who had accidentally cut Nokona's thigh. Nokona never gave any indication that he was wounded or in pain—Jennie's medicine must have worked wonders.

In spite of herself, her gaze went to him, up at the head of the line. Nokona was leader this morning.

And the older man called Windrider was not with them. He must have taken Nokona's place as scout last night and today.

Unfortunately. If Nokona would stay out of camp, stay away from her, she could get some control, straighten her perception, which suddenly seemed skewed and shifting as the views on a kaleidoscope.

But he stayed at the head of their column, his broad shoulders gleaming copper in the sun while he pushed relentlessly west into the wind, pulling all the rest of them close behind him. Her stubborn eyes kept going back to him, again and again.

At least she knew he was human now. They had actually talked to each other.

That was what she needed to think about—how to talk to Nokona, how to persuade him to inquire about Hannah and take Abby to Santa Fe without forcing her into his bed. She could do that. Thank God he spoke English.

Thank God he had set her onto Chester's back and turned away as if she'd been an animal he'd been petting. He hadn't had the same, strange, hot yearning that she'd had.

Nokona had women every day. She had only reacted so violently because she'd never known there could be so much pleasure in a man's touch.

Most likely, he would never touch her again. She would simply remember that and stop remembering the way he had made her feel. That would be the sensible thing to do.

But her treacherous memory brought back the low vibrations of his voice.

You would if I wanted you to.

An uncontrollable trembling took her.

He had all the power. She must work like two women in every camp they made so that she could pay for her keep in that way.

That's what she would do. And she would forget the wild sensations that had danced through her body at the brush of his fingertip.

But her memory betrayed her again.

Shy Woman.

She closed her mind to the sound and turned her eyes away from the sight of him. No more. She *would* not remember any of that anymore.

Finally, after an endless day of hard riding across the plains, which were brightening now with the first, faint sheen of green spring, Abby let herself watch Nokona ride off ahead into a brown ribbon of trees. They were the sign of a creek, that much she had learned about survival.

Quickly, he came back into sight, signaling that that would be their camp. Everyone rode in and dismounted.

The adolescent herdsboys had just taken Chester with all the other horses when Jennie came over to Abby to suggest a place beside hers for her bedroll.

"I've missed you today, Abby," she said, smiling at her. "But I thought you were enjoying Wanaru and Mota and I know they were thrilled to be making friends with you."

She shook her head wonderingly as she shifted her parfleches onto her other shoulder.

"Times have really changed the *Nermernuh*," she said. "When I came to them all those years ago, the Comanche women tested the courage of every white or Mexican woman with whippings and beatings. Now they make friends with newcomers for distraction."

Abby looked at her, a tiny, flaming-haired woman who looked as content as Mama had in the midst of her family. How had she done it? How had she accepted capture and rape and years and years of life lived in a way totally foreign to her upbringing? Life in which she was forced to be a wife in a polygamous marriage?

Jennie's lively green eyes flicked to something over Abby's shoulder. Abby turned to see Wanaru and Mota, arms full of wood, smiling and motioning to her.

"Your new friends are asking me to tell you to come build the fire," Jennie said. "It's a mark of acceptance."

"But I don't know how . . ."

"They'll show you. Go to them. I'll go to the creek and carry water for both of us."

Abby put down her packs and went toward the place her new friends had chosen for the fire.

Wanaru and Mota bustled around her, handing her two drawstring pouches made of skin, one about the size of the palm of her hand, the other considerably larger, and pointing at the wood they had piled together. Then, to Abby's consternation, they picked up some other skin bags and, chattering away, walked off in the same direction Jennie had gone.

Holding a pouch in each hand, Abby stared after them.

Then she turned back to look down at the wood at her feet.

A mark of acceptance.

She couldn't betray it. It had given her a warm sensation all day to have those two riding with her and smiling at her, even if she couldn't talk to them.

Besides, this was her chance to work her way to Santa Fe, to show Nokona she was tough enough to pay her way without compromising herself.

So, she squatted down to arrange the pieces of wood into a rough circle. She glanced around to see if anyone was watching her, perhaps ready to offer advice.

But no one was. Everyone seemed to be busy unloading horses or going for water or choosing the best place for the bedrolls. Nokona was deep in conversation with Windrider, who had just ridden in and was standing in the center of the campsite holding a dust-covered horse by the one rein.

One of the boys came and took it away to the herd while she watched. Tomorrow, please God, Windrider would ride with the band and Nokona would scout.

She turned her face back to her work and broke off some twigs and small branches for kindling. This couldn't be too different from building a fire in a stove. She could do it.

When she had a handful of twigs, she placed them carefully in the middle, where the sticks of firewood met. Then she opened the string of the smaller bag and dumped its contents out into her hand. Two pieces of flint and a piece of steel, forged with a handhold that had been wrapped with a strip of rawhide ending in a decorative, beaded streamer.

Papa had started fires with flint and steel on the trail after Hannah lost the box of matches.

Abby slipped her hand through the holder for the steel and struck it against the flint. It made a spark!

But that spark blew away in the wind. She tried again.

And again and again. She went down on her knees and held the bits of fire closer to the kindling, created them in among the tinder itself.

But nothing, *nothing* would catch and burn.

She scooted around to the other side of the wood so her back would be to the wind and her body would shield the fire from the western breeze.

Even that did no good.

Each glimmer died as it was born.

She stirred the brittle sticks and tried again.

The precious spark flared, then went out.

Abby squeezed the steel until the skin wrap bit into her palm and tried over and over again, but she had no better luck. What would she give for some matches!

"Stubborn, stupid wood!" she cried.

Giggles, a bit hesitant, but sounding high and clear, broke out behind her.

She whirled around, still on her knees.

People had gathered to watch her!

Children, it seemed all the six or eight of them in the band. Except for Nokona, looming among them!

She whipped around to put her back to them, her heart pounding.

Drat his heathen hide! Didn't he have anything better to *do*? How could she pay her keep by working if he saw that she couldn't even start a fire?

"Stubborn and stupid *wood*?" he drawled, in his low, rich voice, and then said something, probably the same thing, in Comanche.

The children's laughter pealed out into the wind.

Abby's fury ignited as the kindling refused to do.

"Stop insulting me!" she cried, scrambling to her feet to turn and face him. "Get down here and do it yourself if you know so much about it!"

She stamped her foot and pointed down to the circle of wood with a quick, sweeping gesture that ordered him to do as she said.

The children understood that even if they didn't understand her words. They burst into even louder giggles.

Nokona stepped forward and, still laughing, they fell back to let him through.

He muttered at them in a mock growl and ruffled the hair of two of them as he passed.

His irritating grin broadened as he reached Abby and her would-be fire.

He arched one black eyebrow and looked from it to her, ruefully shaking his head.

"If this is how your work pays your way, I believe you'll have to come away with me."

Abby felt a huge blush roll up into her face in a heated wave. She must be turning a bright, flaming red!

"How can you *say* such a thing in front of these children?"

He gave her a profoundly sensuous smile.

"Come away with me and I'll say it in private."

His eyes, deep and dark as forest pools in autumn, smiled at her, too. They made her limbs go weak.

They made her feel his strong hands spanning her waist again.

They made her wonder what it would

be like to touch just the curve of his full bottom lip.

She took a step toward him, then realized what she had done.

Merciful heavens! Was she losing her senses?

She shook the flint and steel at him, much to the children's growing delight, and shouted, "I *can* build a fire!"

"Then do it," he said, and stamped his foot, one fist on his hip, gesturing angrily from her to the wood as she had done to him. It was a perfect imitation.

The children screamed with laughter.

Abby glared furiously at him.

"Wanaru and Mota will help me when they get back from the creek!"

"If they don't, and if I don't, this is the sun we'll finally starve and go over into the After-World."

He glanced back over his shoulder at the children and translated.

Their laughter and giggles rose into shrieks of pure glee.

"You're heartless and cruel," Abby cried, "humiliating me in public this way!"

"You're heartless and cruel," he mimicked, "refusing to come away with me."

"So you can humiliate me *alone*?"

Abby felt her aggravating blush actually get hotter, like a rushing fire.

"*You* can't make those twigs burn, either!" she shouted. "No one can! Not without matches in this wind!"

He turned and grinned at the children, translated for them, then slanted a sly glance at Abby with his hot, dark eyes.

A trembling ran through her, as if he'd touched her again.

"You don't care one whit for my feelings," she said. "And that's a terrible example to set for these children!"

He ignored that.

"What's in the other bag?"

For an instant she couldn't think what he meant.

Then she remembered the larger skin bag on the ground at her feet. She snatched it up.

"Of course!" she said, "this must be tinder . . ."

She pulled at the drawstring, looked inside.

"N-o-o," she said, doubtfully, "it's fur . . ."

She stuck her hand in. "No, feathers . . ."

"By the Sun Father!" he roared. "Give me that!"

The children screamed with laughter again.

Abby clutched the bag to her, held it away from his reaching hand.

"*I* started out to build this fire, and *I'm* going to build it!" she said, and threw him her fiercest frown.

He answered with an exaggerated shrug.

"Not without help, you're not. Little Otter can tell you that and he has only six summers."

He repeated that in Comanche for the children and a whole new wave of giggles began.

Abby turned her back on him, squatted down, and dumped the contents of the bag onto the ground in front of her. The aroma of cedar rose to fill her nostrils, a scrap of the feathers or fur or whatever it was floated upward to tickle her nose.

The rest of the small pile was unfamiliar to her—it seemed to be, perhaps some moss, maybe some bark. A handful of something else, dry and powdery. Downy, short, blue feathers. They *were* feathers instead of fur.

Whether they were meant to start a fire or not, she had no idea.

If they weren't, she'd soon know because the hateful Nokona would ridicule her mistake. And so would all these aggravating children.

But that was all right.

She gritted her teeth. She would endure any amount of humiliation before she'd give him the satisfaction of asking him.

Forcing her hands to be steady, she took a little of each of everything that had been in that bag and added it to the twigs. If she let him get the best of her now, he'd torment her forever.

She wouldn't look up, but she could feel his eyes on her.

And a half dozen other sets of eyes on her back.

More than either, though, she could feel Nokona sitting on his haunches beside her. She could smell his scent of sweat and dust and horse and something else, some other masculine aroma that she knew instinctively was his alone.

She knew it from that morning.

She knew it the way she knew the shape and power of his hands around her.

Her breath came short.

Trembling now, the slightest bit, she arranged two of the fluffy feathers on top of her kindling, took the flint into her left hand and moved it against the steel in her right.

Instantly, the fire sparked.

The feathers caught it.

Abby cupped her hands around the tiny flame, bent over, and blew on it until it grew. And grew.

The moss, or whatever it was, began to burn. The twigs caught fire.

She straightened her back, shakily pushed an escaping tendril of her hair out of her eyes, and looked up at Nokona.

His dark gaze was waiting for hers.

In the depths of his eyes, she thought she saw a glimmer of something new. Could it be respect?

But he only flashed her the most infuriating grin and said, "Good thing I suggested you look in the other bag."

Abby's jaw dropped.

"You are taking credit for *my* success?" she cried.

The corners of Nokona's mouth twitched while he translated for the children, then he added his deep, rolling laugh to their cries of delight.

Nokona laughing!

Even in her fury, Abby could hear what a wonderful sound it was—what a deep, rippling celebration.

It changed his face in her eyes forever.

From fiercely handsome to wonderful.

From hawklike to winsome. Beguiling. Wonderfully beguiling.

It lit a fire in his chocolate eyes that melted her all the way to the bone.

Fighting against it, she forced her trembling legs to lift her to her feet.

"I'm perfectly capable of building a fire, and I've just proved it!" she said, when the laughter had died down some.

Nokona watched her full lips curve, saw her mouth move, he knew she was speaking, but he didn't hear what she said.

Shy Woman's face was one to hold a man's eye. Her pale skin could turn to the color of dawn in a heartbeat and when that happened, her large eyes changed color, too, from the pale gray-brown of the trees in winter to the shimmering golden lights of autumn leaves. Then they—those wide eyes that missed nothing around her—exactly matched her hair.

Her hair, if she would let it swing loose, would be a curtain of sunlight.

"My Chief!" one of the children called. "Shall we bring the cookrack and the pot? Shall we see if the white woman can cook?"

"Yes, yes!" some of the others answered. "We're hungry! Cook the food now!"

The shrill voices brought Nokona back to himself.

What, in the name of the Sun Father, was he doing, anyway, even looking at this woman, much less *thinking* about how she looked? That made him a terrible husband, disloyal, a traitor to his delicate, beautiful Tope.

It also made him a traitor to his people. This white woman was the worst kind of intruder—she had come here deliberately to try to destroy the religion and the customs of the *Nermernuh*.

He would *not* let it happen again.

He turned away from her.

"Run on, now," he said, and, without giving the white woman another glance, strode past her toward the eager little faces.

"Get your bows and as many arrows as you can find," he said, fixing all his attention on the children. "The women can't

105

cook if we don't hunt some meat before Father Sun goes down."

Those words were tragically true. If the hunt brought them nothing, then there wouldn't be enough food for the adults in the band to eat tonight. The pemmican was gone since everyone had eaten in the saddle in the middle of the day. All that was left were a few strips of jerked beef and a handful of the cornmeal they had traded for from the Wichitas long ago.

That was in no way enough to sustain fifteen—no, sixteen counting the missionary—people riding such a hard trail.

Worry for his people flogged his back as he waved away the last child who clung to his side and went to catch a fresh horse. It would be pathetically poor hunting around here, he knew that from experience.

That was what he should have been doing, instead of trying to create some fun for the children. They were the reason he'd spent even one word or one breath on the white woman, Abby, they were the reason he'd even noticed her at all. He had been feeling so bad about their sad faces that he'd seized on the chance to tease her so he could hear their laughter again.

The children were the only reason he'd delayed his hunting duties, the only reason he'd even spoken to the missionary.

Missionary.

His blood rose hot and high from just thinking the word.

Was there no end to the means the intruders would use to try to destroy his people?

He slipped the rawhide lasso from his shoulder and sent it whistling over the heads of the horse herd, whirling in circles like his angry thoughts.

First traders, then Texian Rangers, then buffalo destroyers too wasteful to deserve the name "hunter," then soldiers and settlers, now missionaries. And he, Nokona, helpless against them all.

He had done no more good than a weak old woman, right there in front of his entire band, when Tope was killed. The memory tortured him while he caught a horse, bridled it, threw himself onto its back, and set off down the creek, scanning the trees for the movement of game.

For the time of one breath, when he lifted his horse into a lope, his anger against himself flared. He tried to grab onto it, to nurture it, to make it grow strong, strong enough to hold his sorrow at bay.

But it crumbled.

The movement of that soldier, turning away from Nokona, riding straight at Tope, the horse's shoulder knocking her down, the iron-shod hoof striking her head, happened all over again in his mind and he knew that those actions had taken place so fast that no one, not even the swiftest man ever born, could have stopped one motion of that terrible chain.

Even if he, Nokona, had at that moment been mounted on the legendary swift white stallion, *Kwahira*, he could not have saved the small, sad Tope.

The Tope he'd spoken to so harshly only a little while before she was killed.

Regret turned in his belly like the heated blade of a knife.

Keen, bitter, constant regret that would be his companion for the rest of the long seasons that he would draw breath.

Wanaru and Mota smiled and praised Abby's fire so much that she felt almost competent again. All the time that they set up the rack for the big, iron cookpot, filled it with water and then with the roots, berries and small amounts of cut-up meats that different members of the tribe brought in, they showed Abby what to do and let her help. She *did* feel capable—for the first time since the attack.

The attack.

Memories came over her, full force, and set her flat onto the ground from her kneeling position beside the fire.

A sickening regret pumped like a poison into the stream of her blood. She would never get over it. Never. She'd never get over not taking care of Hannah, not even if she held her in her arms again tomorrow.

"Sister!" Hannah had screamed, in the shrill terror of a child caught by the very devils of Hell. *"Help me, Sister!"*

A hand dropped onto her shoulder.

Abby jumped and knocked over the wooden bowls beside her with a great clatter.

It was Jennie.

"Abby, are you all right?"

"Y-yes," she stammered.

Jennie looked down at her, her brow creased with worry.

"Do you want to help me hand these around?" she asked, and Abby scrambled to her feet, already reaching for something to do, grabbing for work to comfort her.

For the first time, she noticed that people were gathering around the fire, eager to eat.

"These are stiff pieces of hide we use as plates," Jennie explained as she handed them over. "Give them to the adults."

Abby did so, walking back and forth from the stew pot, where Mota dipped up the food, putting it into each eager hand as everyone sat down, cross-legged on the ground. She hurried past Nokona, handing him a plate without looking into his face, but he was so deep in conversation with Windrider, sitting beside him, that he didn't even notice who gave him his food.

Jennie helped, and then, when everyone

was served, she sat down on the other side of the fire and motioned for Abby to join her. As soon as Abby sat down, Windrider took a bit of his meat and put it into the fire.

Jennie murmured, "He's feeding the fire as a gesture of thanks."

Abby barely heard her. Suddenly, the aroma of the soup was rising from the plate in her hands to fill her nostrils. It filled the air. It filled the world. It made her stomach growl in desperation.

Hungrily, Abby dipped her horn spoon into the hot, chunky mix of meat and roots, took a bite and then, quickly, another. It was delicious!

Everyone else seemed to think so, too, for they ate heartily, and, after assuaging their first hunger and seeing the children's stomachs finally filled and the youngsters off to play, several of the band accepted second helpings. They lingered over them.

A general conversation sprang up. Abby listened carefully. She didn't recognize a single word, but she heard a sad tone to the talking in spite of the full stomachs.

Jennie got up and refilled Windrider's bowl, then Nokona's. With a questioning lift of her eyebrows she reached for Abby's.

Abby nodded her thanks and accepted.

When Jennie was sitting beside her again and a lull fell in the conversation, Abby spoke to her.

"I can't believe that we just threw to-gether whatever everybody could find and this soup turned out to be so delicious!"

She took another bite.

Then she glanced up.

Nokona's dark gaze was fixed on her face.

The corners of his mouth were lifted a little, and his eyes held a glint. He was about to tease her again, to make her blush in front of everyone.

She met his look head-on.

"I helped make this soup," she said. "After I started the fire."

He flashed his crooked grin that, some-how, always surprised her.

"Working your way to New Mexico?"

"Yes, I am!"

His dark eyes flicked to the meat on Abby's plate and then up again to meet her gaze.

"Well, you'll have to do more than build a fire and help cook a stew to earn a deli-cacy like this," he drawled.

"What delicacy? Roots and wild onions, some nuts and berries and a rabbit or two?"

His steady look held hers.

"And rattlesnake. That's a rare treat."

Abby's stomach lurched and turned.

"Rattlesnake?" she cried. "No one eats snakes!"

Then she remembered his rolling laughter, his egging on the children's giggles.

"It's no use," she told him, sitting up stiffly and drawing all her dignity around her. "You needn't think you can torment me *all* the time. I don't believe you."

"I'm not lying."

His dark eyes continued to hold hers. He looked perfectly sincere.

"You've been making fun and laughing at me all day!" she cried. "*All* day! You can stop it now."

She whirled around to look at Jennie.

"This isn't *snake*, is it? It can't be!"

Jennie's sympathetic green eyes were twinkling.

"Yes, Abby, I'm afraid it is."

"I killed it myself," Nokona said, his low, calm tone barely covering a rising chuckle. "It was one of the biggest rattlesnakes I've ever seen."

Abby felt her eyes flare wide. She stared at Jennie, then, swiftly, at other faces around the fire, begging *someone*, *anyone*, to say it wasn't true.

No one did.

Naturally. None of them spoke English.

But forcing that logical thought into her head, trying to concentrate on it, didn't do one bit of good.

She could feel the snake wiggling inside her, crawling up out of her stomach and into her throat.

112

She clapped her hand over her mouth and fought it down as she scrambled to her feet.

Nokona muttered something in Comanche and then burst into his deep, rolling laugh. A whole chorus of loud guffaws welled up to join him.

Abby picked up her skirts with her free hand and ran headlong over the rough ground, trying to reach the privacy of the trees that grew along the creek.

7

Nokona's gaze brushed past the Fire Flower's, then came back and caught there.

She, out of all the camp, was not even smiling. She leaned around Windrider and beckoned Nokona to bend toward her and listen.

"Go and make amends to her," she said, quietly, in English. "I heard how you and the children teased her about building the fire. Abby's going through a hard time and, since she isn't used to our ways, she may think you're trying to hurt her feelings."

Every muscle in his body tightened in resistance.

"She wouldn't *have* to get used to our ways if she'd stayed among her own kind," he said.

"Her own kind is the human race and you are included. Go see about her."

His lips parted to refuse the request.

But she forestalled him.

"Nokona," she said, "I'm asking you. Please."

"I'll talk to her, all right," he said, stood up, and strode away from the fire.

The anger in his belly made him feel just as hot as when he'd sat beside it. Meddling missionary! Whining woman!

Next the Fire Flower would be wanting him to carry Abby in front of him in his saddle to keep her from feeling lonely! Well, coddling wouldn't get her to New Mexico, where she was evidently determined to go, since she'd stuck to their band like spines to a prickly pear.

Why, in the name of the Sun Father, hadn't he sent the missionary woman back to Fort Sill?

Straight ahead, he caught a glimpse of shining, golden brown hair and pale blue cotton dress disappearing into the trees. He would talk to her quickly and then get back to his supper.

He followed her tracks through the low-slanting sunlight, then he heard the sound of gagging and moved toward her.

She was bending over the low-hanging branch of a big hackberry tree, throwing up. She vomited until there couldn't be even a scrap of anything left in her stomach. The violence of the retching shook her slender body and made the sturdy limb dip down and then tremble upward until the whole tree was quaking.

Keen regret cut him. He should have kept his mouth shut and let her keep her supper. Too late, now.

He had told her the meat was snake, which was true, just to see the astonished look on her face, to bring a laugh into the camp, to try to make it more like the old, happy days. How could he know she would have such a violent reaction to that bit of teasing?

She'd better learn to be tougher than that if she was going to ride with this band.

But he hated having done this to her.

Even if she was an intruder.

He glanced toward the creek, thinking of getting water to splash on her face, but she chose that moment to stop throwing up. Slowly, she placed both her slender hands on the suppporting limb and straightened her back.

Nokona stepped toward her.

"Well," he said, lightly, to distract her from her misery, "I had decided that you'd lost your head. I couldn't see it anywhere."

She whirled to face him, turning loose of the tree so fast the discarded branch bounced up and down behind her.

"Leave me *alone*!" she screamed.

The wild desperateness in her eyes was that of an animal trapped. An even sharper arrowhead of remorse stabbed into him.

"How *could* you hide and watch me in such an embarrassing, private condition?"

Locks of her hair had strayed from the knot at the nape of her neck, swinging down on each side in smooth curves that cradled the oval shape of her face and brushed her prim white collar. They caught both the gold of the late sunshine and the chestnut brown of the shadows thrown by the trees.

"You are the cruelest, most heartless, un-civilized savage alive!" she cried, her cheeks flaming red. "*Why* won't you leave me alone? Dear God in Heaven, *following* me here, *laughing* at me for being sick!"

Throwing him a look like she wanted to kill, she whirled away from him so fast that her full skirts tangled around her feet. She grabbed the cloth up in both hands and ran, headlong, toward the creek.

Nokona went after her.

She threw herself prone onto the shallow bank and began slapping water onto her face. Then she rinsed her mouth and drank from the cup she made of one hand, stopping only to bathe her face again and again.

Nokona walked up and stood over her.

She came scrabbling to her feet like a she-panther bent on revenge.

"Get away from me!"

She stopped and swallowed hard, trying to rid her voice of its trembling.

"*Stay* away!"

She didn't quite succeed. But she raised her chin defiantly anyway.

He had to admire that.

And the fact that she lost all her shyness and attacked him head-on.

"You've made fun of me all day long!"

"No, I haven't."

"You have! Even to saying I'd be your . . . concubine if you wanted me to."

Her voice sank to a husky whisper.

The blood rose into her cheeks, pink as the light from the setting sun. He took a step toward her.

He needed to touch her. Just once. Only to brush one shining strand of her hair away from her flushed face.

"Abby . . ."

She took a jerky step backward, drew herself up with the dignity of an old war chief, and made a great show of looking around and behind him. Then she fixed her huge, gleaming eyes on his face.

"Where's the crowd? I'd think you'd have brought the herdsboys or the warriors or the women or the children—or perhaps the whole band at once to join in the fun of laughing at me!"

Her voice stayed steady, but underneath he could hear her deep hurt.

The Fire Flower was right. This woman wasn't accustomed to The People's ways.

And she *had* been through a lot lately. In fact, she, too, was in mourning. The same

119

hyena's teeth of sorrow that tore at his guts with every heartbeat were tearing at hers.

"Our ways are ..."

"Savage and uncivilized," she said, bitterly, "which I can endure if you'll help me find my sister. And I can work to pay my keep."

Her voice broke a bit, and she stopped to clear her throat. She took a shaky step toward him.

"If I have to do your work and take your orders to find Hannah," she said, "I will. If you inquire about her and take me to her, I'll build your fires and prepare your food. But I will not submit my body *or* my pride. No more ridicule."

Savage.

Uncivilized.

But somehow, coming from her, the words were not insults.

They were only marks of ignorance.

And now she was setting out the terms of an agreement between them as if she held all the power to enforce it. When he, Nokona, held her very life in his hands.

That, too, showed how naive she was.

"Do we have an understanding?" she asked. "Will you stop ridiculing and tormenting me?"

Her huge, golden brown eyes filled with tears. They spilled over and trembled on her lashes.

Suddenly, he wished he could cry, too.

Wished he could weep until his body was nothing but an empty husk that would blow away in the wind.

There was too much sadness already in this new, coming season of the spring, and he had added to it, though he'd only been trying to make laughter. Some had laughed, but Shy Woman had cried even more inside.

Guilt slashed at him.

Guilt at the way he had treated an *intruder*?

His anger flared up again.

She had no valid reason to even *be* here, and none at all to be jerking his emotions from one extreme to the other like camp dogs with a marrowbone.

"Buck up," he said, harshly. "If you ride with the *Nermernuh* you'll have to learn to take teasing."

"There's a difference between teasing and ridicule! Why do you have to make me a laughingstock? Just leave me alone! Ignore me and let me work in camp in return for my food and your help in finding my sister."

Her voice cracked apart this time. She was shaking all over as if she had a fever.

"My . . . sister," she repeated, in a low, pitiful tone, as if talking to herself.

A chill ran through him. Abby was weak and accustomed to living in houses. The attack on her family, the loss of her sister,

121

the hard riding and scant food on this trail were breaking her body.

And he had broken her spirit. At least, partly.

The least he could do was give it back to her.

"You'll never find your sister."

The breath went out of her as if he'd punched her in the stomach with his fist.

"You *are* cruel!" she cried. "You don't have to say such a thing!"

"You don't have the strength to ride even one more day."

"*You* don't know how much strength I have! I'll never stop until I find Hannah!"

"You'll stop when you faint from hunger and fall off your horse."

Her eyes, like her hair, shone with fire here and fell into shadows there.

Sorrow cast the shadows.

Anger lit the fire.

She was consumed with rage and grief, he realized, with a sudden, strong lurch in the pit of his stomach. Mostly grief.

Just as he was. He might be looking into a mirror at himself.

They must recover their balance, both of them, before they lost it completely.

He repeated his challenge.

"You'll stop when you faint from hunger and fall off your horse."

"Don't you wish I would! So you could just ride away and leave me there to die!"

122

She glared at him, clearly determined not to be the first to look away.

Her whole body was trembling, just as he himself was shaking inside.

But she didn't break the stare.

Neither did he.

Because he would not let her grief take her. Nor her impotent rage. He'd give her anger, clean anger, and something she could do about it. Anger to give her strength.

"I can leave you to die whenever I please," he said, scornfully, "but I don't need to bother because you'll starve yourself soon."

"You *are* cruel!" Abby shouted. "It would've been kinder of you to kill me as soon as you saw me. Right after you killed the soldier who was only trying to get away."

He closed his ears to that. His own sorrow he would deal with later.

"Game and water are scarce between here and El Rancho del Cielo," he snapped. "When we must eat snake or cactus or prairie dog, why don't you refuse it instead of wasting food that could nourish somebody else?"

"Because I have decided to eat it and keep it down," she said, "to nourish myself."

She narrowed her eyes and looked at him straight.

"Because I intend to survive to find my sister."

"Of course," he sneered. "I can hardly wait to see it."

"You don't have to wait."

She stepped closer to him, kept giving him that same, sharp, golden brown look.

"Come and watch while I eat another rattlesnake supper."

Abby swung away from him and began to march out of the trees toward the camp, leaving him standing still. Well, he could stay right there on that same spot until his feet put down roots, for all she cared.

How dare he follow her out here to taunt her when he knew she was sick?

You'll never find your sister.

You don't have the strength to ride even one more day.

Abby heard his rough, arrogant tone all over again. She savored it. She would make him eat those words if *she* had to eat every snake on the plains.

How in Heaven's name had she ever thrilled to his hands, wanted him to touch her again? Well, that would never happen anymore.

She walked faster and faster toward the cookfire. Her legs trembled, but she made them carry her anyhow. Her hands shook, but she held them down by her sides. Her backbone felt like jelly, but she kept it ramrod straight.

He was following her again now. Every pore, every nerve in her body screamed that he was right behind her, although he moved so silently that she could hear nothing but the sounds of the children playing around the edges of the camp and the murmurs of voices near the fire. Nokona was right on her heels, ready to laugh at her again.

Well, she'd be laughing at him this time. He had done his best to destroy her but he'd made her so mad that he'd saved her instead. The joke was on him.

She ignored the swirl of dogs that ran out from the fire to meet her, stalked to her place beside Jennie, retrieved her plate and horn spoon, then moved straight to the pot hanging over the fire.

"Abby?" Jennie said. "Can I find you something else, maybe some plain berries to eat?"

"No, thank you."

Abby picked up the ladle and dipped it into the pot.

When she had filled her plate and glanced up at Jennie again, Nokona was standing behind her, his eyes narrowed to shining, dark slits.

"Nokona doesn't believe that I can eat this stew and keep it in my stomach," Abby announced, looking all around the circle of copper-colored faces, pantomiming so that everyone would understand her. "I will prove that I can."

Then, with a great flourish of her horn spoon, she dipped up a bite, put it into her mouth, and chewed.

It is sweet, it is delicious, it is giving me strength.

She repeated those words in her head like a chant while, standing in the middle of the camp with all eyes on her, she determinedly ate the whole serving. When she was done, she stared defiantly at Nokona and then, with a great flourish, turned the dried-hide plate upside down to prove that it was empty.

A congratulatory shout burst from one throat, then another, then all of them. Laughing cheers and waves of applause surrounded her.

But they sounded to be from a far distance.

Nokona's steady gaze filled all her senses. His face told her nothing, but his eyes held a heated spark.

Respect? Had her determination made him admire her against his will?

The cheering died down. Nokona spoke.

"That's rattlesnake," he said, and paused for a moment, watching her, as if waiting to see if the word would have the same effect on her as it had had the last time. "We'll see if you can eat grasshoppers when *that* time comes."

She met his challenging look while fury rushed through her veins. It surged up into her cheeks like a river of heat.

But her stomach didn't turn, didn't even lurch.

"You can't admit you've misjudged me, can you, Nokona?" she said. "Save your breath. Nothing you can say will move me now."

But she lied. And she knew it.

Just the sight of him, standing there, moved her.

"Good for you, Miss Abby," he drawled, in his most derisive tone. "But you still have a long way to ride. One meal of snake meat doesn't make you tough enough for that."

He loomed there in the dim light of dusk, flashing his eyes, arrogant as the Archangel Gabriel. No! He was Lucifer!

All the animosity, all the anger that he roused in her came swirling even higher in the windstorm in her heart. He had so little regard for her, so little respect—she might as well be a grasshopper herself.

She would change that, she vowed in that moment. Somehow, if she had to eat a bucketful of rattlesnakes, she would change that.

They started riding again at sunrise the next morning, after a scanty breakfast of leftover stew. Abby ate her share and kept it down, but Nokona wasn't there to see it. He had already gone out to scout.

Once the whole band was mounted and on the trail, Jennie settled her mare into step beside Abby's mount.

"Thank you for letting us use Chester to carry the tipis," she said. "Wanaru's packhorse is so lame he can't take the weight."

"You're welcome," Abby said, reaching down to stroke the neck of the little bay mare Jennie had loaned her. "I like Ohapia just fine. What does her name mean?"

"Bay Mare."

They both laughed.

"Now, that's what I call a plainspoken, well-fitting name," Abby said. "Who gave it to her?"

"Nokona. He named her a long time ago."

Jennie leaned over and patted Abby's hand.

"I'm so glad you're with us, Abby," she said, "you make Nokona laugh. He hasn't laughed much for a very long time."

Abby just looked at her.

"He doesn't strike me as the laughing kind."

"But he is. Fun and happiness are great in his nature."

Abby shook her head.

"He laughs *at* me, ridicules me. That's different from fun and happiness."

"The Comanche way is to tease and correct and comment in public on one's behavior," Jennie said. "He's only trying to bring some laughter into this pitiful band."

Abby stared at her, frowning, trying to think if that could be so.

"When he teased you about building the fire he was only trying to give the children some fun. They're very sad because they all loved his wife and she loved all of them—she had no children of her own."

"Did he want any?" Abby blurted, and then had no idea at all why she'd said such a thing.

"Yes. Very much. But they never came.

"Nokona wants laughter and fun for himself, too, although he wouldn't admit it," Jennie said. "For a long time before his wife died, she was desperately sad because she saw no hope once the old, wandering ways are lost forever."

"What do you mean?"

"We're leaving Comancheria, our home hunting grounds. The buffalo are gone, we have nothing to eat, and if we stay, we'll be forced onto the reservation."

"So you're going to Santa Fe?"

"To a *rancho* near there. My daughter, Ysidora Pretty Sky, and her husband, Don Rafael, have offered us a home."

Shocked, Abby stared at her.

"You and Nokona have a grown daughter? Tope ... no, I shouldn't speak the name of the dead. I mean, Nokona's first wife had no children but you did?"

Jennie stared back at her, frowning in puzzlement.

Somewhere, ahead of them, a horse's hooves thundered over the prairie. Closer by, a child's voice called.

But neither woman turned her head to look toward the sounds.

"Abby, whatever are you talking about?"

"You and Nokona! I saw you, that day the boy cut him with the knife. The two of you were alone and very intimate while you doctored his wound."

Jennie's green eyes flared wide as she took that in.

"I understand," Abby said, quickly. "I know that it's a custom of the Comanche to sometimes have more than one wife. That's one of their practices that my Papa aims to stop."

Jennie kept looking at her.

"I've wondered, though," Abby went on, "is it sometimes the custom for a woman to have more than one husband? I've noticed you seem close with Windrider, too."

Jennie threw back her head, then, and laughed, her curly mane of red hair bouncing until the silver streaks in it glittered in the sunlight.

"I'm Nokona's *mother*!" she cried, when she could catch her breath.

The word stunned Abby. It sounded like

a foreign language in her ears. All she could do was repeat it.

"His *mother*?"

"Yes!"

Abby shook her head in bewilderment.

"I thought you were forced to be his captive wife. You touched him so gently and kissed him when you bandaged his wound . . ."

"And you thought I couldn't naturally, voluntarily, love a Comanche man? That since I'm white, I'd have to be a sex slave *forced* to touch him?"

Abby felt her face go hot.

"White or red makes no difference when it comes to love, Abby. I have loved Windrider, Nokona and Sky's father, for almost forty years—loved him with all my being, as I could never have loved any other man."

Abby stared at her harder, trying to make her mind work, willing it to absorb what she'd heard.

"You've been with the Comanches all these years of your own free will?"

"By the *determined* will of my heart and of Windrider's," she said. "Texian Rangers found me with The People and took me back to San Antonio. Windrider risked being shot on sight to come into the town after me and I risked never seeing my mother again to come back to Comancheria with him."

Instinctively, Abby took a deep, shaky breath.

"I can't believe how wrong I was!" she said. "Why, when you said to Nokona that you knew once he'd thought about it, he'd want you to bring me with the band, I thought maybe I was to replace T . . . his first wife."

She stopped, feeling a sudden chill.

"But . . . that could still be true, I guess, even if you are his mother."

Jennie laughed her silvery, little laugh.

"You've heard too many stories of Indians ravaging every white woman they can get their hands on," she said. "What I meant by that remark was that Nokona had said to abandon you and let you starve only because he was wild with grief. He could never be that cruel."

"Yes, he could be!" Abby burst out, before she thought that she was talking to his mother. "I saw him kill the soldier while the man was trying to get away. Nokona ran right along beside him, dragged him off his horse, and murdered him! With no mercy! Just because he was white!"

"No," Jennie said, quietly. "Because that man had just killed Nokona's wife."

Abby gasped.

"For no reason," Jennie said, with quiet fury. "He rode her down as if she were one of these dogs."

She gestured at the spotted mongrels trotting at the heels of her horse.

"She was his only wife?"

The question leapt from Abby's tongue before she even knew that she'd thought it. She bit her tongue. It didn't matter to her if Nokona had a hundred wives!

"Yes," Jennie said, "Nokona had only one wife. Since she had no children, many of the elders suggested that he take another, and even she urged him to, saying that she would share his children, but he would not. He loved her with all his heart."

Abby rode in silence, looking at Jennie, trying to absorb it all.

"As for Windrider, he says that one wife is more than enough," Jennie said, chuckling to herself. "Many of the Comanches feel that same way, many others do not. Your new friends Wanaru and Mota are both married to Brown Hawk—they have been for years."

Abby caught her breath with this shocking bit of news.

"They are? They seem ... very happy ..."

"They are."

"But God doesn't approve of that—it's wrong!"

"Our ways are different, not necessarily wrong. The white way isn't the only way, although most white people think so. That attitude is what makes Nokona so wild sometimes with anger."

Windrider turned and called to Jennie then, but before she went to speak with him, Abby held her back.

"Why didn't you tell me all this before?"

"You weren't strong enough to care about all this. You were crazed and very, very weak, Abby."

"And I'm not crazed now? I'm not weak?"

"No. Last evening, when you ate the stew, I knew you had your strength back. I knew you'd be all right."

She trotted ahead then, to her husband's side.

Abby rode several lengths behind them. She certainly didn't *feel* all right.

How could she?

How could she be all right in a weird, wild world where such strange, *wrong* things as polygamy and murder for revenge were accepted by a *white* woman as normal and right?

And how could she be all right with Nokona prodding and taunting her, thinking up more cruelties every time he saw her?

Poor Jennie. It was only because she saw him through a mother's forgiving eyes that she could say he was a man who loved laughter.

8

All day they rode hard. Abby was glad. She felt like urging Ohapia into a run, smooching to her and calling to her, begging her to carry her out of this strange, barbarous world.

Because her sense of fairness had begun to make her think twice about dismissing Jennie's opinion of Nokona. Maybe it *didn't* come only from a mother's loyalty—after all, Abby had been wrong about more than just the relationship between Nokona and Jennie.

For one thing, he *had* had provocation when he killed the soldier. That hadn't been the wanton, racist murder that Abby had at first thought it.

Also, he wasn't a lecherous, polygamous savage who would force Abby to his bed. He'd given up having more wives and even children of his own because he had loved Tope so much.

That was no small sacrifice. He loved children. He probably *had* been intent on bringing some laughter to the children of the band and not on humiliating Abby when she'd built the fire.

She shifted her sore bottom in the narrow wooden saddle and then stood in the stirrups to straighten the blanket that served as her cushion. Too bad Nokona had gone on to scout, she thought fiercely. He should see that she was so tough and experienced on the trail now that she could rearrange her seat without even slowing down.

He is a good man. Fun and happiness are great in his nature.

Could it be? Could it actually be true?

No. He was cruel to her at the creek, cruel was the only word for it.

You'll never find your sister.

She could still hear the arrogant certainty in his voice.

Abby clenched her teeth.

He *was* cruel.

Unless he was ... canny instead.

What was it Jennie had said?

When you ate the stew, I knew you had your spirit back.

Jennie had seen that the anger which drove her to eat the snake had saved her spirit. Could Nokona have guessed that that would happen?

Could he deliberately have been baiting her for that reason?

136

But why would he care that much?

The questions haunted her all day, held her gaze to the west, looking for him. But all day he stayed too far ahead.

Jennie passed back the provisions—one narrow strip of jerky per person. They ate in the saddle and drank water from the skin water bags. Abby began to think they would never stop, never quit moving, never rest.

Late in the afternoon, they rode up and up a narrowing sweep in the land and over a long ridge. As they started down the steep, quick drop toward a gleaming stream of water, strung out in a rough line, she saw him.

Nokona.

Mounted on his yellow-skinned stallion with the black mane and tail who stood like a statue in the middle of the river.

The setting sun bathed them in fire.

It flashed off the lance Nokona held straight up with his right arm and glimmered along the edges of the round shield he wore on his left. Streaks of blue paint glowed in the middle of it. She saw, as she rode closer, that the streaks shaped a bear's claw.

Her breath caught in her chest.

His skin was painted, too.

As Ohapia reached the bottom of the bank, Abby pulled her aside and stopped at the edge of the water.

137

Diagonally, across half of Nokona's hard face ran black zigzag stripes. Red, yellow, and blue ones, straight up and down, broke the copper color of the other half. His muscular chest, his bare arms, and the lithe trunk of his body wore various symbols: a red hand, a yellow feather, a white arrowhead, a yellow sun, another blue bear claw.

Feathers, perhaps a dozen of them, stood in a ruff down the middle part of his long, black hair.

Regally, he turned his head to the east. As if he'd just become aware of their coming, following him along the trail he had scouted for them.

He lifted his left arm in a gesture of command and the blue paint turned to rich purple in the sunset light. Then he moved the arm across his body in a signal that they should come forward.

A murmur passed from mouth to mouth among the members of the band.

"El Río Gallinas. El Río Gallinas."

Abby knew enough Spanish to know that this was the name of the river, but she'd never heard of it. It might be sacred in their religion or it might be a boundary of some kind, but she couldn't wonder about that now. She couldn't think. All she could do was look at Nokona.

His family and friends rode down to the edge and then splashed into the river. They began to pass in front of him. He sat still as a pagan god and stared straight ahead, not at them, but past them and through them.

The red-gold light poured over him with the same flowing power as the river. It threw the muscles of his upper arms and shoulders, as well as the carved features of his face, into sharp relief. It caressed his naked chest, which appeared to be cut from stone—he sat so still that he seemed not to breathe at all.

His long legs moved, though, the strong saddleman's thighs flexing as if any second he would squeeze the dun into a run. A chill of fear darted through her. Would he leave them? Turn the stallion's head and gallop back the way they had come?

He might do anything. At that moment, he was alone, as removed from all the rest of them as the high, purple mountains far to the west.

At last, Ohapia realized that she was being left behind, that all the other horses were in the water, and she pulled forward. Abby let her go.

Nokona did not move.

Until she approached him. He turned his head and, for an instant, she thought he was looking at her.

But he fixed his gaze on the distance behind her.

His dark eyes burned like a hawk's, his nostrils flared and he stared past Abby at the far, far horizon, into the darkening sky, as if he could see all the way back down the trail they had ridden.

Abby reached him just before he swung around.

His fierce eyes followed the people of his band, touched on each of their backs as they rode their horses up and out of the river, up again to the top of the sloping, sandy bank.

Grief flamed in his face.

His gaze whipped back to meet hers.

His eyes shone black, deep as wells of sorrow, hot as the fury of Hell.

They did not see her.

And she wished she hadn't seen them.

For the first part of that night, while she tossed in her blanket, too jangled by the revelations of the day to close her eyes, until the moment exhaustion dragged her into sleep, Abby dwelt on that look. It mirrored her soul.

Anger filled *her* too, an impotent fury at injustice. And homesickness. Plus guilt, with its constant, tormenting regret.

She hadn't lifted the lid on that cauldron of emotions boiling way down inside her until she had seen them reflected in Nokona's eyes.

She *must* put that lid back on, hold these awful, unfamiliar feelings at bay. Hadn't she lived basically content for twenty-seven years by putting her energies to what needed to be done and ignoring foolish feelings about things that couldn't be changed? What she needed to do now was find Hannah.

That was all. She must put her mind to that and lock away the lurking, sinful hatred and fury that would govern her if she let them.

She clenched her fists so hard that her nails bit into her palms, threw herself onto her stomach, and buried her face in the blanket beneath her.

God must help her! If these feelings ever got loose, she'd destroy the world!

She fought them back, refused to let them into her mind by thinking of Hannah, instead, and how happy she would be to see her. *Abby*! she would cry, and run to her with her plump little arms open for a hug.

And she thought about Jennie. What a shock her disclosures had been!

Fatigue pulled her into unconsciousness, then, and she dreamed that Nokona was her friend.

The next day's ride was even harder and more desperate. Nokona, who had come into camp at daybreak painted in an entirely different way, with more black and more lightning zigzags of yellow and blue, had spent the night alone, meditating and praying, Jennie told Abby. They had entered his sister's *rancho* when they'd crossed the river, and he was mourning. They had left Comancheria forever.

All day he rode behind the band, lance at the ready like a fierce rear guard, pushing all the horses ahead of him. No one ate, because there was no more food. They filled their bellies with water from El Río Gallinas and kept moving.

Toward the home of their kinswoman.

Abby decided that Ysidora Pretty Sky must be enormously rich. They had been riding all day and still had not reached the house.

The house.

The word sounded strange, even silently said in her mind. Abby hadn't been in a house, hadn't *seen* a house, for such a long time.

A time in which her whole world had vanished.

Frantically, she wrenched her mind back from the perilous edge of remembrance.

She forced her paralyzed legs to move, her heels to thud against Ohapia's sides. She moved her closer to Jennie's mount.

"When do you think we'll get there?"

"*Miitutsi!*" Jennie shouted, and, with a sudden, dazzling smile, pointed ahead.

Abby looked and saw nothing except the afternoon sun, starting its journey down in the sky, and the green side of a pine-covered hill. She kept up with Jennie and Windrider as they lifted their horses into a lope and forged ahead even faster. A small smile touched her lips.

Jennie had spoken to her in Comanche. She had forgotten Abby wasn't one of the band.

Then they topped the hill and stopped. Below, in a protected, grassy valley, already turning green, nestled a huge Spanish *hacienda* and its dozen outbuildings—white walls and red tile roofs gleaming in the low-slanting sun. There was an orchard, too, larger than the one at home on the farm, and a vegetable garden laid out in rows.

Horse corrals surrounded one of the barns, with a few horses in different pens. Cattle grazed on the open range behind them.

The rest of the band caught up with Jennie and Abby and crowded into a ragged line along the ridge, looking down. Someone called out and pointed.

Then Abby spotted the two riders coming toward them, halfway between the house and the hill where they sat. They had their arms up and waving—from such a distance they looked like tiny wound-up dolls.

"Petu!" Jennie shouted, "My daughter!"

Before the sounds of the words had died in the air, she had her mount moving. Abby dropped back with the others as Jennie and

Windrider led them down the long, rocky hill.

Toward their relatives.

Everybody here was kin to someone else who was here.

Except Abby.

Her throat closed around the thought. She grabbed the high, fringed pommel of the saddle and clung to it while Ohapia surged down the slope and into the grassy valley in the midst of all the other tired horses.

Tired voices called happy greetings.

Abby fought back the threatening tears. Her family. She needed her family.

Oh, dear Lord above, please let her find Hannah.

Their hosts met them sooner than she thought possible, and almost everyone leapt off their horses into a pandemonium of laughter and chatter, all of it in Comanche and/or Spanish. Abby stayed on her borrowed mare.

She didn't understand a word of it.

But she didn't need to. She knew a family reunion when she saw one.

The Briscoes could never have another one . . .

Mama and Papa . . .

Anguish, pain in its purest form, agony like she had never known, snapped around her heart like the closing jaws of a trap.

She made her mind go still.

There was no strength in her to think about that now. She would think about the present time only.

About the people who were here with her only.

The woman who had ridden out to meet them, the most striking woman that Abby had ever seen, had to be Ysidora Pretty Sky. Her looks were stunning, the most amazing combination of Jennie and Windrider. She hugged them both at the same time.

With her auburn hair, lithe and graceful as a willow tree, and her bright yellow, Spanish-style dress, she stood out like a bright star in a dark heaven among the people crowding around her.

She looked to be about twenty-five years old, but she had to be older because her tall, young companion (now submitting to a kiss on each cheek from the tiny Jennie standing on tiptoe) was undoubtedly her son. He didn't look like her, really, but he had that same quick brightness about him.

Somehow, too, the boy reminded Abby of Nokona. His uncle, Nokona. She turned in her saddle to look for him.

Wasn't he going to dismount to greet his sister and nephew? Evidently not.

He sat on his horse like a suspicious guard—quite a way back from where they all had met—with his fierce face once more set in stone. He tilted his head as Abby

145

watched him and held it still, as if he were listening for something or someone.

Suddenly, the swirling group on the ground was breaking up, each person was picking up his reins and mounting again. Jennie waved at Abby and rode her mare through the group to her.

"I'll introduce you in a moment," she said, turning to look back over her shoulder. "Can you believe that big boy is my *grandson*? Why, the last time I saw him he was no taller than I am and now—why, he's a man!"

Abby's heart turned over. Her Aunt Rose had said almost those exact words when their family had all gathered to tell the new missionaries good-bye.

She slammed the memory away.

"His name is Enrique," Jennie said. "And, of course, he has a Comanche name, too. Isn't he handsome? Just look at him!"

"He is gorgeous," Abby said, and smiled as she turned to look at him again.

With a suddenness that drained her trail-weary soul, she saw, not Enrique's face, but her dear nephew, Seth's, instead.

She turned to face the other way.

Ysidora Pretty Sky was riding over to Nokona, reaching out to silently touch his hand. He looked at her, gave her a trace of a smile.

They *were* close, very close. Like Abby and the brother next to her, John.

Would she ever see John again?

The thought was too much to bear.

She pulled Ohapia's head around and fell into the middle of the band, now riding at a fast trot toward the huge house in the distance, with Enrique leading the way. The thing to remember was that she must think of the present only.

And only of the people she was with.

They rode into the well-tended yard and stepped off their horses into a hospitable new world full of excited, laughing children, sweet-smelling potted flowers and delicious aromas of food.

Beautiful children came running from every direction, it seemed, into the outstretched arms of Windrider and Jennie. They appeared at a glance to be fairly evenly divided between boys and girls, some with black hair, some with auburn, all with dancing dark eyes and creamy tanned skins.

She *was* rich, this Ysidora Pretty Sky, Abby thought suddenly, with a great lurch of her heart. She was rich beyond measure. In children.

Stiffly, Abby climbed down from her horse, closing her heart for the ten thousandth time to the inextinguishable sorrow that she had none.

Long tables, heavily laden, tended by smiling servants, filled the center of a huge flagstoned patio. Red, purple, yellow, white, blue flowers grew in pots along its walls and in more pots in its corners. They had to have been started inside somewhere, Abby thought, in a desperate attempt to distract herself. It was too early in the season, yet, and too cool for them to remain outside.

On the back side of the house, behind the patio, smoke rose from a pit dug into the earth. The fragrance of meat roasting made Abby's mouth water. Near the pit, a big cookfire blazed in a long trench beneath huge iron pots full of more food.

All of it, so much of everything, overwhelmed her senses, drained by privation those many days on the trail. And the children, well-fed, happy children, who made the trail-weary little ones look like ghosts, made her weak with pity.

Her eyes closed against the bright, spinning colors, her stomach tried to rebel from the aromas of the foods, even as it growled to be fed. Uncertainly, she began walking slowly with the others toward the water set out in basins for washing before the meal.

Its cold freshness revived her some, and when she'd laid down the towel, she looked around for a place to sit down. She swerved away from the others and forced her trembling legs to carry her to one of the high-backed, wrought-iron chairs set against the patio wall.

It felt strange, and at the same time comforting, to sit in a chair.

A moment later, someone brought a cool, tin cup and pressed it into her hands.

"Drink some water before you eat."

Abby looked up into the compassionate brown eyes of Ysidora Pretty Sky. She knew, they said. She knew what it was to be homesick.

"I'm Sky," she said. "My mother tells me your name is Abby. Welcome to El Rancho del Cielo."

Abby wrenched her thoughts back to the present, racked her mind for something to say.

"How did you know?" she asked, and took a sip of the cool water. "How did you know to prepare all this feast today? If someone saw us coming and rode in to tell you, you wouldn't have had time for so many preparations."

Sky gave a graceful shrug that made her hair catch fire in the afternoon sun.

"I know things," she said, simply. "I always have."

She smiled. She had a wonderful, warm smile. A mysterious smile.

"What kinds of things?"

"One time I knew there was a treasure," Sky said, ". . . but not where it was."

They both laughed.

Before either of them could say more, a

149

shriek of excitement rose over the sounds of so many voices.

"Papa! Papa!"

Sky turned to look.

"Abby, excuse me," she said, her voice filling with voluptuous pleasure, "my husband is home from Santa Fe!"

Abby sat, holding the cup in both hands, and watched Sky run to the edge of the flagstoned floor and then off into the grass to be caught up in one arm of a man, a tall, resplendently handsome man, who'd just stepped off a gorgeous gray horse. His other arm already held a beaming little girl; two others were clinging to his legs.

In spite of that, he held Sky to him for the space of a long heartbeat. They exchanged a brushing kiss that held as much passion as a fervid embrace. Their eyes met and held for a moment.

Then he went to Windrider and Jennie, to Nokona and others in the band, putting the children down to greet and welcome them heartily.

The family was together again.

Abby couldn't stop watching them. A quick stab of longing pierced her heart.

But, this time, not for her old home.

This time she yearned, with a burning ache in the very core of her, for the new home she'd never had. A home with a man like Sky's, who wore his love for her on his face.

A man whom she could love so much in return that *her* face would light and her voice would go rich with pleasure the way Sky's had just done.

But she had never had even a glimpse of such a love. Every man and boy in the Adirondack community of Tobler's Springs who had courted her in her young, marriageable days had left her heart completely untouched.

She had promised herself at the age of fifteen, when Jasper Risenhoover had come to ask for her hand, that she would die an old maid before she'd enter into a marriage for which she had no feelings at all. She had stuck to that vow through the four or five other proposals that had come to her before the bachelor men throughout the community had started talking of her as being too attached to her family, or too busy running all over trying to help everybody, or too much of a bookworm to be a good candidate for a wife.

If *she* moved like a graceful queen the way Sky did, if *she* had been born as beautiful as Sky with that deep red tint in wavy, dark hair and huge, dark brown eyes in a beautiful face, would her life have been different?

Instead, she had straight, light brownish blond hair and ordinary hazel eyes in a plain face that no one would notice twice.

But she wouldn't want a man who chose

her because of looks. She would want a man who would take the trouble to listen to her and talk to her and care what her thoughts and feelings were. A man who would cause her to *feel* something for him.

A quick stopping of her heart. A thrill running up her spine. A shivery excitement dancing over her skin.

As she'd felt when Nokona held her body between his hands.

A little girl brought her a plate of food, then, a smiling, beautiful girl who was the image of Sky.

"Thank you," Abby said.

"*De nada, Señorita*," the child answered pertly and ran back to her siblings. She was about the same age as Hannah.

Voices rose and fell while people were eating. The family drifted together, plates in hand, and settled near Abby, some cross-legged on the stone floor, some on the benches scattered among the plants and flowers.

Nokona didn't say much, but the others talked eagerly, catching up for all the time apart. It struck Abby that they were speaking English, probably because that gave them privacy—the patio was crowded with all the members of the band. Soon, Sky's children and the new arrivals began running and playing together out on the grass, screaming and laughing.

Abby let the children's peaceful sounds

roll over her, willing them to soothe her. She didn't want to hear the conversations, she realized, as she ate sporadically from the bounty on her plate. She already had too many thoughts to deal with, she didn't need any more.

But then, a sharp note of surprise in Windrider's voice caught her attention, compelled her to listen.

"Crow?" he said. "As far south as Santa Fe?"

"Young warriors, restless to fight, out on a dare, wanting to brag," Rafael said. "I didn't see them, but half the town was talking about their prediction of a big battle brewing for this summer."

"Where?"

"Montana. They say that the Crow and Long Yellow Hair's soldiers will wipe out the Sioux and they've told them so. They can't wait."

"Bastards," Nokona growled. "Siding against their own kind with the white intruders."

Sky chuckled.

"The Crow and the Sioux have been enemies forever," she said. "Like our people and the Apache. Would *you* call the Apache *your* own kind?"

Nokona glowered at her.

"They'll miss the fight running around this far from home," Windrider growled.

153

"We are already into Cottonball Month. Soon summer will be here."

"They've already started back north," Rafael said. "They traded with some Apache for a white captive and hit the trail, hurrying to try to trade her to Long Yellow Hair for a job in his band of scouts."

"*Her?*" Jennie said, quickly. "Did you hear a description of the white captive?"

"A young girl," Rafael replied. "Blond and blue-eyed."

Abby's heart stopped in mid-beat.

It had to be Hannah.

The plate that had been on Abby's lap crashed to the floor and shattered.

"Was she plump? And pretty?"

Her voice rang out impatiently over the clatter of the breaking pottery.

She was on her feet, but she couldn't remember getting up.

Rafael stood up.

"I have told all I heard, *Señorita.*"

Then Jennie and Sky were there, one on each side of her, putting their arms around her shoulders and her waist.

"Her sister was taken by the Apache," Jennie said to Rafael. "Days ago, near Fort Sill."

"She's seven years old," Abby said, eagerly, and took a step toward Rafael. "Her name is Hannah."

He came to her, gave her a slight bow.

"Forgive me, *Señorita,* I wish I could tell

155

you more, but I possess no more information."

Abby's blood roared in her ears.

"I don't need more. I know that child is Hannah! How many blue-eyed, blond captive little girls can the Apache have, anyway?"

She reached out to him.

"It's Hannah and I must go after her. Please, will you give me the loan of a fresh horse?"

"*Mi casa es su casa*," he said, in a voice as kind as the look in his eyes, "and you are welcome to any animal of El Rancho del Cielo. However . . ."

"Abby, dear, you mustn't try such a thing," Jennie said, and held on to her more.

Abby tried to jerk away.

"Yes, I must! Of course, I must! She's depending on me! Who else will save her?"

"The Crow left Santa Fe several days ago," Rafael said. "It'd be hard to catch them now."

"I'll ride fast!" Abby cried, looking over her shoulder toward the stables and the horse corral, starting to pull in that direction.

"Please! Which horse? Which one can I have?"

Her heart was beating frantically, trying to claw its way out of her chest.

And Rafael was no longer answering her.

156

She whirled on her heel away from him, arms flailing, searching for some other help with both hands.

Sky caught them. Abby tried to pull away, but Sky soothed her with her voice.

"You're a sensible person, Abby, I know that," she said, in quiet, encouraging tones. "And you're an experienced rider, having come from Fort Sill all the way here. Think about it. You know that night is no time to take an unknown trail."

Something in Abby's practical mind snapped back to life. She stared at Sky.

"That's true," she said. "But in the morning, at first light, I'm going."

Sky squeezed her hands.

"When the right time comes, if you must go, I'll help you in any way I can."

She meant that. And she could be trusted.

Somehow, Abby knew without a doubt that was true. A great relief washed over her.

"Come, now," Jennie said, putting her arm around Abby once more. "Let's find some rest for you. Won't it be nice—and strange—to sleep in a real bed?"

Abby let her shoulders sag into the embrace, let Jennie and Sky lead her into the dim, cool house and through it to a sweet-smelling room with the breeze blowing through it, let them put her into a hot bath and let a maid wash her hair.

157

"I'll find Hannah soon," she told them, while her muscles and her nerves, her very bones began to give way to the wonderful comfort.

"I'll catch up with them before they get to Montana," she murmured, while she sat on the side of the huge bed and drank the tea another maid brought her.

She gazed drowsily into the low fire in the small, cone-shaped corner hearth.

"I'll save her before anything bad happens to her," she confided.

Then someone took away the cup and saucer. Abby fell back into the softness of the bed.

Blazing sunlight woke her.

A desperate urgency pounded through her body, pulled her up to a sitting position before her eyes had snapped open.

Then she knew what it was.

Hannah. She must follow and find her.

She threw back the covers and set her feet on the floor.

I'll save her before anything bad happens to her.

The window curtains mocked her, rising and falling in the billowing breeze.

I'll catch up with them before they get to Montana.

Outside the tall, casement windows, the greening land stretched on and on. All she could see was, no doubt, Sky's ranch. And beyond that, purple mountains rose against the sky and the whole West waited.

I'll find Hannah soon.

Had she really said all those things and believed them? Had she truly thought she could ride off alone and find the child?

Last night she'd been out of her mind.

She'd have to have help. Someone who could track the Crow. They were days ahead, so she'd need lots of provisions and an extra horse, too.

Money. She'd go to Santa Fe, draw money through the bank, and hire whomever Sky recommended. Sky would help her find a good guide fast.

Abby jumped from the bed and reached for her clothes before she remembered that the maids had taken them away to be washed. Across the heavily carved wooden chair lay a yellow Spanish-style skirt and blouse, serape-striped in blues and greens, as if they'd soaked up the sunshine pouring across them and the earth and the sky besides.

She jerked them on and the leather-thonged sandals waiting on the floor.

The neckline of the blouse fell shockingly low across the swell of her breasts. She tightened the drawstring as much as she could before she ran from the room. Soon her own things would be dry, in this sunshine and wind.

The corridors of the huge house with

their heavy, arched oak doors seemed a maze at first, but as she ran, the sandals slapping rhythmically against the square-tiled floor, she listened for voices and, at last, reached wide double doors. They stood open onto the patio where they all had been welcomed the night before. She ran outside.

The sun glared at her, almost blinded her. Even so, she could see that today, no one was there.

Then she realized. The sun was high, at the peak of the sky.

Oh, dear Lord, she'd already wasted half a day!

She whirled to go back inside.

"Abby!"

It was Sky's voice.

Abby shaded her eyes with her hand and looked toward it.

There, on the east side of the wide yard, in the spotty shade of a grove of budding trees, were Jennie and Sky. Not far from them on the lawn, a dozen or more children played some kind of ball game, screaming and laughing. Those were the voices that had led her out of the house.

Abby picked up the full, tiered skirt in both hands and ran across the flagstones onto the grass.

"Good morning!" Sky called. "Did anyone get breakfast for you?"

"I'm not hungry," Abby called back as she neared them.

They seemed to be working over several piles of equipment, some parfleches, some blankets.

"Thanks for taking care of me last night," Abby said, as she reached the shade and leaned against one of the trees to get her breath. "I think I was out of my mind."

"Everybody is at one time or another," Jennie said, lightly.

"When I woke up this morning I realized that I'll need help to go after Hannah."

"Thank goodness you know that!"

Abby looked at Sky.

"So, Sky, I was wondering . . ."

But Sky had turned to her mother and she spoke at the same time as Abby.

"Will he wait for us to mend this?" she asked, holding up a bridle with a broken strap.

"You know he won't," Jennie said. "You know your brother. He's made the decision to go and he'll be on the trail before this sun goes down."

"Nokona?" Abby blurted. "What decision?"

Jennie turned to look at her full face and for the first time Abby could see that she'd been crying. More tears welled in her eyes.

"He's leaving," she said, her voice breaking. "He won't stay with us. Ever since he painted for war when we crossed the river, I've been afraid he'd push on somewhere, searching for a place to try to live in the old way. And he is!"

"He has to do *something* to lessen his grief—which is worse because he couldn't save Tope," Sky said, bluntly, not even hesitating to use the name of the dead. "He'll come back."

From the frustration in her tone, Abby realized she must have already told Jennie that several times.

"He's here *now*," Jennie snapped. "At last, after so much danger and hardship, we're all here together, and safe. I want it to *stay* that way!"

She burst into a hard sobbing, let go of the blanket she was holding, and dropped her face into her hands.

"Mama!"

Sky ran to her, threw her arms around her, the bridle's rein swooshing wildly through the air.

"He'll come back," she repeated, speaking gently this time, but with an iron edge of sureness in her tone.

Jennie lifted her face.

"Have you seen it?"

"Yes," Sky said, and Jennie's eyes lit with hope. "I dreamed it. Nokona will come back."

A sudden feeling of aloneness swept through Abby.

"Where is he going?"

Sky smiled at her, spoke to her over Jennie's tousled head.

"To the big battle in Montana that the Crow predicted," she said, with a shrug, laughing a little. "Can you believe it? Even though he despises their tribe for scouting for the white army, he believes their prophecies enough to ride for two whole moons or more!"

Abby stared at her.

"Where is he now?"

"Out by the corral, picking his horses," Sky said. "Rafael told him to take the best."

Abby's heart was leaping up into her throat.

Nokona was going to Montana! No doubt along the same trail as the Crow who had Hannah!

"That is the most fortuitous news I have ever had," she blurted. "Thank you, Sky."

She turned and ran for the horse corral.

But before she reached it, she stopped in the shadow of the stables. Her hand reached out to steady her, palm flat against the rough adobe wall.

Nokona was there, yes, leaning on the heavy plank fence, but he was deep in conversation with Rafael.

The sight of them struck her like a blow.

Both tall, both dark-haired, both muscular, both handsome as sin.

Different as sunshine and rain.

Rafael wore finely made clothes, cut to

163

fit his body. The hard-woven, tan fabric of his shirt shone like satin in the sun. His oiled leather chaps gleamed in the sun, like leather armor.

Nokona's skin had no protection, and the way he stood, hipshot and arrogant, proclaimed he needed none. The paint and the feathers had vanished on this beautiful morning, but he still looked ready for war.

In his breechclout, with his long hair flowing loose except for one thick braid swinging from the crown of his head, standing next to his civilized brother-in-law, he was more savage, more fierce, than a panther or a wolf.

Cold fingers of trepidation squeezed her heart.

He would laugh at her as he always did.

He would say she was not strong enough, not tough enough, to keep up with him.

With an enormous effort of will, she drew on the practical side of her nature. Didn't it always overcome her deep shyness?

And wasn't her sensible side always right?

Of *course* Nokona would take her north with him. Why wouldn't he?

He knew now that she could travel and keep up with anyone on hardly any food at all, that she asked for no quarter.

She squeezed her hands into determined

fists. He knew that she could eat snake now and build fires.

He would take her with him.

Finally, a vaquero leading another saddled horse rode up to them. Rafael slapped Nokona on the shoulder, they hugged good-bye, then Rafael mounted and rode away with his cowboy.

Abby's heart rocked in her chest. She stepped out and walked toward him, then began to run.

He ignored her.

He folded his arms along the top of the fence and leaned on it, fixed his eyes on the horses milling around inside the corral.

But he knew she was there.

"Nokona?"

He kept watching the horses.

Abby stood beside him, trying to slow down her heartbeat. Suddenly, he seemed huge. And seething with raw power.

The muscles in his arms bulged tight, another jumped along his jaw.

"Jennie and Sky tell me that you're going north," she said, to his profile.

His incredibly good-looking profile.

She raised her voice over the sound of the wind.

"I want to go with you."

He shot her a slanting, downward glance.

"You cannot mean that."

"You heard what Rafael said last night!"

she cried. "The Crow have Hannah and they're taking her north. I have to go after her!"

He frowned and turned to the horses again.

"Rafael also told you that they left Santa Fe many suns ago," he said, in a tone he would use with an unreasonable child. "There are many trails they could take, or they could take none. You cannot follow them."

"But *you* can."

"I have my own battle to fight and I must ride fast to get there. In two moons, summer season will be with us."

He sounded so final that her heart dropped.

He didn't look at her again.

The wind picked up from the west, brought a whirling storm of dust dancing across the ground.

"You hate the Crow," she said. "For siding with the whites. Why not take their new captive away from them?"

"I intend to take their rotten *scalps*," he said, and the hard line of his jaw changed into a ridge of granite.

"Traveling with me and finding Hannah won't slow you down," she said, quickly. "Two of us can make camp faster than one—you know I can build fires, I can cook what you kill, and I'll eat anything. I promise, Nokona, I'll help you get to the battle."

The words echoed strangely in her ears. Had she really said that?

She, Abigail Briscoe, who didn't believe in killing, would help him get to a battle where he was sure to kill someone. In addition to the one he had already killed.

Yes. And she'd say, and do, worse than that if it would take her to Hannah.

"I know you have a heart, Nokona," she challenged, her heart rising into her mouth for fear this tactic wouldn't work on him, either. "I saw your grief when we crossed the river. And I know you feel guilty because you couldn't save your wife."

His face didn't change, but he tilted his head and swept her with his eyes.

She had a lot of nerve, they said, snapping black fire at her. A lot of nerve even to mention his wife.

Her insides went stiff and scared, but she held his gaze.

"I feel the same way about Hannah," she said, fighting to keep her voice steady. "She was screaming for me to save her when they carried her off into the dark. I can still hear her."

They looked at each other.

The wind lifted the tail of the full, yellow skirt she wore and whipped it against his bare leg.

He looked so implacably fierce she could hardly bear it.

But she made her mouth move.

"Hannah could still be saved, Nokona," she said. "And that would help wipe out both of our regrets."

The horses shifted inside the corral, lifted their heads, and whinnied into the wind.

"You'll have to give her up," he said. "Let her go."

Abby's control disintegrated into a thousand pieces.

To her own consternation, she flew at him with both fists, striking out blindly, pounding at him. His shoulder, his side, his arm felt like a wall of rock to her fists, her blows bounced off them and back into her face, but she kept on hitting and hitting, again and again.

"I won't!" she cried. "Don't say that! I *won't* let her go! If you weren't such a savage, you'd help me—it's the only humane thing to do!"

He set both feet on the ground and turned toward her, her slaps and punches landed on his other shoulder, on his broad chest, on the hard ridge of his collarbone.

To no avail whatsoever.

He caught her wrists in a remorseless grip.

His fingers were so strong they could squeeze her to death. They forced their shapes deep into her skin.

Twisting, pulling back, she shouted into his face.

"Look what you've made me do! You've

made me resort to violence and I don't *believe* in violence! You . . ."

She heard herself and clamped her lips shut.

She would burst, explode, come apart in a million pieces and fly all over New Mexico.

"Savage or not, I *am* helping you," he growled. "The riding we've done since you've been with us is nothing compared to what this trail will be. You couldn't survive it."

"Who are you to tell me what I can survive? I can't survive doing nothing!"

"Then do something. Have some common sense. Go east instead of north. It's too late to help your sister."

He loomed over her like a statue made of wood, not moving one muscle to keep her where she stood, not blinking, not even breathing.

Like the faraway mountains that rose purple and gold behind him.

The sky above them was blue, dark blue, every shade of blue and gray, with white there, too, in layers. Somewhere, inside them, they, too, hid a storm.

"Go back to your home, Abby. There's nothing else you can do."

He was so close she could catch the cedary scent of his breath. His flesh felt warm against her arms.

He wasn't a statue.

Her soul dropped like a stone into a river.

He was real and he was an Indian and he knew this wild country and he believed that for Hannah there was no hope.

She wanted to let go and slide down, into the ground, let the earth take her. She couldn't stand up anymore, her legs wouldn't hold her.

His fingers loosed their grip, his hands shifted on her arms.

For one strange, breathless instant, she thought he was going to put his arms around her.

She needed to be held.

The realization struck her like a cut tree falling.

Her legs ached to take a step toward him.

If she and Nokona shared their sorrow, maybe that would ease its torment.

He set her arms free.

She slammed them down against her sides.

What, in the name of Heaven, was she thinking?

She must not walk into his arms. But she must go with him. She *must*.

"I can't go East," she said, through lips so stiff she could barely form the words, "without knowing I did everything I could."

She stopped and tried to swallow.

"I have enough sense to know that I can't do it alone, and time is of the essence. It would take several days to hire a guide."

170

He didn't reply.

"Please, Nokona," she choked, "will you take me with you?"

"No."

He turned away from her, looked at the horses again, in a way that showed her he wouldn't talk about it anymore.

But still she stood there.

The sunlight, slanting east against the shifting, blue-black layered clouds gathering in the west, traced every motion of the running, kicking horses. Some of them were bucking now.

And the sun outlined Nokona in gold. The rising wind whipped his hair around his face.

Her blood cried in her veins.

The horses whinnied and pounded the hard ground with their hooves; the wind whispered, then shouted, then died again for an instant; the blossoms blowing from the orchard hit against her skirts and bits of wood and dust pinged against the logs of the fence.

Nokona's jaw was hard and set, but the muscles across his wide shoulders and in his powerful arms flexed to rise and fall. Still he didn't speak.

He had told her no and he meant to leave it at that.

10

Nokona stared into the campfire's flickering flames and then lifted his face to the magnificently purple and red sunset sky. Sunset and sunrise were the times when the spirit world was closest to this one, and it was time he finally faced the truth that had been riding with him all day. His spirit was not in balance.

If it had been, he wouldn't even have built a fire—he'd have made a cold camp after riding long into the dark. He should do that every night to reach the north country in time for the great battle.

And to lose whoever was following him.

His mind knew that, intended to do it, but his heart kept pulling back.

He reached out, touched the stiff, painted parfleche on top of the stack beside his saddle. Tope's wardrobe bag. It held her best dress and moccasins.

But grief was not the cause of his uneasiness. She was gone—he had accepted that when they crossed the Gallinas. She was gone forever.

Bringing her things along, however, made him feel that something of her came with him to the north to fight the white intruders, to find a place to live in the old ways after the battle. Because this time, the red warriors would win. That, he knew in his bones.

He pulled the bag to him, stretched out, and laid his head on it.

But still he had no peace.

He couldn't have saved Tope at the moment of her death, he knew that now. But he could have ignored her pleas to keep roaming, he could have led the band to Sky and Rafael's *rancho before* instead of after the Big Cold. And if he hadn't given in to her request to stop at the creek that day, she would still be alive.

It was hard for him to believe, to this day, that he had not heeded his instincts. He had felt a warning when he'd ridden into those trees, probably one sent by his bear medicine spirit, and he had foolishly, stupidly, inexplicably ignored it.

By the Sun Father! And him an old man who had thirty-eight winters! No wonder disaster had struck.

The wind reached in and stirred its fingers into his fire. It flared, then almost died out.

Nokona sat up and fed it another stick.

He felt a wry smile twist his lips. If he had brought Abby with him as she'd begged him to do, he could lie back and watch *her* build the fire.

That was the reason for his unrest on this trail!

The woman called Abby.

His breath stopped.

No. Surely that could not be.

But it was.

Not because he hadn't brought her along—that, too, would have been foolish and stupid. No, it was because ...

He fed yet another stick to the fire and tried to think of the reason.

It was because he felt sorry for her, for her helplessness to do anything about her captured sister—he knew how she felt— even the smallest effort would make her feel better.

This journey would be an enormous effort, though, too big for her. She couldn't hold up to riding this trail for two moons or more. He could still feel how delicate her soft skin and her slender bones had felt beneath his fingers. She was accustomed to a soft life inside of houses.

But she had proved stronger than he ever would have dreamed on the trail to New Mexico.

He pushed the thought away. He didn't

want the responsibility of her, didn't want her slowing him down.

He hit his fist on the ground.

How could he have thought for one heartbeat of taking her where she wanted to go when Tope had died with him dragging her where she *didn't* want to go?

Suddenly, he tried, but he couldn't remember Tope's face.

All he could see in the glow of the fire was Abby's, with her wide, golden eyes desperately pleading. Her wrists had been so vulnerable encircled by his hands.

He leaned to one side, started to stretch out again, reaching for Tope's parfleche.

He had wanted to take Abby in his arms, to ease her pain.

The realization jerked him bolt upright.

That was the reason his harmony was gone.

He wasn't satisfied with giving her anger and the strength it carried the night of the rattlesnake stew. Now he was wanting to ease all her pain.

The woman was a missionary, one of the destroyers of the ways of The People. One of the destroyers that had set him onto this trail alone, away from his band.

Holding her would be the same as holding a stinging scorpion to his breast.

He grabbed his water bag and, with one quick motion, put out the fire. Instead of thinking about Abby he should be thinking about whoever was following him. Somebody was. He'd known it long before he'd stopped for the night.

Tomorrow morning he would stay in camp late to lure him closer, trap him, and make him wish he'd never thought of stalking Nokona.

He gave a great sigh, reached for his blankets, and rolled up in them with his rifle, his knife in his hand.

The only thing he knew for sure was that this enemy had to be somebody new. The old ones were dead at the white men's hands, existing on reservations, or starving on their own lands.

No matter.

He, Nokona, old man, was still fast enough to take anyone foolish enough to try him.

Sky led Kwita, her beloved, favorite mare, toward the wide double doors of the stables just as the sun dropped out of sight and the far western line of the land snuffed out the last of the light. The new foal whinnied as he trotted alongside, following her as much as the mare.

"Do you need me any more with the little one, *Senora*?"

Felipe had stopped beside the path that led toward the bunkhouse.

"No," Sky said, and reached across the mare's back to take the soft rope he had

177

used to help her turn the baby over while she was handling it as a newborn. "Go ahead, Felipe, and have your supper."

She led the mare and baby inside, then into the newly bedded stall and slipped Kwita's halter off.

"*You*," she crooned, to the foal, running her hands over its face and handling its ears one more time for good measure, "you, little one, will wear one of these *mañana*."

She was letting the foal sniff the worn, braided rawhide halter when she heard Rafael's voice, talking to one of the vaqueros outside by the corral. It pierced her heart.

"I must leave you for a moment, my sweet *mamacita*," she said, to Kwita. "*Mi corazón* has come home!"

The mare whinnied after her as she left the stall and latched it, then turned and ran the length of the wide barn hallway out into the dusky night.

"Rafael!" she cried, and threw herself into his arms.

He folded her tightly against his hard, warm self and kissed the top of her head.

"Your mare must still be waiting for her baby to be born," he teased, "or you would have no time to greet me this way."

She pretended to take great offense.

"*When*," she demanded, pulling back to look up at him, "in birthing and raising

178

dozens of foals and six children, have I ever not had time for you?"

He tightened his arms around her waist and looked down at her from beneath the brim of his dust-covered hat. His eyes shone in the dimness.

Her whole body went weak.

"Not ever," he growled. "And you'd better make sure you keep it that way."

"Of course!" she said, briskly. "Now, enough of this silly sentiment. Come into the stables and help me see to this mare!"

His answer, as she had known it would be, was to tangle his hand into her hair, bring his lips down to hers, and kiss her until every wisp of breath was gone from her body. She floated away from the ground, left the earth, clung to him to save her while his free hand slid down her spine and sent tingling thrills all through her.

She made a little cry, low in her throat, and twined her tongue with his.

At last he broke the kiss and began placing small, quick ones on her nose and her cheeks and her chin.

"You tempt me too much, *Señora*," he said. "We are not in our house, in our bed."

"No one is in the stable," she murmured, flirting with her voice as she reached up to stroke his cheek with her fingertips. "Felipe just went to supper."

"But Ramon and Oscar are here in the corral."

"You haven't changed in all these years!" she said, laughing at him over her shoulder as she turned out of his embrace.

They slipped their arms around each other so they could walk close together.

"The Don Rafael de Montoya, after all our seasons together, is still too reserved and proper to make love in the haystack— only because a few vaqueros are around!"

He arched one black brow and gave her a fierce, mock scowl as they walked into the lantern-lit stables.

"And you," he said, "are wild and shameless as the day we met."

She smiled up at him.

"Yes," she said, "and aren't you glad?"

He had to kiss her again before they could go to the stall that held the mare.

When they were walking again, slowly, looking into each other's eyes, he asked the question he always asked when he came home.

"How are the children?"

"Happy. Gone to become *Nermernuh*. They are all in the camp on the river—my parents will have a full lodge tonight."

He chuckled.

"So. Windrider has had enough of houses."

"That's it," she said. "And the Fire Flower doesn't care where she is as long as her grandchildren are there."

180

Rafael chuckled as he opened the door to Kwita's stall.

He stopped short.

"The foal has come!" he said, and turned to her. "Did you know—"

He interrupted himself. "Of course you did, you little fox! You wanted to surprise me."

The foal lifted its head and pointed its ears at Sky.

Rafael stared at it, stepped away from Sky to move quietly around it, looking at the fine head, straight legs, slender neck, the muscled little rump.

"The best one yet," he said.

"I agree. Far Girl and El Lobo's descendants are even better than they were."

He nodded and gave her a look.

"Like ours."

"Ours had better get my mother's mind off Abby," she said, chuckling. "She's 'shocked and furious' with me for outfitting her and encouraging her to go after Nokona when he had flatly refused to take her."

Rafael laughed. "Did that surprise the *Señora* Fire Flower? Has she forgotten what it's like to live with you?"

"I guess so."

He caught her gaze with his smoldering one.

"*I'm* surprised that you didn't grab the

chance for a new adventure and ride off *with* Abby."

"No, you're not," she said, and her words came out in the same rhythm as the sensual slowing of her blood when he looked at her that way.

"Why not? You almost wouldn't marry me because you thought you couldn't bear to live in only one place."

His voice was as warm and gentle as his hands would be on her skin. Soon.

"And now," he went on, giving her that teasing grin that always made the heat rise in her, "in the ironic way life has of changing a person, you have become a nurturer with many children, many horses, and no desire to go away from your one home."

"My husband the philosopher," she murmured, and moved around the head of the mare to get closer to him so that she could touch his face.

"My wife the meddler," he teased, gently. "Did you ever think that Nokona might simply turn around and bring Abby back to you?"

"He won't," she said, and traced his lips with her fingertip.

"If he does," Rafael said, lifting his own finger in warning, "I cannot send any of my vaqueros into danger to take her north, even though I hate to behave in an ungallant way."

Sky felt a smile form on her lips.

"Rafael. My husband the philosopher *and* the gentleman. Ever concerned about the correct behavior."

She pressed her palm to his cheek.

"Nokona won't bring her back, darling. I know that. I know things, remember?"

"Then you know that I love you," he said.

And there in the clean stall, smelling of fresh hay and warm horses, he wrapped her in his arms.

Abby woke with a ferocious start to the sounds of birds stirring in the trees around her camp. Daylight was coming!

She scrambled up, her blood roaring a warning in her ears. He'd be ahead of her, too far ahead, if she didn't get going!

Shaking from the panic of that thought, still awkward from sleep, she reached for Sky's rifle with one hand and her water bag with the other. This was her chance to catch up with Nokona—dawn wasn't quite here yet and she had stopped within sight of his campfire. It wasn't far.

She hurried back and forth through the mists of the early morning, trying to keep her voice and her hands steady so as not to scare the horses while she pulled up their picket pins and tied them to a tree, began loading them with the supplies she'd left packed. The light was grayly dim, as if the day would be cloudy, and the air felt still, as if waiting for rain.

Rain would wash out Nokona's tracks if she lost sight of him. And she would, if she didn't get to him now, because they were heading into a low line of mountains.

She shivered as she threw the packs onto her extra horse and her bags and blankets onto Ohapia, whom Sky had brought out of the herd for her because Abby knew the horse. But she forced her hands to be steady as she mounted and took the reins.

She would reach him in time. Sky had said she knew that she would. And she would.

But the shaky feeling that had clutched her since the minute she woke grew worse. What would Nokona do or say when she did?

A pounding of hooves and a clattering in the trees that sounded like the attack of a dozen clumsy soldiers jerked Nokona to attention. When whoever was following didn't creep up on his camp at the break of dawn, he had let himself drift off into his thoughts again.

Cursing himself for a careless fool, he hit the ground rolling, holding the rifle to his body as he went, and ended up flat on his stomach, the weapon to his shoulder and his eye.

The day was cloudy and gray, mist

floated in the air. Someone could be on top of him before he saw them—if they weren't making such a racket. *Who* could this possibly be?

A shadowy form caught the corner of his eye, to his left, nowhere near the sound of the hoofbeats.

He swung the muzzle toward it, then froze.

A bear was rising from the underbrush, looming higher and higher as it unfolded its huge frame. It hung there in the mist, against one of the scattered pines, facing Nokona, looking at him, appearing to be almost as tall as the trees.

Nokona's breath stopped.

Grandfather!

His medicine spirit. The hair at the back of his neck rose. Had the Great Spirit sent The One Who Owned the Cave with a message because he knew Nokona was out of harmony, was searching for balance?

There was no chance to know.

The noise of running horses came closer, pulled his gun and his gaze in the other direction.

Abby, her hair catching bits of light here and there in the gray morning, came crashing through the trees into his little clearing at an uncontrolled gallop, the packhorse behind her running right on Ohapia's heels. A strange feeling flashed through him.

Had his thoughts brought *her* to him, too, as well as the bear?

Her wide, frightened eyes found him, fixed on him.

"Whoa!" she cried. "Whoa, Ohapia!"

The bay mare stopped so fast Abby's body whipped forward and then back, but, to his surprise, she didn't fall off.

She clung to the horn of the big Spanish saddle with both hands, gasping a little, then threw one leg over and slid down to the ground in a swirling confusion of blue and white skirts.

"It's me, Abby!" she called. "Nokona, put down the gun and listen to me . . ."

She took a step toward him.

A step that took her out from behind the poor protection of her horse and put her between Nokona and the bear.

His bear medicine spirit.

But would Grandfather attack Abby?

Nokona's blood chilled. He couldn't, even if the shot was a clear one, ever fire at the bear.

Yet he'd have to protect Abby.

A huge rage washed through him. She shouldn't have come here. By the Sun Father, did the woman have no sense at all?

"Nokona!" she said, still coming toward him.

"Stop right where you are," he growled, through a throat gone so dry he hardly could speak. "Don't take another step."

A hurt look passed over her face, brought a rush of blood up to pinken her skin.

"You don't have to hold me off with a gun," she said, and the hurt filled her voice, too. "Sky said that if I was determined enough to follow you and skillful enough to find you that you'd take me . . ."

"Do not move."

Her anger began to rise. He saw it flash in her eyes and flow through her limbs to set her stance, feet set apart, hands on her hips.

"If you won't help me, then so be it!" she snapped. "Sky gave me provisions and a rifle. I can go north by myself and I can find Hannah without your help!"

She half turned toward her horses.

"Don't move, Abby," he said, and this time he put a warning into his tone that made her go still as the earth beneath his belly.

All the color drained from her face.

"I'm *going*, don't you understand?" she said, spitting the words at him from between clenched teeth. "You make no sense, telling me not to come any closer, then telling me not to go!"

"That's right," he said. "Don't come to me and don't go back to your horses. Be still."

"Don't be ridiculous!" she snapped back

at him, and spun on her heel in a great swirling of her skirts.

She saw the bear.

Her feet glued themselves to the earth.

Good. If she, and Nokona, both remained completely still until Grandfather decided what he wanted to do, maybe there would be no harm done.

It was good that Abby had frozen in the face of danger.

But the packhorse snorted and pushed backward into the brush while Ohapia, trained by Fire Flower never to move when her rein trailed on the ground, stood trembling, starting a pitiful, terrified crying deep in her throat.

Abby's face went pale.

"Oh!" she said, in a voice strained to breaking by her fear. "He might hurt my horses."

She watched for a long moment.

Grandfather did not move.

Abby made a quick, lunging thrust sideways, as if trying to reach Ohapia without moving her feet, then she was running, hands reaching.

Grabbing for the rifle in the scabbard of her Spanish saddle.

Nokona was up and running before he could think, sliding his rifle into a one-handed carry at his hip, reaching for Abby with his free hand.

"Sky showed me how to shoot!" she

cried, as he clutched her shoulder and spun her around.

She threw the rifle to her shoulder!

His heart stopped.

"Don't shoot," he growled in her ear as he jerked her back against him. "Don't talk and don't move!"

She struggled to face the bear, to level the gun.

Nokona shifted his arm and clamped it against her hard, held it immobile, muzzle to the sky. She was trembling, all the way to the bone.

Grandfather swung his head toward them.

His small, piercing eyes rested on them, looked at them and through them. He stared, never once shifting his glance.

Abby's raw, shaky breaths stopped completely.

Nokona sent his spirit out to speak to the bear.

Give me your message, now, Medicine Spirit, One Who Owns the Chin. Give me the message and go, now. Please.

Grandfather looked at them. From Nokona's face to Abby's and back again.

It was spring! Oh, Great Spirit, help them. Spring season had come. All bears were completely unpredictable in the spring.

Nokona's palm tightened around the

rifle, broke out in sweat, threatened to get so slick he couldn't hold on.

Grandfather lifted his shaggy arms high into the air and for one spellbound moment Nokona thought he would lunge at them.

Then, with no warning and seemingly with no movement at all, he dropped to all fours.

His shaggy back showed above the low brush like a drifting shadow. Once, and then again.

No more.

Grandfather was gone.

Nokona stared at the place where he had last been.

One of Abby's hands clutched his wrist so fiercely that her fingernails cut into his flesh.

Her small, rounded hips pressed hard against him through the folds of her clothes.

"I . . . is he gone?" she whispered.

Nokona stood still and listened to the sounds on the wind, the ones that did not come from the frightened horses beginning to settle down.

"Yes."

Grandfather was gone. And he hadn't given Nokona a message at all.

Or had he?

He looked down at the top of Abby's shining head, smelled the soft fragrance of her skin, sensed the relief beginning to spread through her body.

Had Grandfather brought this woman to him?

Something in his spirit was beginning to think so.

He knew it.

He was to take her north, as she had begged him to do.

A hot wave of fury followed the thought.

Damn it! He didn't want the responsibility, didn't want to be slowed down, didn't want the ... temptation.

He opened his mouth to say that she would have to go back to Sky's.

But he couldn't.

He had felt the danger at that creek all those days ago and had not heeded that feeling. Because of that, Tope had died.

But why would Grandfather bring him this woman?

His heart filled with black frustration.

Why?

11

Nokona jerked his arms from around her so fast that she almost fell. Sky's rifle caught her, its stock jamming hard against the ground, its barrel stiff in the palm of her hand.

It kept her upright, but she had the sensation that she was crumpling into a heap on the ground, anyway.

Because Nokona had turned loose of her.

She could still feel his naked thighs against her buttocks, through her dress and petticoats. She could still feel the steely safety of his arms.

A mad longing for haven, *more* blessed refuge, *permanent* protection, swept through her. Her whole body went weak.

"Nokona . . ."

He had leapt between her and the bear to save her.

She looked in the direction the creature

had taken. Nothing moved in the sparse brush.

Pray God, it was truly gone.

Still helpless, she turned toward Nokona. "Do you think it might come back?"

She hated the way her voice trembled, but her feelings were still running wild.

"Not now."

He was settling her horses, making sure they didn't bolt. Would he set her back onto Ohapia the way he had done on Chester that day, or would he let her stay?

He reached up to caress Ohapia's twitching ears, his arms and hands slow and calm in spite of the bunched, tense muscles rippling across his shoulders. He was so strong.

He had held her so tight!

A great wave of warmth washed over her.

Truly, he *hadn't* been trying to drive her away in the first place—she had misunderstood. He'd been holding the gun because he'd already seen the bear.

Nokona *did* care about her as a person. He would let her stay, she knew it.

He went to see to his own restless horses, briefly, then he turned back toward Abby. But he didn't even glance at her. He strode, fast, to the rock circle filled with the gray ashes of last night's fire, sat down, crossed his legs, and began to build a new one from leftover kindling and wood.

Abby walked slowly, on legs that still trembled, to a place opposite him and let herself sink to the ground.

"Thank you, Nokona. I've never been so scared of anything in all my life."

She drew her rifle across her lap.

"I'm grateful to Sky for giving me this gun and showing me how to use it," she said.

He didn't answer. He didn't even look up.

"Now I'm grateful to you for not letting me fire it. If I'd only wounded the bear, it might've killed us both."

He answered with a quick, inscrutable look.

Then he picked up small sticks from one side of the firepit, laid them on, and sparked a fire that caught immediately. But even when tiny flames had flared up, he didn't look at her.

Reaching to the belt of his breechclout, he untied a skin bag, pushed open the drawstring with two fingers and, one by one, drew out four long, curving objects. He laid them carefully on the ground on four sides of the fire.

Abby didn't dare ask what they were. The way he sat, the deliberate way he made every movement, the distant look on his face clearly proclaimed that he had removed himself from her.

He bent and blew on the fire, made the

flames leap higher, then folded his arms above his crossed legs and stared fixedly into the fire. For what seemed to be a long time.

Then, with a suddenness that shocked her, he raised his eyes and looked into hers. Without looking down, he began touching the curved things, slowly, one at a time.

"These are the claws of our Grandfather," he said, without looking down. "One Who Owns the Den. Chief's Son. Four-Legged Human. You saw him and called him *bear*."

Claws. Those were claws. Of a bear.

The image of the huge one raising his paws up and up into the sky, loomed in her memory.

It could have ripped her open with one fast swipe of a paw. If Nokona hadn't saved her.

Nokona's sharp, hot eyes found hers again, nailed her to the ground where she sat. He didn't seem very glad that he had saved her. He seemed extremely annoyed with her behavior in some way.

"We give Grandfather special names," he said, "because he likes to be called by them. He is closer to human than any other animal. He is a guardian, a healer, a guide. He is my medicine spirit."

Abby stared back into the darkness of his gaze, trying to see into his mind. All the warmth of his saving her drained away. He sounded so cold. Angry.

But why?

"He . . . wouldn't have harmed you? Are you saying that I shouldn't have pulled out the gun?"

A tiny kernel of ice began to form in the pit of her stomach.

Had he jumped between them to protect the *bear*?

"He isn't *my* medicine spirit," she said, pointedly, in a tone of cool reason. "He might have harmed *me*."

Nokona shrugged, a rise and fall of his broad, powerful shoulders that implied he didn't care whether she would have been harmed or not. He spoke in a voice as hot and sharp as those daggers in his eyes.

"I'm saying that I will take you north."

Her heart gave a great, mad leap.

Thank God!

Nokona reached out and fed the fire another stick of wood.

Then he touched the claws again.

"I must go north to find a place saved for the old ways as my wife begged me to do," he said, harshly. "You think you must go north to find your sister."

A jolt of anger shook her.

"Oh! So a place for the old ways is important, but my sister is only a silly whim?"

197

She leaned forward and glared into his face.

His eyes had gone hard as black glass.

"The One Who Owns the Chin came to me this morning at the same time you came crashing through the trees," he said, and a muscle worked along the chiseled bone of his jaw as if he would like to bite those words in two and spit them out.

Abby waited.

"Why do you tell me that?" she finally said, sharply. "I was here. I know it."

"I tell you so that you'll know why I have changed my mind," he said, shortly. "It is not because you followed me to try to force your will on me that I've decided to take you north."

A big drop of rain, heavy as her heart, fell with a hiss onto the fire. Another one followed.

"I resent that," she told him, her voice low and hard with her feelings. "Any reasonable person, any *humane* person, would *expect* us to travel together."

"In your world, perhaps. You should go back to it."

"You've told me that before. I won't."

"Then get ready to ride," he said. "I won't let you slow me down."

Abby's fists clenched, angry words leapt onto her tongue.

Go on. Get away from me. I'll go north alone.

She wanted to say those words so much,

she *ached* to fling them into his face, but her jaw clenched to hold them in.

Because the bear rose in her memory like a mountain of living flesh and blood standing silent out there—ahead of her now, maybe waiting for her, claws uplifted into the air.

Waiting, just as the Apache had been waiting in the trail.

Even if there had been no real refuge in Nokona's embrace, even if he had been protecting the bear from her rifle, he had stood between them. That was better than no one at all.

And the wilderness held many more dangers besides Grandfather Bear.

"You may have muddled Grandfather's message to me by pulling the gun," Nokona said. "And you did it after I had told you not to move. On the north trail, you will do exactly as I tell you at all times. *Always.*"

"I will do my part," she retorted. "Always. I will not be your puppet and I will not be obligated to you."

"You already are. You're too weak, too soft, too ill equipped to make this journey. If you get to Montana, you'll owe me your life."

Cold fury at his arrogance made the back of her neck burn.

"Your *sister* has equipped me, has taught

me what she could in the time we had! I owe her, not you!"

"You will do exactly as I tell you, always," he repeated, as levelly as if she had not spoken. "Start with changing into other clothes—you have some, if Sky has equipped you so well. Those garments you wear are the choice of a madwoman—you need clothes that will breathe in this humid day."

Abby's back snapped ramrod straight.

"*You* choose to go naked, go ahead. *I* choose to wear this dress, which is all I have of my past life. I will wear it until I find my sister."

"A foolish woman's thought."

"No more foolish than riding hundreds of miles searching for a place to preserve the old ways . . . which are already dead."

Anger slashed across his face.

"Not dead yet," he said, his tone a dark fury. "I go north also to fight in the last great battle. Against your kind."

A chill of fear chased up her spine.

For an instant, although he never moved, she thought he would stand up and strike her.

But he stayed still.

"It's a white world now, Nokona. There's nothing you can do except learn how to live in it."

"Don't try to flay my ears with your missionary talk. Remember you go with me only because of *my* religion—the sign from my medicine spirit."

He touched the bear claws again.

Reverently.

Rain, coming harder now, ran off his shoulders and down over his powerful arms, making his naked, copper skin gleam in the mist.

Abby couldn't take her eyes off him, yet she itched to get up and run.

Dear God in Heaven, what had she done?

The bear was his medicine spirit.

She had ridden miles out into the wilderness to be alone with a naked savage steeped in a heathen religion. He cared no more for her than for one of the horses. Not as much. The horse was more useful to him.

What might he do to her? Any idea he was a refuge for her was nothing but a desperate delusion.

But she had to go with him. He was her only hope to find Hannah.

Nokona picked the claws up and, slowly, rhythmically, began putting them back into the leather pouch.

The rain slapped Abby in the face with a half dozen, huge, pelting drops, then the heavy skies opened up and it began to pour.

For the next few days, they rode so fast and hard and so far apart, in spirit and mind, that when they did stop their only words concerned what had to be done to make the brief camp.

Except for that first night, when Abby sat for a long time before sleeping, shaking from exhaustion, drying her dress by the fire.

Nokona's low voice came floating to her from out of the dark.

"Good thing Sky gave you that blanket."

The sardonic tone was so . . . intimate, somehow, that she let go of her dress with one hand and clutched the blanket tighter across her breasts.

"Otherwise," he drawled, "you'd have the choice of wearing that dress until it dried or going *naked* like me."

Abby shot words back at him like defensive bullets.

"Sky gave me a skirt and blouse."

"Buckskin?"

"Yes."

"But you are too stubborn to wear them, even when they're more suited for the trail. Too . . . civilized, perhaps?"

"What I wear or don't wear is none of your concern!"

Abby bit her lip to keep from saying more. Her raw nerves tightened. Ignore him. She had to ignore him. Otherwise, she'd be too angry to sleep. Already, she was almost too tired.

He was silent for the space of two heartbeats. Then he spoke in that same, sarcastic way.

"You haven't told me how you got away from my mother," he said. "She must've been too wrapped up in her grandchildren to notice your leaving. Did you tell her good-bye?"

The uncanny insight sent a shiver over Abby. And a fierce resentment.

"I'm supposed to do everything you tell me, *always*, and then share my deepest feelings, too? You don't demand much of your traveling companions, do you, Nokona?"

Then, before she could stop, she muttered the answer to his question, to herself, very low.

"Sky's going to explain to Jennie for me."

He heard her.

"Sky's a bad influence," he said. "She's never missed a chance to get into trouble herself and now she's helping you do the same."

"I'm not in trouble!" she cried, and dropped her dress to whirl around and glare out into the darkness toward the sound of his voice, holding the blanket to her skin like armor.

"Except for being trapped on the trail with a nosy, arrogant, *bossy* person who has nothing better to do than to *carp* at me!"

Her fingers dug into the fine weave of the blanket as she waited for his contemptuous answer.

To her great shock, he burst into laughter.

The rich, melodious sound of it rolled to her and past her and out into the night.

She grabbed up her dress again and held it so close to the flames that it began to scorch and she had to snatch it away again.

Nothing, nothing in the whole crazy world was the least bit fair!

Nokona could guess every thought she had before she even thought it, but she'd never understand him if she rode with him for a million years.

During the next few days, though, she did understand that he was utterly determined not to miss the great battle. He pushed them mercilessly, stopping only for a few moments at a time, riding into the dark every night.

At first, she had protested.

"I don't like to ride in the dark. What if the bear's waiting out there somewhere?"

"If you're scared, turn around and go back to the *rancho*," he had snapped. "Or better yet, back to your home."

She clamped her lips shut and never mentioned her great fear again.

After they stopped each night, Abby forced her exhausted limbs to keep moving until she had meticulously taken care of her own horses and performed her share of the chores. Which usually wasn't much—more often than not, they made a cold camp, mainly only to sleep for a few hours. They lived on jerky and tortillas, eaten in the saddle.

Spring burst over the land in a riot of green grass and newly leaved trees, plus the bright blues, pinks, and purples of wildflowers, but Abby was able to see all of that only intermittently. Most of the time, she watched Nokona's broad-hipped little packhorse moving in front of her or the rump of his yellow dun with the sweeping black tail.

She tried to keep her eyes off Nokona himself. When she let them rest on his broad, bare shoulders gleaming in the sun or on the glossy blackness of his long, swinging hair, her treacherous body remembered how she had felt when he'd held her tight against his own long, hard one.

The warmth of his lips against her ear.

The feeling of refuge from the bear.

She didn't want to remember any of that, nor the way the thrills had run through her when he'd picked her up that time in the middle of the horse herd. She *wouldn't* remember it.

She'd keep her mind on Hannah.

The sun was straight overhead and blistering, in spite of the high thunderheads piling up in the sky to the west, when Nokona led them down into a narrow valley where the wavering wind couldn't reach. The air was so sultry it sucked away Abby's breath.

Her stomach was an empty hole. Her bottom, her legs were worn completely out from sitting in this saddle.

"Nokona . . ."

She clamped her mouth shut.

On this whole trip, she hadn't complained once, except about riding after dark, and she wasn't going to do so now. She wouldn't give him that satisfaction.

She *was* tough enough to ride this trail with him, and when they got to the end of it, she intended to make him admit it.

A quick movement in the brush, caught in the corner of her eye, suddenly made her gasp.

"The bear?" she called.

That fear rode with her all the time.

"Nokona, I just saw something move over there!"

"Will you *stop* worrying about bears?" he called back, without turning around.

And this wasn't a bear. The brown flash in the green gave a high, graceful leap, showed a glimpse of white.

It held her gaze as a streaking star would in the night, moving so fast, so effortlessly, that it made her cry out.

Nokona turned in his saddle to call back to her.

"Antelope!"

He circled the buckskin on the narrow trail and in one long, graceful motion, threw the leadrope of his packhorse at her.

"Hold this horse."

He pulled his rifle from the beaded scabbard beneath his leg and thundered away.

A whole herd of antelope burst out of the tangled copse and bounded ahead of him, their lithe bodies leaping high and long over the still underbrush. Then Abby lost sight of them all while she struggled to get hold of the rope and ride ahead of both the extra horses, jostling for position on the trail behind her.

Just after she got them strung out to follow, the sharp crack of a shot tore the air, echoed down the valley. The horses jumped, but she held on to them.

Her heart twisted.

That antelope had been so beautiful!

But probably Nokona hadn't been close enough to get that first one she'd seen.

All of them had been beautiful, though.

She'd rather keep eating jerky, she thought, as she lifted the horses into a long trot and rode toward the sound of the shot.

She saw his buckskin first, standing in the middle of the trail, sides heaving a little from the run.

Then Nokona's voice came to her, floating out of the bushes near the horse, at the side of the trail.

He was speaking Comanche, in formal

207

tones that rose and fell in a vibrating rhythm.

She rounded the bend and rode up on him. Ohapia stopped; so did the extra horses, with their noses at her hip.

Nokona was standing over a fallen antelope, looking down at it. He was speaking to *it*!

He finished, glanced up, and saw her.

As if he'd been waiting for her, he dropped in an easy motion to his haunches, took the antelope by its small horns, and turned the head toward Abby. Then he stood and looked down at it again and began to speak, this time in English.

"My brother, forgive me," he said, and she knew he was repeating what he had just said in Comanche, because the tone and the rhythm were the same. "My name is Nokona and I speak for me and my companion, Abigail."

A frisson of a thrill ran up and down her arms.

Strange. This seemed so very strange.

But at the same time, it seemed right. Indisputably right.

"Both of us will need fresh meat and more food before our long journey is done. We take your life for that purpose and we thank you."

Transfixed, Abby stared at him, then looked again at the antelope at his feet.

Nokona's words repeated in her mind.

Her heart felt warm. He had spoken for her, too.

He had called her his companion, had treated her as his equal. And he had repeated the Comanche ritual in English so she could be a part of the blessing.

She felt his eyes on her then.

"Thank you," she said.

She stopped and swallowed hard, for her voice was filling with tears.

"Never again," she said, "even in anger, not even silently in my mind, will I call you a savage."

12

The soft words opened a great hole inside Nokona, moved into it, and settled there.

He looked at her.

Her face flushed pink from the humid heat. And from her feelings.

The shine in her amber-colored eyes held his gaze still.

She truly felt the blessing.

Sudden anger filled him. Why did he care? Her remark was an insult. He was *Nermernuh*, one of the Lords of the Plains. Why was he feeling this stupid gratitude?

He dropped his hand away from the antelope's horn and stood up.

"Call me whatever you like," he said, harshly. "The opinions of whites about my people are nothing but whistles in the wind."

A look of hurt came over her face, but her gaze didn't waver.

She took a handkerchief from her pocket and wiped at the sweat on her forehead.

"I didn't mean that the way it sounded," she said, awkwardly, and he noticed as she patted the scrap of cloth against her neck that her hand trembled.

From exhaustion, no doubt.

A great wave of frustration rolled over him. She wasn't strong enough to ride as hard and fast as they'd gone this morning—she ought not to be here, damn it!

And she ought not to be his responsibility! He'd be lucky to get her to Montana all in one piece.

"It's ... just that I had called you a ... savage ... before," she explained, carefully, "but then you acknowledged the spirit of the antelope and that's such a thoughtful, *civilized* thing to do ..."

Confusion made her blush even pinker.

"I'm sorry, Nokona," she said, simply.

But his resistance, all his contradictory, churning emotions pulled him away from the new closeness that had sprung up between them for that one moment.

"I don't want to hear the word *civilized*."

"Well, I meant it as a compliment! And you've certainly applied enough words to *me*!" she cried. "*Weak, soft, ill-equipped!*"

"All true," he snapped.

He turned back to the antelope, then strode toward his horse to get his skinning knife.

"I'll help you," she said, and started to get down.

"No."

"I intend to do my part!"

"Go water the horses. There's a stream on the other side of those trees."

She made a furious, incoherent sound and turned away from him, the leadropes of the two packhorses clutched together in her slender hand.

A sudden, sharp feeling of loss came over him. He didn't intend to, but he stood and watched her go, her back straight as the barrel of his rifle, her waist tiny in the tight confines of her dress.

He knew exactly how she felt between his two hands.

And how clean and fragrant her hair smelled.

The unwanted memory deepened his fury.

By the Sun Father, he wished she'd ride East all the way to the horizon!

He held on to that thought while he prepared the meat and loaded it onto the horses that she led back to him.

He kept thinking it, slamming it into his brain every time his contrary heart wished that she would talk to him as they rode up out of the valley and headed toward the river.

"We'll camp early," he called to her over his shoulder. "To cook the meat."

213

"I'll do it," she called back, her voice tight. "When this is all over, you'll never be able to say I haven't done my part."

She sounded a bit strange.

He glanced back at her.

She wasn't quite so flushed now that they had climbed up out of the valley, but the air, even here, on the side of the mountain, was heavy and still.

Abby needed rest. Her shoulders slumped a little and she held on to the saddle horn.

She should never have come.

Some perverse part of him couldn't resist trying to give her comfort, though.

"It isn't far to the river," he called, above the clanking of the horses' hooves against the rocks.

And when they rode into the scattering of newly green trees that grew along the east bank and she dismounted and went straight to gathering wood for the fire, that same part of him covertly watched her while he unloaded the horses. She was a gallant one, he had to admit.

Without even taking a drink of water or stopping to get used to walking instead of riding, she moved in and out of the sunlight that fell into the little semicircle of a clearing, getting things ready to build the fire. The full, heavy skirts she wore pooled against the ground, covering new grass and old tree limbs, when she bent over.

214

Then they lifted to barely brush the earth when she straightened up and took her gatherings to the spot she had apparently chosen for the fire. Tired as she was, every motion she made was full of dignity and grace.

She had heart. That was a quality he could never resist.

Nokona dropped the packs beneath the tallest pine and went to find some rocks to use in making the firepit. He'd do that himself.

But before he'd found even one suitable stone, Abby called to him. Her voice sounded strange, weak as a baby bird's cry.

He wheeled to look at her.

"Nokona?"

His name was a question to ask what was happening to her.

She was standing up straight but her whole body wobbled precariously. She held out her arms, seeking for balance.

Then her bright eyes closed.

He dashed forward and caught her as she fell.

In his arms she was limp as a child lost in sleep—he couldn't feel her body move, not even to breathe. Raw fear grabbed him by the throat and he fought it as he ran to the tree with the deepest shade.

She *couldn't* be really sick. Somebody as stubborn as she was wouldn't be brought down by riding hard.

But she wasn't used to the food, and, despite her eating to keep up her strength as she'd declared on the occasion of the snake stew, she didn't eat enough.

He knelt in the grass, laid her down.

She *was* breathing. He touched the pulse at the base of her throat to make sure, unbuttoned her collar to get to it.

He brushed back her hair, felt her forehead. Sweat stood on her temples.

It was the heat, heat and exhaustion combined, that was all that was wrong.

Quickly, he began to unbutton the bodice of her dress, fumbling with the tiny buttons all the way from the collar to below the waist, and when that was done, he pulled it open, peeled it from her skin at her shoulders and down her arms, past her waist and off. Then he sat back and stared at her in consternation. She wore still more layers of clothes.

He set to work at the tied strings and laces, finally made the corset fall away, jerked the thin layers beneath it off over her head. At last!

She lay naked to the small breezes that were moving in the air.

And to his hungry eyes.

She was wonderfully beautiful, her limbs long and lithe, her skin pale and soft. He could still feel it, everywhere his fingertips had been.

Her breasts would exactly fill his hands.

216

He tore his gaze away, got up, and went for the water bag he'd hung in another tree.

"Abby," he said, as he bathed her, as he tried gently to put some of the cool liquid down her throat.

She turned her head, gave a great sigh, as if to say that at last now she could rest, but her eyes stayed closed. Nokona stopped trying to rouse her, cooled her temples again.

Her skin gave off the delicate scent that belonged only to her.

Desire, so strong it startled him, stirred his loins.

He set his jaw, took his eyes off her, and tried to harden his heart to the vulnerable picture she made.

Hadn't he told her and told her about wearing those layers of stupid clothes?

He put down the water bag and strode to her packhorse, to the parfleches full of things that Sky had sent with her. In the second one he found a skin skirt and blouse.

She'd wear these whether she liked it or not.

Wrapping her in the skirt, pulling the blouse over her head, he tried not to look at her. But he did.

And those soft words of hers stirred inside him again.

Never, ever . . . will I call you a savage . . .

This time they didn't make him angry.

They made him cool, cooler than the water he'd poured on her skin. Cool with recognition of something in himself.

That hadn't been gratitude that he'd been feeling when he'd first heard them. It had been happiness!

He went still, holding Abby's shoulders up with one hand while the other settled the blouse around her. His fingers knotted themselves into its fringe.

Gently he laid her back down.

He'd been *happy* that she'd joined the antelope blessing with an open heart. It was true that others' opinions of him and the *Nermernuh* meant nothing—*except for her*.

The realization rocked him back to sit on his heels, to stare off into the trees toward the crashing sound of the fast, rocky river. But he didn't let her fringes slip from his fingers.

Somehow, and he had no idea why, he needed Abby, the meddling missionary woman, to understand his people and their ways and to know that they were good.

"Abby. Abby, listen to me. You must wake up and eat."

Nokona.

That was Nokona calling to her. He was close by, nearer than the sound of a rushing river somewhere beyond.

She went to him, floating on the sound

218

of his sensual voice, lifting one arm to reach out to him as she opened her eyes.

His face was hovering over hers.

She looked up into it, dreamily taking it in.

He was handsome, so handsome. Handsome enough to make his smile clutch at her heart.

The curve of his lips was even more sensual than his voice.

"I've been doing your job for you," he said, in a slow drawl that matched the rhythm of her sleepy pulse. "I made the fire."

Abby raised up.

"I told you I would do that . . ."

His eyes were wide and dark. Dark and soft. Soft and warm.

Warm as his low, rich voice.

"But you took a nap instead."

She caught the cedary scent of his breath. His mouth was very near hers.

"Did I faint?"

"You fell and I caught you. But I think you were only pretending to faint so I'd have to do all the camp chores."

She smiled.

"Well, did you do them all?"

He shrugged, a slow rise and fall of his massive shoulders that made her want to run her hand over the muscles beneath his bare skin.

His hair, shining like black silk in the sun, swung against the hard line of his jaw.

She wanted to touch it, too, run her fingertip along the chiseled bone.

He was talking, though. She lifted her gaze to his eyes and tried to listen.

"I took care of the horses and started cooking some meat."

"Not rattlesnake, I hope."

The unexpected jest made his eyes gleam, lifted the corners of his mouth.

His wide, firm mouth with its full lips.

Lips that must taste like . . . warm honey?

His dark gaze dropped to *her* mouth.

"If it was, you'd be brave enough to eat it, wouldn't you?" he said. "Brave Abigail. And beautiful, too."

Beautiful.

The word broke open her slow-beating heart.

No one had called her beautiful, ever. Plain was the word for Abigail. She had always thought she was plain.

But Nokona's eyes, dark and intent, roamed over her face, loving to look at her.

He thought she was beautiful. He really did.

Her mouth drifted closer to his.

His skin smelled of the fire, and of horse and of sweat.

His lips touched hers.

And then his mouth took hers, fast and hard and eager, started her blood leaping

220

and tumbling like the noisy river out there somewhere.

She touched his face, just once, before her strength was gone and her trembling hand fell down.

Onto the incredible power of his naked arm.

With a low, incoherent sound, he pulled her closer, cradled her head in his hand, deepened the kiss.

A quick, traveling shock went through her.

He was tracing the seam of her lips with ... his tongue?

Did men and women really do such things?

Wonderingly, she let her lips part and met the tip of his tongue with her own.

She didn't care what anyone else did.

This was she and Nokona.

Then every thought was gone, her mind gone forever into the melding of their hungry lips and tongues, into the mingling of their breaths.

Abby dug her fingers into the muscle of his arm to keep from falling out of her grassy bed and off the face of the earth, then she kissed him back with all her heart.

His mouth was her world, her sun, all the heat she'd ever need.

No, she needed his hands, too. His fingertips that were setting a trail of fire down the side of her neck.

And his huge, callused palm burning the skin at the small of her back.

He pulled her closer. The tips of her breasts sprang up, high and hard, tingling, *hurting* to touch him, to brush against his bare chest.

They rubbed against skin.

The shock of the sensation stunned her.

She felt naked! Was she? What had happened to her?

Where were her clothes?

She tore her mouth from his, looked down at herself, frantically ripped her hands away from him to feel what she wore.

"How did I get into this?" she cried.

She grasped his huge wrists and pushed them away from her body. He let her go.

"Abby, what's wrong?"

"You undressed me!"

His low laugh started deep in his chest, rumbling like the noisy river.

"Of course I did. How else could you have changed your clothes?"

"All the way down to my *skin*! Nokona, you took off my *underwear*! I have nothing on beneath this buckskin."

"I know," he said, with a beatific smile. "I saw you."

She froze, staring into his amused, dark eyes, still languid and hot from the kiss.

"You *saw* me!"

222

Both hands flew to her face. The rushing heat of a deep blush rolled into her cheeks.

"That is *despicable*! You took my clothes off me when I was unconscious! Nokona, you took unfair advantage of me!"

"No. I took care of you."

"And just how do you figure that?"

"You passed out from heat prostration," he said, his eyes laughing at her. "Because you wouldn't listen to me when I told you to get out of those ridiculous clothes."

She set her fists on her hips and glared at him.

"No. You changed my clothes because you told me to do everything you said, *always*, and I never would wear what you told me to wear. So you are determined to make me!"

He just looked at her, still smiling, cocked his head, and lifted one eyebrow. He let the challenge stand. He was agreeing that what she'd said was true.

Embarrassment—pure, bitter chagrin—filled her.

On its heels rushed a grim, steadfast determination.

She pushed her hands against the ground to steady herself and stumbled to her feet.

He stood, too.

"I may have no choice but to travel with you, Nokona," she said, tilting her chin to look straight at him, "but I'm neither your

doll nor your slave . . . nor your concubine!
I will choose what clothes I wear."

He nodded. He tried to appear to be taking her seriously. But his eyes twinkled and
the corners of his mouth twitched, wanting
to smile.

And, fool that she was, she wanted to
kiss him! In spite of her upset, in spite of
the *fit* she was in, her throbbing lips ached
to rush back to his. She could still taste
him.

Frustration and fury overwhelmed her.
She felt tears spring into her eyes.

"I didn't mean to kiss you!" she cried.
"And I never will again!"

She turned on her heel with all the dignity she could muster, rushing away to
look for her dress.

"That's too bad," he said, to her stiff
back. "Because you are one who likes to
kiss."

She faltered a bit.

"And kissing is a civilized thing," he
teased. "Not at all native to the
Nermernuh."

And, fool that she was, God help her, she
wanted to laugh!

This man was making her crazy!

She plunged away from him, kept going,
dashing on her bare feet through the grass
toward her precious, familiar garments he
had thrown over the low limb of a pine

tree. Her thoughts moved as fast as her shaking legs.

He was right—she did like to kiss. At least, she liked to kiss *him*.

Oh, she had behaved in the most outrageous way! The most scandalous, disgraceful way that she could ever have imagined!

With a man who had taken off her clothes. Dear Lord, he had seen her completely *naked*!

Scariest of all, in one way that thought stirred her desire.

She snatched the dress, then the petticoats, down from the limb and clutched them in her arms.

"I'm only teasing you," he called, gently. His tone was serious now. "Abby, you need not run away."

Yes, she did need to run.

Her pulse was racing like a storm wind, her very breathing was choking her, sensations and memories whirled like wild, scattered birds through her head.

And her treacherous body was still yearning for his touch.

She needed to run far and fast, needed to take the north trail alone.

But the instant the thought came, her practical self shouted into her ear.

Hannah! Think of Hannah.

Without his help, she'd never make it to Montana.

"I'm not running away!" she yelled at him back over her shoulder, "I'm changing my clothes. In private!"

She ran toward the sound of the river.

Tears blurred her eyes as she came up on it, but she sensed the edge of the high, rocky ledge and turned to run along it, in the same direction the riotous river was rolling. It was a long way down from the top of the bank to the water, *such* a long way it made her dizzy to look.

So she wouldn't. She'd go far enough away from Nokona to think what she was doing, far enough away to be truly alone, and change into her own dress and get her wits about her.

And she would never faint again!

Hot, impotent tears welled up in a rush from deep down inside her. She would never give Nokona another chance to say she was too weak to endure this journey.

Nor another chance to take off her clothes and lure her into such wanton and shocking behavior!

She flew even faster over the scattered rocks cutting at her feet. The least he could've done was to put some moccasins on her when he'd taken her shoes!

In the next instant, with the next running step, she came down on a patch of small, loose gravel that started sliding beneath her. She reached with her other foot to catch herself and found earth, but that earth was already moving.

Toward the river.

A scream, one frantic, agonized, high, swirling shriek, tore itself free from her throat without any conscious effort.

"No-ko-na!"

And then she was falling, turning over and over into empty air with only the bundle of cloth in her arms between her and the rocks of the swift-running river. It was miles and miles below her.

But the next moment, another endless one in which she couldn't draw any breath, took her plunging to the water.

It slammed her helpless body through the emptiness and into the waiting cold depths where the sucking undertow reached up and got her.

She had time only for one, deep, shaking gasp full of air before it pulled her under.

13

Lost.
She was lost.

The water swept her downstream, tumbling her over and around with a giant's hand.

But only for an instant.

The giant relented, let her have a mouthful of air, let her slow enough to draw it into her lungs.

Then he turned cruel again and pulled her into a relentless, dizzying circle, a mean child's game. He swirled her, lifted and dropped her, dragged her head under, let it up for a second, dragged it under once more.

Her lungs burned like live coals in her chest.

Her arms tried to move, to grab for a rock, to push out of the circle, but her strength, even the strength of pure panic, was pitifully gone.

No!

Her only thought was *no*. That was all. She hadn't time or hope for anything more.

Then something slick slid along her arm and another monster ripped her bodily from the first one's grasp. Air, blessed air, came pouring over her face. Her nostrils strained to take it in, her mouth started spitting out water.

The behemoth turned her facedown, then the water was draining away and she was gulping life into her lungs.

Something rough struck her across the stomach, something wonderfully solid. She moved her feeble arms enough to drape them over it.

It was a log.

But the water still pulled at her feet and legs, tugged at her thighs.

It couldn't get her now, though.

Something else was holding her. Something solid, something smooth and strong, had wedged itself against her back.

It moved.

Someone, not something.

Nokona.

He took her face between his hands, which were cold as the river, and shook her a little. But his lips against her ear felt warm.

"Spit *all* the water out," he said, pushing each word separately from his mouth as if he'd run a long, long way.

Of course! He'd been fighting the river, too—in order to come to her!

If Nokona hadn't saved her, she would have drowned.

She tried to find breath to thank him, but she couldn't draw in enough air to make speech.

He held her over the log, facedown, and pushed on her back until more water ran from her mouth.

At last, he scooped her up and held her hard against his chest. Still gasping, she collapsed into the safety of his arms and buried her face in his neck.

He started carrying her out of the danger.

He could have walked through fire. Or on top of the water.

Nokona had saved her from the river.

She clung closer, pressing her cheek to the muscles rippling beneath the wet silk of his skin, drawing the scent of him into herself.

The hollow of his neck held the heat of his body; she nuzzled into it and felt the strong pulsing of his blood.

He started up the steep bank. She raised her head and glanced back over his shoulder at the rushing water still flaunting its power. Drops of it trembled on her lashes— she blinked them away.

The sun lit the fast, swirling currents.

And showed her her blue dress riding on top of them.

The river taunted her with it. It dipped the dress under, then lifted it up over the water like a banner waving against a stormy sky.

Every drop of her already-chilled blood turned to ice.

Her dress!

Oh, dear Lord! It was being swept away! Soon it would be gone.

She tore her arms loose from Nokona and lunged back toward the water.

But he was too quick for her, too strong. He held her fast.

"My dress!"

She was screaming. She knew that, but she couldn't stop.

"Nokona, turn me loose, I have to get my dress, that's the last thing I have that *my mother made me!*"

Her voice rose to a shrill shriek and she kicked and clawed at the embrace that had changed in the blink of an eye from a cradle to a trap.

But Nokona was as impervious to her voice as he was to her fists and feet and he just kept climbing on up the bank, carrying her away from her clothes with huge, fast strides while the river snatched her dress away and carried it out of sight around a bend.

It was gone.

Mama and Papa were gone, too.

The thought fell into her mind with the

same, straight, inevitable drop that had carried her, falling, into the river.

She would never see them again. Mama and Papa were dead.

Nokona stepped over the top edge of the bluff not too far from where she'd gone into the river. Now he held her high above it.

But a great, awful sinking dragged her eyes back to it, pulled her bones toward the hideous, swirling depths.

"I am *not* letting that river have my only dress!" she cried, beating at his shoulders with her fists. "Take me back there. I'm not letting it have my dress!"

Nokona threw back his head and laughed.

"They say, sometimes, of children, that they have so much spunk they'd try to stop a buffalo stampede," he said. "But I never heard of one who'd fight a whitewater river."

While he laughed, he carried her away.

Numbly, she watched the spring-laden trees and then the leaf-littered ground move past her. Mama and Papa were dead.

Nokona stopped and set her down on her old grass bed.

"You need to get out of those wet skins," he said.

She only looked at him.

He touched her dripping hair before he turned away.

Blindly she watched him go to the foot of a huge pine tree, squat down, and pull at the rope on his pack. He jerked something from it, stood up, and came back to her.

"Take off the skins and wrap up in this blanket."

She heard him speaking, but her ears wouldn't take in a word he said. Mama and Papa were dead.

The next thing she knew, he was sitting on his haunches, shaking her gently by the shoulders.

"If you don't want me to undress you again," he said, "and see you without your underwear again, get out of those wet skins and wrap yourself in this blanket."

She held out her hand for it.

"Do it now," he said, thrusting the pile of soft wool into it. "I'll leave you."

And he did.

At first she couldn't make herself move.

Then she remembered his threat. He would undress her *again*.

Every single bit of this was all his fault.

If he hadn't been so high-handed and *rude*, so dictatorial and *bold* as to actually rip the clothes off her body, she would still have her dress!

She sat up straight and ripped at the wet knot holding the skirt around her waist, pushing the blanket aside so she could use both hands, but her fingers were too numb, her hands were shaking too hard. Finally, she managed to loosen it enough to stretch the whole top of the garment and push it down off her hips, then she tore the blouse off over her head and threw it on top of the skirt.

This was all his fault! If he hadn't embarrassed her so much and made her run toward the river to change her clothes, she would never have fallen in.

She snatched up the blanket and wrapped it around her, as tightly as she could.

The rushing noise of the river taunted her. It ran too far below the bluff for her to see it, but that didn't matter—the picture of the blue dress on the glittering waters vibrated in her mind.

Nokona might as well have ripped it off her body and thrown it in!

"That blanket looks good on you."

His teasing tone came from directly behind her.

She whirled around.

"I wouldn't have to wear it if you hadn't made me lose my dress!"

The word broke in half as she spoke it.

But she wouldn't stop. She couldn't.

"Every bit of this is all your fault!" she cried, surprising herself at the venom in her voice. "I don't have one thing left from home anymore, and your interfering arrogance is the very cause of it!"

A shocked look crossed his face, then it closed to hide his feelings.

She took a step toward him.

"You are an insufferable dictator, Nokona. Just because you're the war chief you think you own everybody else. Well, maybe the Comanches can accommodate that, but I can't!"

She advanced on him again.

"If you'd left my dress on my body where it belonged, you tyrant, I'd still have it!"

Anger flashed in his eyes.

"If I'd left *you* in the river, you'd be dead by now."

The calm, hard words stopped her cold.

"That current's strong as a dancing devil wind," he said. "It was all I could do to get to you."

Once again she felt the undertow pulling her down. It had had the strength of hundreds of horses, far more than that of any man.

But Nokona had fought it to save her.

Bitter chagrin filled her veins, suffused her face with heat. She hadn't even thanked him.

Instead, here she was, giving him an unforgivable tongue-lashing. Sorrow had destroyed her reason.

"Forgive me," she said.

She took another step toward him, a slow one this time.

"My mama made that dress for me. It was all I had left."

Her lips trembled with grief, but she talked anyway.

"My papa said I looked pretty in that dress. He was the kindest, gentlest man who ever lived."

Nokona didn't say a word.

Abby took another step.

"Nokona," she said, and her voice sounded hollow as a stick hitting a piece of wood, "Mama and Papa are dead."

He opened his protecting arms.

She walked another step, and then they were around her, bundling her up in the blanket, pulling her to him.

Gathering her in.

"But *you* are alive," he said, and pushed back her loose, wet hair from her face.

He wrapped his arm around her neck and held it in the warm crook of his elbow, brought her cheek to rest on his bare chest.

"How can I be?" she cried. "I need my family!"

"I know," he crooned. "I know."

He pressed his lips to her forehead, just at the edge of her hair.

The deep, warm solace of the kiss spiraled down and down inside her until it touched the center of her cold grief. Just once, like the brush of a bird's wing.

It was not enough to melt the ice she had become.

237

He knew that.

He held her closer.

He began to sing.

Her body stiffened with surprise, but Nokona only cradled her head against him with one huge hand. And he sang to her.

The sad melody spoke of all her pain, drew the memories out of her and into the air, lifted them onto the fragile breeze, let them live there, instead.

And let her tears begin to come.

The cold knot at the core of her grief started to melt and, for the first time since Papa had driven around that bend into the arms of the waiting Apache, she could cry. Nokona held her.

He picked her up and carried her to the soft grass where she'd lain before, sat down cross-legged and cradled her in his arms while the hot tears poured down her cheeks and over the naked skin of his chest.

"Mourn," he murmured. "Make the sorrow give you strength. Weep for your family. They are gone."

He hummed the melancholy melody and held her close.

Abby clung to him and cried out her heart.

When, at last, all the tears were ended, Nokona lifted a corner of the blanket and dried her face, poured water from his skin bag into a gourd, and gave her a drink.

The cool water in her throat, in her stom-

ach, was real. T...
smooth as glass a...
real.

But Nokona was mo...

His strong arms, his w...
ing muscles were a whole,

His fingers closed over h...
bowl of the gourd.

"You've come a long way," he ..., "and
you can go on. You have life and you must
live it."

She had always been here, held in his
arms.

This was her only remembrance, all the
others were gone.

"I have life because of you," she blurted,
and lifted her gaze to his. The look in his
dark eyes, like his words and his voice, sent
strength into her.

"Thank you, Nokona."

"I had to save you," he drawled, and the
corners of his mouth lifted a little. "Who
would build my fires?"

His voice dropped sensuously low on the
last word and his gaze drifted to her lips.

Fires. Yes. There was more than one kind
of fire. She had learned that from his kiss,
that flame in her loins.

She smiled at him as she let go of the
cup.

"And all the while I was thinking that
you saved me to share rattlesnake stew."

"No," he said, and his dark eyes grew

his sensuous lids dropped lower, it was because I didn't want to ride such a long trail alone. If the horses could talk, I wouldn't have bothered."

The sudden tension in his voice belied the words.

He wrapped her closer, held her hard against the heat of his wet body coming through the thick layer of wool.

"Abby," he said, the word bursting from him in a raw, new voice, "I was so scared."

She twisted in his arms to look up at him. His eyes burned into her.

He cared for her! He cared that much.

Her blood danced in her veins.

"So was I," she said. "But I knew you would come."

He pushed the blanket out of his way and thrust his fingers into her hair, held her head in both his big hands as he bent down to kiss her.

She let go and leaned into him, let herself dissolve into the hard shape of his body, let her lips melt into his. Their hot sweetness seared her.

He smelled clean and wild, like the treacherous river. Yet he felt solid as the earth.

She slipped her arms free to wrap them around him.

And let the blanket fall from between them.

A shocked surprise speared her, surprise that she would do such a thing, but she couldn't make herself do any differently. No more than she could stop kissing him.

His naked chest brushed her bare breasts. An overpowering pleasure poured through her.

And a wanting for more.

Nokona moaned and deepened the kiss.

She pressed herself against him, shameless in the throes of such wonderful, new sensations.

New sensations. This was what it was to be a woman.

His mouth devoured hers.

She found the thrilling tip of his tongue with hers, then left it, again, and then again, tantalizing him, loving the way he always pursued her. Loving her new power.

Finally, he entwined his tongue with hers and took control, took the very soul from her body and kept it for his own.

Abby dragged her sated mouth away at last, but got no farther than the hollow of his collarbone. She kissed him again, there, and held her lips still where the blood pulsed hot and slow beneath his skin.

While the rhythm of his heart beguiled her, coming steady and strong against her yearning breasts, she touched her tongue to him. She tasted the salty sheen of his sweat.

She moaned. Then licked him.

He shivered and grasped her upper arms hard in his hands.

"Keep that up and I'll be seeing you without your clothes again."

She tilted her head and looked up at him.

"I dare you to make good on those words."

His fingertips dug into her flesh.

"Be careful what you dare," he warned, scorching her face and her neck, then her breasts with the dark heat of his eyes.

She smiled, dropped her lashes and then slid down in his arms, pressed her open mouth to the cunning, curving place in the middle of his chest where his massive muscles met.

He gasped, a quick, wild intake of breath, and she felt his hard manhood against her hip.

"Look here."

"No," she said, and caressed his long thigh, "don't talk. Just hold me."

"Just hold you!" he said, and his voice was hoarse. "I *can't* just hold you, Abby. Not like this, not with you with no clothes . . ."

She felt the heat of the blood rushing up into her face, but she felt no embarrassment. She ran her palm over his chest, over his standing hard nipples.

"*You* never wear clothes," she said, and glanced up to tease him with another, innocent smile. "So why should I?"

He pulled her closer, slid one hand sinuously down the side of her body to cup her hip. He held her against the growing pressure of his maleness through the blanket still between them there.

"So I won't be compelled to do this . . ."

This time he stopped his own words and took her mouth with his.

In a brand-new, in a different kind of kiss, a kiss that held a power like the rushing of a storm wind, a shining strength that tore loose all the vague yearnings that she'd never known how to name and set them surging wildly in her blood.

She locked her hands behind his neck and kissed him back until she was dizzy with the sweet danger.

The tips of her breasts sprang up harder, reaching for him, rubbing against him, desperate for more. More, yes, and something else, but she could not know what that was and she couldn't stop kissing him to ask.

He put one hand on her bare rib cage, slid it up to cup one of her breasts.

She gave an incoherent little cry of delight.

He broke the kiss and looked down at her with his eyes burning, their lids heavy, heavy with desire.

Desire for her.

"You might regret this," he said, and his voice shook with that passion. "Abby, do you know what you're doing?"

"Yes," she lied, and pressed her throbbing lips to the magic place in the middle of his chest again.

He groaned and tangled his fingers into her hair, tried to pull her away, but pressed her mouth closer instead.

"I know what I'm doing," she said, then, softly, lifting her gaze to meet his. "I'm loving you, Nokona."

Suddenly, the words took on a life of their own and floated, shimmering, there in the air between them.

True. They were true.

He cradled her head in his hand with the quick power of lightning and kissed her again with a desperate exhilaration that stopped her heart. Then he put one arm around her back for protection and held it beneath her, put her away from him so he could lay her down.

The other fanned the blanket out behind her, threw it to the ground.

Then she was stretched out and lying on it, floating between the deep, scratchy wool and Nokona's hot, smooth skin.

Reaching for him with a heavy, thrilling thunder pounding in her blood.

Her greedy hands slid over his shoulders and down his back, fumbled at the barrier of his breechclout.

She made a little noise of protest.

"Ah," he said, pushing his face into her hair, nuzzling hard at her ear and her neck, melting her bones with every touch of his lips and his tongue, "I thought you wanted me to wear more clothes, not less."

"Not ... now," she said, gasping as his mouth dropped a quick caress at the base of her throat and started a slow, slow journey downward into the valley between her breasts.

"I'm glad you lost your underthings," he murmured, between kisses. "It is what you would call a sin for such to cover these."

He cupped her breast and brushed his callused thumb over its taut, straining nipple.

His lips began to travel slowly up to it.

Never, ever, had she known such agony ... such *pleasure* existed.

"I ... didn't know you knew the word *sin*," she panted.

Then she bit her lip in fear that her words had distracted him.

He could not stop now. He could not.

But he did. He raised his head, threw back his hair, and looked at her from beneath his languid lids.

"In-deed! Why, Missy, me own mother will tell you that I am nae sinner," he drawled, "but I know that word and many more, too, in your language."

The unexpected, broad Irish brogue and the incongruity of its coming from the mouth of a long-haired, bronze Comanche warrior made her laugh.

"What other words?" she murmured, and arched her back beneath him so he wouldn't forget her body, now weeping with need.

"Like beautiful," he said. "Surpassingly beautiful."

A frisson of delight ran through her.

"You said that before," she murmured, through swollen, heavy lips still longing for his. "You're the only one. Everyone else has always said I was plain."

His incredulous look lit bursting flames inside her.

His heavy-lidded eyes caressed her. First her face and then, slowly, all of her.

"Everyone else is a fool," he growled. "When the light hits your hair it turns to gold. To match your eyes. You are like sunshine. Daughter of the Sun."

He leaned down and kissed her then, on the mouth, hard and deep, as if to seal the name to her. Then his lips moved to her breast, back to finish what he'd started, to enclose the begging, budding peak of her breast.

To melt her bones right into the ground.

This, *this* was the best pleasure of all. This was what she had been waiting for without knowing what was possible.

But then a new, hard, satin heat came against her leg. His callused fingertips moved up her thigh and into the very core of her, stole away her breath and her very ability to think.

He shifted up and loomed over her then, huge and powerful, his copper shoulders dappled by the drifting branches of the trees, and drove that primitive heat inside her, a silk-sheathed lance that impaled her body and her heart.

This, this was best of all.

For he was part of her and she of him.

Loving. They were loving each other.

"Abby," he murmured, with his hot lips against her neck, his face buried in the hollow there. "Abby."

The deep timbre of his voice saying her name made her tremble with that sensual pleasure.

Happiness flowed through her; she wrapped herself around him and followed his lead.

Moving with him in an ancient rhythm that swept them up and held them high on a mountain above the lonely river where its rage could never reach.

14

A horse desperately whinnying pulled Nokona from sleep. He opened his eyes to early sunlight.

And to a woman in his arms.

Abby.

A sweet, soft warmth ran through him.

He clasped her closer, just for one heartbeat, buried his face in her hair. Maybe he'd only been dreaming. Maybe they could lie here for a little while.

But the high, nervous neighing came again, shrill and piercing over the low roar of the river.

Abby started.

"Wha-a-t?" she cried. Then she relaxed and sank deeper against him.

"Wake up, Abby," he said, shaking her a little as he moved her head gently off his arm and untangled his legs from hers.

He threw back the blanket and grabbed for his breechclout and moccasins.

"Something's spooking the horses."

She sat up.

"Nokona?"

She smiled and reached for him, then scowled at him fiercely for moving away. Tousled and sleepy, reaching slowly, with her long, graceful arms, for the blanket to pull up around her, she made his whole body ache to lie back down.

But the danger was no dream.

"I'm going to see. Get the gun Sky gave you and get behind that tree."

"I'm going with you!" she cried.

"No, you're not. Do as I say."

He ran for his rifle, snatched it up, and started toward the horses, keeping to the best cover, trying to imagine what was scaring them.

His buckskin wouldn't panic over nothing. Neither would Ohapia.

Then it hit him, the visceral knowing that would have come to him sooner if his mind hadn't been full of Abby.

He looked at the ground.

There were no tracks until he reached the narrow, open space between their camp and the river. There, in an unbroken line between the trees and the water, parallel to the river, stretched the huge, curving footprints of The One Who Owns the Den.

The hobbled horses were settling down, starting to graze again.

Nokona stood still and listened.

Occasionally, one of the horses gave an indignant snort between bites. The day birds called and whistled, flew down from their nests and started to feed.

Underneath that ran the rumble of the fast water.

Nothing else.

He stared at the tracks for several long minutes. Each of them shone clear—the grass had a sheen of dew and the bare spots of earth held some moisture. The imprints of Grandfather's feet were unmistakable.

Nokona backtracked him to the edge of the sharp cutbank and looked down.

The bear had come up out of the water and headed north in a straight line, halfway between the river and the trees.

Nokona followed his path.

It began to veer toward the water.

A long lance's throw later, Grandfather had stopped at the top of the bank and left a set of four footprints. They showed he'd been standing still, at an angle, facing northwest, his head out over the water.

That was the way Nokona had planned to take after he and Abby crossed the river.

However, The One Who Owns the Chin had turned and made another clear set of standing tracks facing northeast. The two sets formed a vee shape, the image of a fork in a trail.

Grandfather had taken the right-hand

one. He had left the river behind and angled away from it.

Nokona dropped to his haunches and tested the depth of one of the footprints. Grandfather had been moving at a lope.

Squinting into the bright, eastern sun, Nokona started trotting alongside the trail. It stopped where the trees began.

Searching ahead, into and on the other side of the pines, revealed nothing.

He came back to the last track, squatted, and ran his fingers into the marks of the bear's claws.

It was the last one.

Right here, Grandfather had disappeared.

Nokona sat there for a long time, feeling the morning around him, waiting to know for sure the meaning of this visit from his medicine spirit.

Finally, he stood up, cradled his rifle in his hand, and, moving fast, started back upriver toward their camp.

"Nokona!"

Abby was running through the trees to meet him, clutching the blanket to her with one hand and waving her gun with the other. Her hair was flying wild, almost catching on the low-hanging branches.

"What are you doing?" he called.

He ran to her to try to keep her from seeing the tracks, to keep her fear of the bear at rest.

"Didn't I tell you to stay in camp?"

She ignored his question.

"What was scaring the horses? Are they hurt? Are they still there?"

"They're all right," he said, and caught her elbow to turn her back toward camp. "Maybe a hungry wolf trotted by on his way up the river."

"I just had a terrible panic when I thought we might be afoot," she said, breathlessly. "Oh, Nokona, if we lost the horses, we'd *never* get to Hannah!"

"We won't lose the horses."

She walked beside him, keeping pace, carrying her rifle across her body tangled into the edges of the blanket.

"I was so scared that it was the bear."

He didn't answer.

"While I was hiding and waiting for you to come back, I was thinking about when we find Hannah," she said, and shot him a confiding glance that struck at his heart. He was a coward for hiding the truth from her.

The truth about the bear and the truth that she probably would never see Hannah.

"I'll be ready now, to find just her," she went on. "Up until yesterday I'd been living in some kind of dreamworld that, when we got to her, Mama and Papa would be there, too."

He slowed his pace and looked at her.

She stopped. The familiar blush climbed into her cheeks.

"I know it sounds crazy," she said, "but

253

I kept seeing all three of them together when I would imagine our reunion—I couldn't let myself believe they are really gone."

Abby leaned against the trunk of a tree to hold the blanket on her back while she shifted the heavy gun to get a better grip.

He reached out and took it.

She smiled her thanks, then wrapped herself into a wool cocoon and hugged herself with both arms, looking up at him with huge, trusting eyes.

"It's hard, Nokona, but you're the one who gave me the courage to face the fact that Hannah is the only family I'll find."

Guilt struck at him again, but he couldn't discourage her quest now. Not when she was looking at him that way.

"We won't find her unless we get on the trail," he said, starting them walking again toward camp.

Even through the blanket he could see she still shivered. From letting herself remember that her parents were dead and from being afraid that Grandfather had returned.

"When I saw you running out with your gun, I thought you'd come to save *me*," he said, lightly, to distract her. "But I guess you only care about the horses."

Frowning, she flipped back her hair and gave him a slanting, golden glance.

"The bear wouldn't hurt you, it's your medicine spirit," she said sharply.

Then she came out of herself and realized he was only teasing.

"It's the *horses* who are carrying me all the way to Montana," she said. "I've always been known as a most practical, sensible woman."

She threw him a coquettish smile. It made him wish he had his hands free.

He held her gaze with his.

"*I* would say you should be known as a most passionate, sensual woman."

He was rewarded by her deepest blush.

"Not *known* as! Nokona, you have no shame!"

She sounded indignant, but she smiled at him again.

"I'm not the one wearing my bed instead of my clothes."

She pretended to slap at him. The blanket swung open, she gasped and grabbed at its edges, laughing a little.

Good. For now he had made her feel better.

Later, at the end of this trail, there would be time enough for sorrow.

When they reached camp, he stopped by the packs to lay the guns down, then dropped to his haunches to pull out the empty parfleches for the strips of smoked antelope.

"I'll build up the fire," Abby said, "and

make some hot mush to go with the meat.
We need breakfast if we aren't stopping in
the middle of the day."

"We aren't," he said, his mind going
back to Grandfather's message. The One
Who Owns the Chin was saying that time
was important, as well as direction. Nokona could feel it.

He thought about that while he stacked
the painted parfleches at his feet.

Abby's dismal wail pierced his musing.

"What'll I wear? Nokona, these buckskins are still sopping wet!"

"Wear this," he said, as his hand fell onto
the *natusakuna*, which had been wedged
into the pack by the other hide cases. "We
need to be riding."

He pulled it out and tossed it to her.

She caught it and stepped behind one of
the trees.

He smiled. Shy Woman. Even after last
night's passionate sharing, she wasn't
going to dress in sight of him. He shook
his head in wonder.

How could she be the golden Daughter
of the Sun, hot and shining in his arms,
saying, *I'm loving you, Nokona,* and be Shy
Woman, hiding from him the body he had
held next to his all night long?

He went to the smokefire, which had
burned almost out, and began swiftly to
put the meat strips into the bags. He was
tying them closed and knotting their raw-

hide straps to his packsaddle when Abby came back.

"Nokona."

Her voice trembled with a breathless excitement.

The sight of her pulled him to his feet.

She stood among the trees like a shaft of sunlight in the soft yellow buckskin dress. Its brilliant bands and medallions of beads, its rich fringes, long, leather, beaded thongs, each called to his eye in turn as she slowly, slowly turned on her heel for him to look at her.

Then, suddenly, all he could see was the buckskin decorative flap, not fringed like the front one, that hung from the neck down the back of the dress. It was covered in the symbol ⌐, painted in dark blue over and over again, one for every war honor that he had ever earned.

Wearing that symbol was the privilege of a brave warrior's number one wife.

That was Tope's dress.

But that was Abby wearing it. The dress and its matching, beautiful, beaded moccasins.

Tope was gone.

Every inch of his body went cold.

He had saved this missionary woman's life, but not Tope's.

"Nokona," Abby said, again, and turned around to walk toward him.

Her tawny hair swung like gold silk from

a part down the middle. She had found Tope's bone comb.

"I can't believe you brought all this along for me," she was saying, smiling the way she had smiled at him last night.

"You knew I would follow you! When you left me at the *rancho's* corral that day, telling me that you wouldn't take me north with you, you already knew that you would!"

Her wide, golden eyes glowed as she turned her face up to his.

"I can't believe that you know me that well!"

He did not know her at all.

Yet, he did. He understood, at this moment, exactly how she had felt when she realized that her beloved blue dress was gone forever.

He was looking at what he had lost.

His eyesight blurred.

The soldier's horse moved across his range of vision again, unexpectedly fast and relentless. It headed straight at Tope, who was kneeling on the ground.

It drove over her.

Tope was gone. He couldn't even remember her face.

"Thank you, Nokona," Abby said, and came to him, stood on tiptoe to kiss him.

His arms went stiff—he used them to hold her away from him. A thousand wild feelings tore at him, feelings that he needed Abby to understand.

"That dress belonged to my wife," he blurted. "I brought it along so that a piece of her could go with me to a place where the old ways can live on—there's nothing else I can do for her now."

He stopped and swallowed hard, groping for more words to catch the thoughts chasing each other through his mind.

"I *couldn't* save her," he said. "I didn't even have a chance to move from where I stood before she was dead."

The buckskin melted into his palms. The beads stroked his fingertips.

Then they ripped at him as she pulled away.

"Oh!" she gasped, her voice tearing with pain. "So *I* am only taking *her* place!"

Her translucent skin blushed furiously red.

"You give me her dress to wear, her comb to use—you saved my life just to make up for not saving hers. I mean nothing to you, Nokona, nothing but a substitute!"

The words cut into his thundering heart like so many enemy arrows.

"No! Abby, you . . ."

She drew herself up to her full height.

"Oh, how I wish I had never made love with you! I should never have lain with you—I'm old enough to know better!"

Those arrowheads drew blood.

"You don't mean that!"

Her eyes blazed, hot enough to burn him.

"I most certainly *do* mean that! I'm still not a real person to you—after all our passionate night—any more than I was when you used me as an object of fun to make the children laugh! You care nothing for me."

Anger sprang to life inside him, a tight-woven rope of fury to wrap around his heart and staunch the flow of his lifeblood.

He snapped at her.

"How can you say such foolishness?"

"*I'm* not the one talking foolishness! *You're* the one riding hundreds of miles hunting for a place that doesn't exist only to please a woman who is dead and gone!"

"That is not the only reason . . ."

But she would not be stopped.

"You ought to face reality, Nokona. As I have done. My Mama and Papa are dead and when I find Hannah, they will not be with her. We'll never be a family, at home together, ever again."

He crossed his arms and glared down at her. The rope tied itself into a knot, jerked tight and hard around his wounded heart. But still, it bled.

"And Tope will not be coming back to you, no matter *how* many women you put into her clothes and take into your bed!"

She held her ground and returned his glare.

"There *is* no place where the old ways can live on, don't you see that?" she cried. "White settlers are everywhere! Besides, Nokona, even if you did find such a place, what good would it be to you? Your family wouldn't be there, and everybody has to have family and someone at their side to love and help them!"

He slammed his heart shut against those words.

But she hit it again, like an enemy striking coup.

"I know that circumstances are forcing me to make a *different* life for me and for Hannah," she said. "Why can't you see that you have to make a different one, too?"

She was telling the truth, a truth he already knew.

And hated.

He tried to shut out the words, but they pounded their way through his ears and into his head. He flung them back at her.

" 'Things are in the saddle and ride mankind'?" he quoted bitterly. "Mr. Emerson is a white man. His thoughts are those of a helpless coward, not those of a warrior of the *Nermernuh*."

Narrowing his eyes, he took a step toward her.

"I go to the north not only to find a place

for the old ways, but to *fight*. To fight your kind."

He spun on his heel.

"Pack up and mount," he said, hurling the order at her from over his shoulder.

He started at a trot for the horses. He was a fool to stand here and listen to her.

And he'd been a fool to lie with her and open his heart to her.

He would never do that again.

Abby rode behind Nokona all day, fighting to keep her eyes on the trail he broke and off his broad, bare shoulders and muscular back. Her palms could feel those muscles beneath his coppery skin and her mouth could taste him if she looked at him.

Worse, the sight of him broke her heart right in two.

Oh, dear God in Heaven, she wished she could leave him and end that torture for good! If she did, though, she'd never find Hannah. She'd never even survive.

One good thing—he was pushing on as if furies were after them, eating and drinking as they rode, and she didn't have to face him or talk to him at all.

For the thousandth time, she swung around in her saddle to see if the wet buckskins spread over her packs in the sunlight were dry enough to wear.

That dress belonged to my wife. I brought it

*along so that a piece of her could go with me
to a place where the old ways can live on.*

The bald words beat again at her heart,
battered it like incessant, icy stones of hail.

But how could that be? She cared no
more for him than he did for her. Of course
she didn't.

She had gone into his arms because of
her loneliness, because of her pain.

That was all.

She would not allow such a thing to happen again, nor would she bare her feelings
to him in another angry exchange. From
now on, she would insist upon a neutral,
formal relationship with him as her guide,
only her guide.

Ohapia tossed her head, made the Spanish bit jingle. Absently, Abby loosened the
reins and fixed her eyes on the mare's
small, pointed ears to keep them off Nokona. Shifting to a fresh position in the saddle, she went back to her pondering.

She should never have set her deepest
feelings loose. That wasn't her way, it never
had been—she was sensible Abigail, always
the one to keep her mind on whatever
needed to be done. Instead of her loss and
her own sorrow—and the incredible, sensual closeness that Nokona had made her
feel—she should have kept her heart set on
finding poor little Hannah.

Now, at this moment, what needed to be
done was setting new perimeters for the

rest of this journey. She put her heels to her mount and caught up to Nokona.

"I want to reiterate that as soon as we find Hannah and take her to a town, I'll pay you for your trouble," she said, in the most authoritative tone she could muster.

He whipped his head around to look at her with hard, dark eyes.

"Oh? Have you decided to pay money instead of doing your share of the chores?"

The look and his sarcastic tone obliterated her resolve to control her feelings. Fury raced through her.

"I've decided that ours is to be a businesslike relationship and nothing else," she snapped.

"What about the next time you fall in the river and scream for help?" he said. "Shall we negotiate a price now so I won't have to hesitate when I need to save your life?"

Stung, she blurted, "You won't! I'll be extremely careful from now on."

"And so will I," he said, with another dark look, a look as vindictive as if *she* had been the one to seduce, then betray, *him*.

Abby stiffened.

She would *not* be drawn into another argument. And she *would* put this relationship on a different footing. After all, they had miles and miles to go, maybe a month or more to be together.

"We can't argue all the way to Montana, and we certainly can't continue any sort of personal connectedness," she said. "So let's find some other topics of conversation."

He scowled at her.

"We could simply not talk at all. Have you thought of that?"

"Yes, but for such a long way that wouldn't be practical," she said, coolly, refusing to let herself scowl back at him.

She raised her chin and gave him her most dignified look.

"I was surprised to hear you quote Mr. Emerson this morning," she said, in the formal tone she would use with a new acquaintance at a literary gathering. "How did you come into contact with his work?"

"A warrior of my people took a book Mr. Emerson had written from some of your white people, Texians, during a raid," he said, mimicking her manner, making it sound very prissy and pretentious. "I don't know whether or not you are aware of it, but books are greatly prized among the *Nermernuh*."

"I didn't see any books the whole time I was with your band!" she retorted, hotly. "Besides, how many of your people can speak English, much less read it?"

"Oh, we don't *read* the books," he said. "We're savages, remember? We use them as padding between the layers of our shields."

Abby stared at him.

"They are perfect to deflect the arrows of our enemies."

She couldn't think of a reply.

A raid. In Texas. Against white settlers.

Like the Apache raid against her family.

The first time she ever saw him he was killing a man.

That was an act that she could never, ever commit.

They were of two different species.

How could she even have *thought* of loving him?

15

Nokona pushed ahead, day after day, fast, as fast as if he were leaving enemy territory driving a whole herd of captured horses. But speed didn't help.

His lonely heart stayed right with him, heavy in his breast.

And Abby stayed right behind him, stiff in her shell.

Every time she spoke to him in that distant tone of voice, every time she tried to start some stupid conversation with a remark like, "Have you read any other works of Mr. Emerson?" he felt enough fury to punch a hole through a cliff face with his fist.

Fury with himself.

Of course telling her that that was Tope's dress at the very moment she had decided he'd brought it along for her had hurt her feelings!

But her reaction had been devoid of all reason.

How could she be so illogical as to jump from that fact to the idea that he had saved her life because he couldn't save Tope's?

How could he even *talk* to somebody like that?

Yet he wanted to. He longed for the close companionship they'd had for such a little while.

He wanted her back again—Abby, Daughter of the Sun.

Finally, in the middle of that long afternoon, they rode around the end of the mountain they'd been climbing. The true northeasterly direction he'd been holding now led them down a sloping incline through a stand of lodgepole pines and into a high, mountain meadow.

"Oh, Nokona, *look!*"

For the first time in days, she sounded like the Abby he had held in his arms.

She rode up beside him and they stopped the horses.

Flowers filled the world. They danced in the sunlight shining through them, preened themselves in the wind, spilled red and blue, yellow and gold and white, pink and purple all over the earth like spirit-painted stars.

And they tore down Abby's aloofness.

She looked at him, her big eyes shining. "Let's stop early today," he heard him-

self say. "We'll camp here—there's a creek
at the bottom."

They got off the horses and ran downhill
through the shifting waves of color, looking
and looking to fill their eyes. Without need-
ing words, they secured their mounts beside the chattering, clear-running creek and
ran up the mountain again, into the strong-
est sunlight like people just let out of a
cave.

"I've never seen so many beautiful
flowers!" she called.

I've never seen such a beautiful woman.

Abby stood tall and straight, with her
head thrown back, the curve of her throat
graceful as an eagle's wing against the blue
sky. The wind swept her hair back from
her face.

She was wearing it loose now, not tied
back in a knot the way she had done.

Nokona bent down and began to pick a
bouquet.

"They smell so wonderful!" she called,
without looking at him. "Some spicy, some
sweeter than honey."

"But none better than a good snake
stew!"

She laughed, for the first time in days,
and held out her arms to the breeze. The
fringes on the buckskins Sky had given her
swayed against her sides.

Tope's dress was tucked back into its
case again and forgotten.

He hoped.

If they crossed the path of some band other than Crow, he'd try to trade out a change for her in case this dress got wet again.

He straightened up, and, with a quick, silent prayer, strode toward her, offering the flowers he'd gathered.

She turned and gave him a startled glance, then looked down at the bouquet.

As she took them, her fingers brushed his with fire.

"Thank you, Nokona."

Then, with the airy abandon of a child, she threw herself down and pulled up her knees to wrap her arms around them. She clasped the bouquet in both hands and buried her face in it.

He dropped down beside her in the soft, flower-strewn grass.

"These are to say that I'm sorry, Abby," he said, in a voice so raw it scraped his own skin. "I never would intentionally hurt you."

But she shook her head. She didn't want to talk about it.

"Have you ever seen anything so beautiful? Ever?"

"Yes," he said, bluntly. "You."

She glanced at him sideways, gave him a small, appreciative grin.

But her eyes didn't smile.

"That's why the only flowers I have put

into your hands are yellow and golden," he said, gently. "Flowers for the Daughter of the Sun."

"Thank you," she said, again.

"You're welcome."

She was quiet then, and he waited.

Sweat broke out in his palms. But he couldn't push her. He couldn't take that chance.

He stared down the hill at the four horses, moving slowly in their hobbles, choosing this spot and that to bite off some grass.

"Your intentions are not the question," she said, in the tone of a beginning, and his heart leapt high in his chest.

Just as he had hoped, they would wipe out the distance between them with flowers and words!

He bent his head to listen, watched her full mouth as she spoke.

"You didn't intend to hurt me, I know that," she said, with her most sensible air. "You only told me the truth. But the bigger truth is that you and I both need homes and families in them to stand by our sides."

Nokona waited some more. She hadn't finished yet.

She turned and looked at him directly, her amber eyes wide and frank. Swallowing hard, as if working up her courage, she clutched the flowers tighter in both hands.

"I must find my sister and go to live in a whole new way and you must go to fight and then to find a place to live in the old ways."

Nokona reached out.

"Abby . . ."

She pulled back just as his fingertips grazed her shoulder but her straight, honest gaze never left him.

"Nokona," she said, and his hopeful heart hit the bottom of his chest with an echoing thud, "the biggest truth is that we are so different we should never have lain together at all."

He stared at her, as stunned as if she'd slapped him across the face.

How could she say that? How could she deny such a magical, loving night?

Especially in that practical, matter-of-fact tone? She might as well be discussing the weather.

He continued to sit beside her silent and still as a stone.

His pride would not let him answer.

Nor get up, as he longed to do, and stomp away from her in disgust, get onto his stallion, ride off, and leave her.

Don't worry, we never will lie together again.

He would not say that, either. He was a warrior of the *Nermernuh*.

He would not let her know that that night had meant something to him since it had meant nothing to her.

272

She glanced back over his should
way they had come and then looked a

"Are we heading toward the place whe
the Crow said the great battle would be?
Do you think that they'll go straight there
with Hannah?"

His blood stopped cold. As cold as this
woman he'd thought was so warm.

Here in this meadow full of flowers, she
was telling him not only that she regretted
having made love with him, but also that
the only reason she was still riding with
him was so he could take her to her sister.

He set his jaw.

And looked straight at the spot where
her gaze rested, on the line of quivering
aspen trees that marked the winding way
the valley took as the creek cut in and out
between the mountains. He wouldn't worry
any more about her feelings. She was
tough. She'd just proved that.

"We must be," he said. "We're going
straight in the way that Grandfather set
for us."

"*Grandfather?*" she gasped. "You mean
the . . . bear?"

He glanced down at her.

"Remember the morning the horses
woke us whinnying?"

He watched her quick blush come.

Good. He, too, remembered that that was
the morning they'd waked in each other's
arms.

273

ed.

...rightened by The One
...n. He had come in the
...s for us to follow—tracks
...a straight, northeasterly

...en riding this way for all of
these da... ...e cried. "Following the *bear*?
He was *there*, prowling around us that
night and you told me it was probably a
hungry wolf scaring the horses!"

"Yes, so as not to frighten you," he said,
and stood up.

"But I'm telling you different this day because now I know how much you love
the truth."

He looked down into her upturned face.
Her eyes widened with shock, and then
narrowed against the pain, as his sarcasm
soaked in.

Angry as he was, hurt as he was, he
hated himself for it.

What a silly, childish effort to hurt her!

Now that he had done it, he didn't want
that at all.

He wanted this useless arguing done.

He wanted her back. With his arms
around her.

He wanted her as his close companion
again.

He wanted her to make him laugh. He
wanted to see her smile.

274

Then get her back, Nokona, War Chief of the Nermernuh.

The Great Spirit whispered those words into his ear.

And much *puha* came flooding through Nokona's veins.

He reached down and lifted her to her feet.

"You talk of what cannot be changed," he said. "But we *can* change this waste of sunlight and flowers."

She stared up at him in stunned surprise.

"Nokona," she blurted, "we can never—"

"Do not think about whether we should have lain together," he blurted, "nor about what we will each find at the end of this trail. We humans and our animal brothers must truly live one sun at a time or we do not live at all."

She lifted the flowers, brushed them against his chest as her eyes searched his face.

"That," she said, finally, with the little catch in her voice that he loved, "is the biggest truth of all our truths today."

She stood on tiptoe and kissed the side of his neck.

"How many suns do you think we'll have on this trail?" she whispered.

He rested his chin on her bent head and stared out across the creek to the next mountain, bursting with spring.

"All of this New Spring Moon," he said,

as he silently calculated time and distances, "and part of the Flower Moon."

"Then we will live them, every sun," she said, "while we follow the Grandfather Bear."

His blood leapt in his veins.

She was accepting his medicine spirit, believing that he was showing the way!

Could it be that they might *not* part at the end of this trail?

He closed his mind to the thought and carefully took Abby by the shoulders.

They had just made a pact and he would not break it. He would keep his spirit in the present and let the Great Spirit hold the future.

He drew in a great sigh of the fragrance of flowers, bent his head, and kissed Abby's hair.

She lifted her face to lay her cheek against his.

They pushed hard the next day and every day after that, because neither could forget why they rode north.

But they did not speak of it.

The urgency was simply there, inside them, Abby thought, like their heartbeats and the rhythmic motions of the horses.

Outside them, there was peace. Majestic mountains with their aspens and larches, flowers and sparse grasses took her and Nokona into their fold. They let them see deer leaping the fast-running creeks and bounding across the meadows, white eagles soaring through blue skies above snow-covered peaks, let them hear the wind sighing in the pines and the howling of the wolves in the dark.

Every night, they lay in each other's arms and listened, looking up into the star-spangled black of the sky.

Nokona gave her herself as a woman.

In those sweet days, strung one after the other on the thread of the invisible trail that they followed, they became part of each other. Abby wrapped herself in that closeness and caught herself praying that this mystical time never would end.

The days were getting hotter as they crossed the North Platte River and veered east for a path between the Bighorn Mountains and the Black Hills. They avoided Fort Fetterman, as they had done all the other forts and the well-traveled roads and trails, but still the tracks of other people began to cross theirs.

All heading north.

"There *is* a great gathering," Nokona said, "just as the Crow told it in Santa Fe."

A cold, terrible hand squeezed Abby's heart.

She swallowed twice before any words would come out.

"Do you think there'll also be a great battle?"

"Yes."

Then he lifted his eyes from the faint marks on the ground to look at her.

"We have some few suns yet to go," he said.

"I know."

But the agreement was broken.

Hannah—the image of Hannah in the hands of the Crow who were carrying her somewhere up ahead on the fronts of their saddles—filled Abby's mind and her heart.

The terror closed her throat then, and she could speak only in a croak that sounded more like a frog's.

"What if she isn't there?"

"We'll look someplace else."

She stared at him, across the narrow space between their horses, and held his gaze.

"You have to fight, whenever they have the battle. What should I do if we don't find her before then?"

"If this is the biggest summer gathering, ever, of all the Northern Indians, then someone there will have seen Hannah or heard some word of her."

He clamped his lips shut and turned from her quickly, though, supposedly to look for more tracks to identify.

She knew him too well, now, for him to fool her.

He still doubted that Hannah had survived to come this far.

It might be that they had ridden for hundreds of miles and dozens of days only to find that no one at the big gathering had heard of her sister.

She might never find Hannah.

Yet, she looked down at the ground, followed Nokona's gaze, and found the shallow place beside a river where dozens of hooves had come from two directions to meet and churn up the mud.

They all pointed in the same way she and Nokona were going.

Some of them might have been made by the horse that was carrying her baby sister.

Seven suns later, a half circle of young braves rode down the valley to meet them on a grassy bench of the Little Missouri River, in the middle of a long afternoon. The sight of them froze Abby in her saddle

They appeared out of nowhere, just as the Apache warriors had, back then a lifetime ago.

Abby's breath stopped as she kicked Ohapia in the side and made her duck back behind Nokona.

She had to blink and look twice because the sight of any other people after all this time in a world of only the two of them was too strange.

They were real. Real as those murdering Apache had been.

But their faces weren't painted.

And they weren't sitting still as evil spiders, waiting for innocents to fall into their web.

They rode their ponies forward, each waving one arm in the air, looking the newcomers over with quick, black eyes, shouting in challenging voices. Nokona held up his hand.

She managed to say, "Whoa," in a semblance of her normal voice and pulled her horse to a stop.

But he wasn't signaling to her, he wasn't even thinking of her. He was greeting their challengers, riding ahead to meet them.

She stayed where she was and tried to listen, not sure if he was speaking in his language or theirs. All she could really hear, suddenly, was Hannah's pitiful screaming, floating back from her captor's galloping horse.

Abby! Abby, help me!

Oh, dear Lord, what shape was Hannah in now?

Abby clenched both her hands around the horn of her Spanish saddle.

Oh, dear God, Hannah *must* still be alive! She had lived to be in Santa Fe many, many days after she'd been taken. Surely, surely, she could live until Abby found her.

She *must* still be alive. *She must be.*

The new Indians stopped their horses and so did Nokona, keeping his mount between her and them.

He spoke again, adding signs to his

words this time, and the spokesman answered. His companions cast curious glances at Abby and circled their horses restlessly while Nokona and their leader talked for what seemed to be forever.

Then the strangers wheeled their horses and started back upriver.

Nokona rode back to her.

"They're taking us into a big encampment," he said. "They say it's the biggest village they've ever seen in all the seasons they've been alive, but it's still not the Big Gathering. That is forming farther west on the Tongue. They're on their way to it."

He stood in one stirrup and leaned out to reach for the rope of his packhorse.

"I told them that you're my wife."

The word shocked her. Was that true, according to Indian ways?

She wished. Right now she wished it was true.

He caught the lead.

"Feelings are running strong against whites right now."

Her heart dropped. He'd called her his wife to protect her. That was the only reason.

Then she forgot all about that.

Whites. Whites and Indians.

Abby lost her breath.

If Hannah *had* made it this far ... what had happened to her?

281

16

Abby sat stiff in the saddle, still barely breathing, as she rode behind No kona up the bank of the river. On her right, it flowed, wide and rolling, muddy with the melting of spring. On her left, the high plains stretched west, all the way to the mountains, purple against the bright sky.

Ahead of her lay the big Indian camp—noises of children and dogs were already drifting out to them.

In that camp, *maybe*, was Hannah.

She opened her mouth, tried to speak, but her voice was gone.

The third time she tried, the words came.

"Did you ... did you ... ask them about Hannah?"

"No. They're wary of me, of any other Indian who might be scouting for the United States Army. I asked for Tall Bull, a chief of the Miniconjou Sioux who has long been a friend of my father's. They'll ask him if it's true and then they'll take us to him."

As he spoke, they rode around a bend.

The camp spread out before them, spilling down the west bank of the river in an endlessly long chain of crescents made out of tipis. The half circles all opened to the east.

At the southern edge, very near to them now, sat three of the young braves who had ridden down to meet them, facing downriver, waiting for them. Their horses pricked their ears and watched Abby and Nokona as closely as did their riders.

Nokona rode toward them, amid roiling children and dogs running out to see the strangers. Abby could barely make herself follow.

She hadn't been among this many people since her family had come through St. Louis on their way west. For all these weeks, these nearly sixty days she'd marked on a stick that was her only calendar, she hadn't seen another human face but Nokona's. Now there were thousands.

A weary shaking spread from her hands through her whole body. She had ridden so far for so long. What if Hannah wasn't here?

The yellow and tan of the tipis stretched as far as the eye could see north and west, dotting the green of the spring grass, mixing with the pale pink of wild roses near the river. The camp was teeming with people. It came closer and closer and swallowed Abby up.

Their escorts led them at a walk on a winding way through the lodges and around cookfires, among women carrying loads of water and wood. Grown men sat in front of every lodge, working on weapons or sitting and smoking. Children played everywhere.

Abby turned her head from side to side, trying to see every one of them.

Would they let Hannah be with them if she were here?

Could she possibly be lighthearted enough to play?

No head full of golden curls showed among all the sleek dark ones.

At last, they stopped in front of a lodge set a bit apart from the others in its crescent, a tipi painted all the way around with blue-and-red running buffalo. An old man sat beside the door-opening.

The young warriors stopped their horses and got down to speak to him.

This must be the Miniconjou Chief, Tall Bull.

He looked up, finally, squinted his rheumy eyes at Nokona, and made a sharp gesture. Nokona dismounted.

Tall Bull gestured for him to sit down, picked up a long, carved pipe from its place across his lap, and offered it. They sat and talked, then smoked, for a long time.

The old man called several others to join them, but no one spoke to Abby or suggested that she dismount.

She was glad. A terrible dizziness had overtaken her; she'd not be able to stand.

Soon, though, a group of women materialized around her horse, pulling gently at her, smiling, gesturing that she should get down. She wanted to refuse, but then she realized that she mustn't offend them and make feelings against the whites even more bitter.

So she went with them, with a last glance back over her shoulder at Nokona, who sent her a slight nod of approval. The women sat her down near a cookfire built a stone's throw from the tipi where he talked with the old man.

Gradually, the sunshine and the solid ground stopped her shaking.

But she could not eat the food they gave her—she merely sipped at the broth so as not to seem rude—and she could not keep from looking, constantly searching, in every direction for Hannah.

Her only comfort was to think of how kindly they were treating her. Surely, if Hannah was here, she was all right.

Finally, using a combination of signs she made up as she went, she began making her own inquiries about her sister. She put on a questioning expression, spread her hands, and looked around to ask *Where?*, pointed to a girl about Hannah's size, touched her own hair and then the yellow skin dress of a Miniconjou woman, after that, the yellow paint on one of the water bags.

They understood her. They made enough signs in return for her to know that they did.

But they shook their heads sorrowfully and shrugged, showing her their empty hands.

Abby thought she couldn't sit there, impolite or not. The smells of smoke and cooking meat, the sounds of talking and laughing, the sight of so many people moving and milling around her made her want to jump up and run.

Run to every one of these thousands of tipis that stretched up the river and look inside for Hannah.

She turned and glanced over her shoulder at Nokona, who was watching her. Finally, with one last passing of words and signs back and forth between him and Tall Bull, he stood up and came toward her.

"Thank you, thank you," she said to the women, and put down her bowl. Then she jumped to her feet and went to meet him.

Relief lessened her tension, but only for an instant.

"We're invited to stay here," Nokona said. "Tall Bull is sending runners to the

287

Oglala, the Santee, and the Hunkpatila of his own people to inquire about your sister."

"Let's go, too!"

He waved that away as silliness.

"There are Assiniboine and Shahiyena on the other end of the encampment, too. If the Crow did bring her north, someone here will surely know something."

"I can't sit around anymore!" she cried. "Please, Nokona. Let's go look for ourselves."

"We can't refuse their help and their hospitality—that'd be an insult."

He glanced over her shoulder at her hostesses.

"Be polite to these women," he said.

To Abby's consternation, he walked away, to a group of men gathering around Tall Bull.

The women tugged at her arms to say she should sit down again, so Abby did.

When what she wanted to do was to ride at a gallop up the river, screaming Hannah's name.

Two small boys came and took away her and Nokona's horses. He stayed with the men and said no more to her.

She thought her heart would burst from her body. She could not bear this waiting.

The sun dropped lower and lower in the sky, gradually went down. People came and went, talking and laughing. Music started up and dancing began.

The beat of the drums, the sound of the flutes, scraped the inside of her skin like an edge of flint. Abby closed her eyes and wove her fingers together, prayed that she'd be strong enough to hold herself all in one piece.

"Abby," Nokona said, from behind her.

She was on her feet the instant she opened her eyes.

"I sent a boy for one of our horses," he said. "We can ride double—it isn't that far."

Her blood stopped running.

"Hannah?" she whispered, trying to see his eyes through the dusky dark. "Have the runners found Hannah?"

"We'll have to go see in the next camp circle over, which is a band of the Hunkpatila Sioux," he said. "A few days ago, as they traveled West, they met two Crow scouts riding toward Yellow Long Hair's fort. The Hunkpatila killed them and took their horses and captive—a little white girl with blond hair."

Abby's breath didn't come again the whole time they waited for the horse, Nokona helped her up onto its bare back, and they rode at a long trot through the night up the river. But even without air in her body, she managed to whisper over her shoulder to Nokona.

"Hurry, please hurry!"

A little white girl with blond hair. It had to be Hannah! Who else could it be?

Joy, pure joy, erupted from a lost spring deep inside her, warmed her very bones.

Only Nokona's strong arms around her, and his smooth bare thighs pressing the backs of hers, kept her from flying apart.

They were there.

Suddenly the horse was stopping. They were there.

With a little shock, she realized that the boy who'd brought their horse had been guiding them. She hadn't even seen him until now, when he stopped his pony beside their mount and they all three slid down to the ground.

In front of a lodge, a large one, with smoke coming out of the top and the door-flap closed.

It lifted and a woman came out of it.

She went straight to Abby, said something unintelligible, then reached out and patted her on the arm.

It was good of her, Abby thought, as her feet began flying forward, her back already bending to fit through the low door. This woman, a stranger, was congratulating her on finding her sister.

The close air in the tipi almost knocked her down. It was stifling hot, so hot that sweat started running down the small of her back.

The fire—why didn't they build the fire outside, the way the Miniconjou had done?

Then the glint of blond hair caught the light from the flames and Abby found herself on the other side of the lodge without even being aware of going around the firepit.

She fell to her knees, pulled back the covers, caught the small face in her hands, and turned it toward her.

The joy bubbling through her body caught her spirit and carried it, soaring, through the skin walls to the sky.

"Hannah!" she cried, and her voice rang loud in her ears. "Oh, thank you, God, it *is* Hannah!"

Then the fear hit and choked off her words.

Hannah's skin, dry as paper, burned her palms. The child was hot with fever, hot as the coals in the center of the pit that held the fire.

Abby sat flat down on the ground, gathered Hannah into her lap, and stripped away the robes and blankets piled on top of her.

"Darling . . . Hannah, sweetheart, it's Abby!"

Hannah wore only a breechclout, her poked through her skin beneath hands. Even here, in this sweltering here wasn't a drop of sweat on her. 't an ounce of fat.

"Wake up, sweetie, wake up. Sister's here."

But the big blue eyes stayed tightly closed.

"She's so thin!" Abby cried, running her hands down the sticklike arms. "Oh, Lord, she's so thin!"

She glanced up to find Nokona beside her.

"She doesn't even look like herself!"

Every inch of the child burned with the fever.

"The air in here's too hot!" Abby cried.

She folded Hannah into her arms and struggled to her feet.

"Please, Nokona, help me get her out into the fresh air!"

Bent beneath her burden, she swung around and started toward the door-opening. The woman whose lodge it was barred her way, speaking fast and earnestly to Nokona. Her hands and arms threw huge shadows onto the tipi walls as she signed to him.

"She's afraid you'll kill her by taking her out into the shock of the night air," he said to Abby. "She was trying to sweat her and break the fever. Why don't you stay here with her while I go back to Tall Bull and arrange for a place to take her?"

Abby nodded and sank to the ground where she stood. She clutched Hannah to her, tucking the bedraggled blond he into the hollow of her shoulder while she kept up a stream of desperate talk, begging Hannah to wake and talk to her.

She didn't.

The woman talked to her, though, chattering fast in a tone of protest as she went to the bed and started straightening it, making gestures for Abby to lay Hannah down again.

"I can't!" Abby cried. "I can't turn loose of her—I've looked for her many days, many moons!"

The woman stared at her, her round face wrinkled in frustration, her bright eyes glinting in the glow from the fire.

In the sudden quiet, Abby noticed Hannah's breathing. It grew until it filled the tipi.

It filled the night.

A sick terror spread through Abby's veins.

"Water," she croaked to the woman, looking around as if Nokona were still there to translate for her. She turned pleading eyes back to her hostess.

"Please! Get some *water*!"

Numbness threatened to paralyze her, but she managed to clasp Hannah tighter in one arm and make gestures of bathing her with the other.

The woman shook her head and pointed to the bed, signing that Hannah should be in it, under the covers so that she'd sweat.

Abby clutched her closer and tried to think. Which worked faster to bring down a fever? What would Mama do?

Oh, dear God in Heaven, if only Mama could be here now!

"No," she said. "Bathe her. We must bathe her now."

She lurched up to her knees with Hannah still in her arms, looking for the water bag everywhere. Where did people usually keep the water in a tipi?

The Hunkpatila woman came brushing past her, heaving a disgusted sigh.

"*Wa-ter*," she said, and stuck her head out of the door opening to call to someone in her language.

In an instant the tipi was teeming with three additional women, one spreading a skin onto the ground by the fire, another adding sticks to the flames, another carrying in hide bags full of water.

At their direction, Abby laid Hannah on the hide and took the piece of cloth one of them handed her. Her hostess worked on Hannah from the other side, still frowning and clucking her tongue. They bathed the bony little body over and over again.

Abby kept her gaze glued to Hannah's face, which did not change in the slightest way. Her eyes never opened.

The Hunkpatila women worked in silence, keeping the fire so hot that Abby's own skin felt scorched, keeping the wooden bowl of cool water full from a succession of pouches that someone else kept bringing to the door. Abby knelt and wet her cloth, squeezed the cool water over Hannah's forehead and face, down over her pitiful body.

They worked until the grassy floor was soaked.

The fever burned on, untouched.

Finally, later, she had no idea how much later, Nokona returned, took Hannah from her arms, and led Abby out to his horse. Bareback again, with Abby sitting behind him, holding on to both him and Hannah, they wove through the lines of tipis and cookfires back to Tall Bull's lodge.

Nearby, two new ones had been set up.

"Tall Bull provides me with a lodge for myself and one for you and your sister," Nokona said, as he threw one leg over Maanu's withers and jumped down.

"Don't leave us!" she cried.

"I'm not," he said, gently, and he reached with one hand to steady her as she slid down from the buckskin's warm rump. "It's custom for a warrior to have his own lodge—Tall Bull wants to show every hospitality for the sake of his friendship with Windrider."

The terrible tension in her eased the slightest bit. Nokona wasn't leaving her. Yet.

She walked close beside him and held Hannah's hand while they took her inside.

"Tall Bull is sending these women to help you, too," he said.

There seemed to be a host of them, coming in with shy greetings, robes and food, backrests and wood for a fire. Nokona dealt with them.

Abby could see nothing but Hannah, hear nothing but her painful, dragging breath.

It had to be pneumonia—Uncle Jonah had sounded just that way.

Before he died.

The thought turned her stomach cold, set it to churning.

But acknowledging at last what she had instinctively known from the minute she'd first heard Hannah's labored breathing also steadied her somehow, cleared the haze from her mind.

Do something, she had to *do* something!

"Tell them we must keep trying to break this fever," she said, turning to Nokona. "Is there any pennyroyal or ague root near here, do you think? And sassafras root! I'll make some tea and we'll try to get that down her!"

She hurried to the fire and stirred it up, even though someone was already doing that.

Then she ran to the bed that another woman was making by the tipi wall, grabbed the robes with both hands, and started dragging them toward the fire.

"The bathing didn't drive out the fever, and neither did taking her out in the night air," she said, wiping her streaming forehead with her fringed sleeve. "So we'll go back to trying to sweat it out of her."

Nokona spoke to the women and they began bringing out herbs and medicines. He told Abby which to use to make poultices, which to use for teas.

She began preparing everything at once, spread the salve on Hannah's poor, sunken chest with her own fingers, held her head up with her own hands to try to dribble some tea into her throat.

While she waited to see if any medicine would work, she washed the child's limp hair and tried to crimp some curl back into it with her fingers. The curls wouldn't hold. It was as if her hair, like the rest of her body, was already half-dead.

Abby talked to Hannah, sang to her, recounted memories she'd rather not recall to try to bring her out of her stupor. Nothing helped. She stayed the same.

Finally, Nokona caught both Abby's shoulders in his big hands, gently led her away, and sat her down beside the tipi wall.

"I will use some of Grandfather's medicine," he said.

He walked back to Hannah, stood over her, and began to sing.

This was different, a much different song from the one he'd sung to comfort Abby in her sadness. But this song, also, went straight to her feelings and drew them out of her body. It held a gravity, an imperativeness, like the urgency that had ridden with them on the trail.

For a moment it was gone from her.

She was free of responsibility for a little bit, while all of it rested on Nokona's broad, beautiful shoulders.

> *Hana nina i a*
> *ha ni na in a ni na*
> *hi ni na i a*
> *ya hi ha*

While he sang, he opened the medicine bag he wore at his waist, took out something and unwrapped it. It looked like some kind of root.

Still singing, he turned and held it to the four directions. He touched it to his own tongue, then dropped it into the pot of boiling water that bubbled over the fire.

He sat on his haunches beside Hannah and sang, took out the bear claws he carried and placed them around her in the four directions. He poured one of the herb teas onto cedar limbs warmed by the fire and laid them against her head.

Finally, his face came into sharp relief as he bent over the pot that sat in the fire and dipped a gourdful of liquid to hold over her sister.

Abby gasped.

But he cupped his free hand to catch any drops that might fall and continued singing while he let it cool. At last, he supported Hannah's head and dribbled some into her mouth.

Abby's heart stopped.

Hannah drank it. And she kept it down.

After a few more sips, Nokona dipped his fingertips into the gourd and bathed her head, her eyes, then her chest, up and down over her clogged lungs. He stopped, put down the gourd, and came back to sit beside Abby.

"What was that root?" she whispered, without taking her eyes off Hannah.

"Bearroot. I am not a shaman but since the bear is a healer and also my medicine spirit, I have *puha* to use his herbs."

They sat for an age with silence between them, listening to Hannah's breathing over the crackle of the fire and the murmurs of the women huddled on the opposite side of the lodge. Soon her rasping quieted.

"Feel of her now," Nokona said.

Trembling with hope, Abby crawled forward, reached out her hand. She brushed back the damp hair and laid her palm on her sister's bony forehead.

She brought it back covered in sweat.

"You're better! Oh, Hannah, your fever's broken! Talk to me, can you talk to me, Baby Sister?"

She grabbed the limp, little hands and massaged them, patted both of Hannah's hollow cheeks.

The fever was gone.

It was *gone*.

But everything else was the same. She couldn't wake Hannah, couldn't get her to talk, to open her eyes, to respond to her voice.

"Nokona!" she wailed.

He appeared right behind her, touched Hannah to judge for himself.

Then he pulled Abby to her feet and turned her into his arms, swayed with her, while he cradled her weary head against him.

"Let her rest before you try to wake her," he said. "She needs sleep. So do you."

He led her to one of the beds laid out beside the wall. "Rest."

Tears rushed through her defenses, poured down her cheeks until she couldn't even see him.

"She'll live now, won't she?" she begged.

He helped her gently down onto the folded robes.

"Her fever is gone," was all he would say.

Abby tried to beg him for more, to urge him to reassure her, but as soon as her body stretched out, sleep took her.

17

Voices, two different male voices sounding a low chant, woke Abby. One of them was Nokona's.

She opened her eyes and, in that instant, she remembered everything at once. Sunlight poured through the walls of the lodge, filling her with a terrible, translucent hope.

This morning, Hannah would be well. Or, at least, much better.

That thought danced in her veins as the motes of dust danced in the air. This morning, Hannah would wake up.

She scrambled up and stumbled toward her sister's bed.

She *was* better! At least, the sound of her breathing wasn't nearly so loud.

"Hannah," Abby said, falling to her knees beside the pallet, reaching out to turn the thin face toward her. "Hannah?"

Miracle of miracles, Hannah opened her eyes!

The blank, dull eyes of a stranger. A pitiful stranger.

"Sweetie!" Abby cried, and gathered her up into her arms.

"It's Sister, darling! Don't you know me?"

At least the fever had not returned—Hannah's skin was dry, but fairly cool. And she moaned. Yesterday she had made no sounds at all.

Abby cradled her head in the crook of her elbow and met those stranger's eyes again.

"I have searched and searched for you!" she crooned. "It's Abby. Your big sister has found you at last. Everything's going to be all right now. Everything's all right."

Hannah stared up into her face with an absolutely flat expression.

The look made Abby's throat tighten in horror.

Something was terribly wrong besides pneumonia. Her breathing was still strained and she was weak from that and the fever, but something else was wrong.

Had the horrors she'd been through damaged her mind?

Oh, dear Lord, what if they'd destroyed it?

What if the child *stayed* like this?

Well, she would not let that happen!

She grabbed the skinny little body up against her, squeezed it to her chest, and

304

rocked back and forth, sitting cross-legged on the ground.

"Your big sister has got you now, sweet Hannah. I'm going to take care of you. I'll get you to a doctor and he'll make you well."

Hannah made no sound, gave no response at all.

Abby pulled back and peeked at her face. It gave no clue whatsoever that Hannah had heard.

The next instant her mouth was open and she was screaming, making a sound so sudden, so high and piercing that it couldn't be real. But it was.

Her whole body went rigid, as if from a seizure, and Abby bent forward to lay her down.

But Hannah clasped her around the neck with the strength of a grown man while her eyes rolled to one side.

"No-o-o-o!" she yelled, in the raspy, trembling voice of a very old person. "Indians! Papa, it's Indians! No! No! No-o-o-o-o!"

Abby managed to turn just enough to get a glimpse of Nokona and another man standing behind her.

Then Hannah was dragging her farther down until her face was almost in the bedrobes, butting her head into Abby's shoulder, pulling at her with a steadily lessening strength.

"Go away!" Abby cried, but Hannah drowned her out.

Her screeching rose to an alarming pitch and she began scratching at Abby with her long, ragged fingernails until Abby thought she'd claw her skin off her body.

"She's afraid of you, can't you see that?" Abby yelled, as she finally broke Hannah's death hold on her neck. "Back off. Nokona, tell that man to get out of here!"

Hannah's arms fell away, her whole body went limp, and her eyes dropped closed.

Abby scrambled to her feet, whirled on the two men.

"Can't you see she's scared to death of Indians? Please, Nokona, you two get away from her!"

"This is White Cloud, shaman of Tall Bull's band of the Miniconjou," he said, his low, calm voice rumbling to fill the tipi. "He is here to make a curing ceremonial for your sister."

"That won't do any good!"

"He has medicine from The One Who Owns the Den—more of it than I do."

"Bear medicine!" she shouted. "What Hannah needs is *real* medicine."

She glanced over her shoulder to see her sister. Hannah lay perfectly still.

"Where's the closest white doctor?"

Abby took a desperate step toward Nokona.

306

"Is there a fort anywhere near here? The soldiers will have doctors with them. It's her mind, Nokona, something is wrong in her mind. That needs more than *bear* medicine!"

He stepped away from the shaman, met her in the full sunlight streaming down through the smoke hole.

"The medicine of the Grandfather brought you to your sister. The Four-Legged Human guided you to this river and this valley out of all the rivers and valleys in this high plains country!"

He made a great, sweeping gesture of one arm that was as angry as his voice.

"Maybe so!" she cried, her own anger rising like a gorge in her throat. "But now don't you see that finding her isn't enough? She's sick, she's really bad sick, and we have to take her to a doctor!"

His face turned into a mask.

"I have brought a doctor to her."

"A medical doctor," she said, slowly biting off each word, "is what I'm talking about. This child has to have a *real*, medical doctor. A *white* doctor."

His dark eyes hardened until they were thin chips of black rock.

"So," he said, "you no longer trust me. I, with the help of Grandfather, brought you safely over hundreds of miles of hard trail, straight to the camp where your sister lay. But now you do not trust me."

His tone slashed at her, sharp as forty knives.

"I trust you. But not in this. Just not in this bear medicine to treat my sister!"

"Bear medicine drove out your sister's fever."

That stopped her.

But only for an instant.

"A fever's different. The loss of her mind is worse—and harder to treat."

She wrung her hands.

"Please, Nokona. Please understand. I know you're mad at me right now, but put that aside and help me get her to a white doctor. Where's the nearest one?"

He turned away from her without answering and spoke to the Miniconjou shaman. The old man made a gruff reply, turned, bent his head to duck through the door opening, and went out.

Nokona glared at her.

"The nearest white doctor is at Fort Lincoln, Long Yellow Hair's fort, three suns' hard ride from here. He and his soldiers will be marching out of there any sun now to try to drive all these Sioux and Shahiyena onto the reservations. They will find the great battle."

"Oh, then we must hurry! We'll get to the fort before they leave or meet them on the trail—the doctors will be with the soldiers, won't they?"

He stared at her and made no answer.

"Oh! You needn't show yourself, No-kona. They might mistake you for a Sioux. Just take me and Hannah close enough that I can hail them down."

His dark eyes burned in his face. They didn't waver.

"No," he said. "I'll find you an escort you *can* trust."

He turned and left the lodge before she'd absorbed what he said.

The sound of his voice drifted back to her from outside the walls, just as it had done when it waked her such a short time ago. His low, rich, beguiling voice.

It hollowed her out like a melon scooped by a spoon.

But her anger flooded back to fill her again.

He ought to understand! He was being completely unreasonable, stubborn and blind. Couldn't he see that Hannah's health was the important thing right now?

Couldn't he understand that she needed a doctor from her own people?

Her heart dropped into the earth. He didn't *try* to understand. He didn't care about her one bit. Not a bit.

The door-flap lifted, and, for a short, glad instant, her heart jumped back into her chest.

But it wasn't Nokona.

It was the women Tall Bull had sent to help her with Hannah, slipping quietly into the tipi, one after another. They greeted her with shy smiles and went straight to their tasks.

Abby spun on her heel and went back to Hannah. Her breathing was more labored. She had not moved.

All day Abby vacillated between hovering over Hannah and trying to talk to Nokona again. They needed to be on their way to the doctor this instant, yet she knew preparations had to be made. He was probably making them now.

He was probably planning to go with them, too.

I'll find you an escort you can trust.

Those dry, sarcastic words kept ringing in her ears. Surely he hadn't meant them. Surely his anger would have cooled by now and he would listen to reason.

Why, she couldn't travel for three suns trying to take care of a sick child when she couldn't even communicate with the people riding with her! Nokona knew that.

And he cared for her! He did! He couldn't have held her so tenderly in his arms all those magical nights on the trail if he didn't.

Her heavy heart turned over. Pray God, Nokona cared for her. She cared for him. How could he even *say* that she didn't trust him?

But she had to put Hannah first right

now, even if that separated her from Nokona forever.

She cupped her shaking hands around
the child's thin face.

What was she thinking? She and Nokona
could never *be* together forever, even without Hannah.

It would behoove her to realize that fact.

The thought pierced her heart. But she
couldn't be selfish and think about her feelings now.

She reached for the scrap of cloth in the
bowl of water that the Miniconjou women
kept filled, and bathed Hannah's face for
the thousandth time.

"Talk to me, Baby Sister. It's Abby. Darling, these Indians are friendly. Abby won't
let anyone hurt you."

Hannah's eyelids never fluttered. Not
once.

Hours had passed, now, since morning,
when she'd opened them and said those
few words.

Abby's stomach constricted. Hours and
hours had passed while she waited for Nokona to come back and say that the horses
were ready.

What was he *doing*?

If this went on much longer, Hannah's
mind might leave her completely. Since the
doctor was so far away, they should already be on the trail!

She got from her knees to her feet.

"Please watch her closely and come to find me if she shows any change," she said, gesturing to her helpers so they'd understand.

Abby ran to the door opening, bent down, and went through it.

The camp lay quiet in the spring afternoon. Children played down by the river, out of earshot; women watched them while they worked over their sewing. A few were beginning to stir up their cookfires.

The sun was dipping low in the western sky, beginning to throw light behind the distant mountains from purple to red. It was later than she'd thought!

Her blood chilled. Had they lost a whole day that Hannah could have been traveling toward help?

"Nokona?" she said, stepping out into the pathway that wound between the tipis to accost the first person passing by, a woman with an armload of wood.

Abby mimed the word *where* and said it again, loudly, "Nokona?"

The woman turned and pointed at a lodge she'd just passed, which was the buffalo-painted one of Tall Bull's. Smoke was coming from its smoke hole, the low rumble of voices sounded inside.

Abby started toward that tipi.

Before she'd taken two steps, Nokona came out of its door-opening.

"Oh, Nokona, I'm so glad I found you . . ."

"Hush!"

He took two long strides and met her, grabbed her by the arm, pulled her with him toward the lodge set to the west of the one Hannah was in. He thrust her unceremoniously in through the flap.

The tipi was empty, except for a few robes stacked neatly on one side and Nokona's packs and bags on the other. Low flames burned in the firepit. This must be the private lodge Tall Bull had provided for him.

The next thing she knew, he had her by both arms and was turning her around so he could lecture into her face.

"Don't *ever* interrupt a Council. I heard you asking for me . . ."

Her tense nerves snapped.

"A *Council*? I'm agonizing over Hannah's condition all day and praying she'll hold on until I can get her to a doctor, and you're sitting around in a *Council*?"

He tightened his grip, gave her a shake.

"These people are insulted that you turned away their shaman! I had to explain, beg them to understand your determination to take your sister to a lesser doctor."

He dropped his hands and stepped back, his face etched with disgust.

"After that, the young warriors Tall Bull chose to escort you to the fort objected that they might miss the great battle. It takes time, Abby, when you give offense to people, to talk them into giving up what they want to do to help you do something useless!"

"But I thought *you* would relent and take us to Fort Lincoln! I know you were angry with me, Nokona, but you know it's not true when you say I don't trust you."

"You don't trust me or any Indians, but you'll have to trust Seven Ponies and Rides Swift. You can't get to Fort Lincoln alone."

"I *know* that!" she said, hotly, but inside she was cold. Cold as death. He wasn't going with her.

"Please, Nokona, come with me. I can't even *talk* to Seven Ponies and Rides Swift. What will I do?"

"Keep silent. Be glad you're getting what you want. Pray that the army doctor can cure your sister."

But at that very instant she couldn't think about Hannah. Not with Nokona talking to her in that flat, irrefutable tone.

Not with Nokona standing an arm's length away.

With his heart as far away from hers as the moon.

"You'll be on the trail at first light, don't worry!"

"And where will you be?"

"Here. And when you are at Fort Lincoln I'll be on the Tongue or the Powder, getting ready for the great battle."

His dark face blazed.

"After that, I'll be on the Little Bighorn, where the Crow left the breadbox prophecy."

"What prophecy?"

"Some Crows scouting for the white soldiers left an empty breadbox in that valley. They covered it with drawings telling the Sioux they'd be wiped out, and stuffed the cracks with grass to show it would happen in the summer.

"That is where I'll be fighting your people."

Abby's feet froze to the warm grass on the ground.

"Oh, dear Lord!"

She breathed the words as a prayer.

"You might be hurt in the fighting."

"I might be killed."

She could only look at him. She couldn't speak.

"But not before I've made some white men wish they'd stayed in their own land."

"No," she said, slow as the movement of her blood. "No. Do not go into danger, Nokona."

"Why not?"

Silence filled the lodge. It grew so long and deep that she could hear the beating of his heart.

And hers. The heart where all her life she had kept her true self locked away.

Until Nokona had set her free.

"Because I love you."

The look on his face didn't alter, but the ice in his dark eyes melted.

The low-slanting sunlight poured in through the western wall, enclosed them in its warm, red haze.

"I'll never see you again, Nokona," Abby said, surprised that the bitter words came so clearly off her tongue, "and I'll never love any other man."

He reached for her with one huge, hard hand.

But she stayed where she was while he slipped it into her hair and cupped her cheek. Because she wanted to watch him, she had to see his face.

The golden red glow of the sunset caught his high cheekbones, traced the handsome shape of his nose, the arch of his brows. The sensual strength of his mouth.

His mouth.

She took a step toward him.

The light washed his naked shoulders and his chest, made them gleam like polished copper. His skin was a sleek smoothness over their hard muscles, she knew that. The tips of her breasts remembered that. They tingled at the memory.

Her whole body thrilled to his.

This would be the last time. She would live the rest of her life on this.

She reached up and touched his lips, traced the shape of them with one fingertip.

His eyes blazed.

"Abby," he whispered.

Then he pulled her hand away, held it down to her side with his callused fingers like sweet shackles around her wrist. He jerked her to him and consumed her with his kiss.

He set his feet apart and brought her hard against his hot maleness, wrapped her whole body with his.

I love you, Nokona, I love you!

Every pore in her body, every nerve ending, every inch of her skin shouted that silent message to him. And her lips and her tongue told him so, too.

She stayed very still where she stood, urging him, begging him, compelling him with slow, long caresses of her tongue and tiny, faint moans low in her throat to make this kiss last for the rest of their lives. His mouth told her *yes*.

And his hands promised that, too.

He moved them over her shoulders, palms flat and hot, out from her spine as if stroking sleek wings.

He slid them down her arms and back up again underneath her fringed sleeves.

He found her bare waist and spanned it for one long heartbeat, taking possession, laying his claim.

Then he slipped them up over her rib cage and cupped her breasts. Which, every time, fit exactly into his palms.

Because she and Nokona were made for each other.

This was the only time left to them. She must fill herself with him.

She leaned forward to rub against his chest, but he forestalled her with his thumbs, brushed their roughness back and forth, barely skimming her taut nipples to set her body on fire. She tore her mouth from his.

"Get this off," she whispered.

He lifted the blouse off over her head and threw it away.

She took a step forward, grazed the sleek skin of his chest with the tips of her breasts. Thrills raced along her skin.

"Abby."

He growled her name like a warning.

She did it again.

He kissed her like a wild man as he drove her down.

Into the sweet-smelling grass, into the stormy haven of his arms.

"Remember this," he said, his voice raw with his passion. "Abigail, promise me that you will remember this."

She caught his face between her hands.

"I will. I promise you, Nokona."

His dark eyes looked into her soul, there in the sunset light.

And hers into his.

"Will you?"

"Until the moment that my spirit leaves

my body," he vowed. "And always in the After-World."

He bent his head, then, to find the thong that held her skirt and untie it, to undo his own belt and let his breechclout fall away.

"Lie still," he said.

For one, empty moment he left her. Then he was there again, picking her up, carrying her, laying her down. Her naked back sank into the deepest, softest of buffalo skins.

"Lie still," he said, again.

And he came onto the skin with her, knelt between her legs.

He smiled at her, there in the red-gold glow of the sun.

Then he bent and kissed her flat belly.

The shivers ran through her all the way to the bone.

She reached down to touch him, tangled her fingers into the silk of his hair.

"Nokona."

The word was a moan, a slow cry for mercy.

But he gave her none.

His lips pressed another hot kiss, then another, at random onto her trembling flesh.

At random, but moving ever downward.

To the weeping center of her womanhood.

Her hands fell away, limp and helpless onto the robe.

But she didn't feel it. Nokona, Nokona was filling her senses.

His mouth left her then, left her bereft.

But only for a moment.

His fingers licked traces of fire along her skin.

He took her hips in his hands and she arched up to receive him, to take him into her and love him again.

For the last time.

Tears poured down her cheeks like rain.

Until Nokona found them and kissed them away.

Then time did not exist.

Nor separation.

It could not be.

For they were wholly a part of each other, coming closer and closer, already one.

Moving slowly and sweetly, powerfully sure in the rhythm of their lifting hearts, knowing perfectly well how to make their pleasure together.

"Nokona," she whispered, and turned her lips to his cheek. "Nokona, I love you."

He wrapped her tighter to him, to his sweat-tinged skin.

"What is truly felt is never lost," he said, hoarsely, and carried her infallibly into the winds that would pull them apart.

Lightning flashing in their blood, they unleashed a more irresistible storm, willed it to rip them free of the restricting arms of earth. It carried them, clinging together, riding gale after gale that couldn't tear apart, up out of the valley and over the mountains.

Until, whirling and flying, they burst into the sky and raged across the heavens like a hot shooting star.

18

"Abby, these two warriors will take you to within sight of Fort Lincoln. From there, you'll have to hold Hannah on your horse and ride in alone."

I'm already alone! With you right here!

Her lips parted, but her voice wouldn't come.

How could she even answer him when he sounded like a stranger? And acted like one.

He hadn't come close to her, hadn't touched her, since she'd left his lodge to prepare Hannah for the journey. In this black time just before the dawn, she couldn't even see him—he was only another dark form moving among the horses and the other men outside the tipi.

"I can carry her," she said, raising her voice a little to carry over the snuffling, creaking sounds of the horses.

He didn't reply.

*Come with me. Please, Nokona, I can't
leave you.*

"Nokona," she said, fighting to keep her
teeth from chattering, "please thank these
warriors for me."

He muttered something to the young
Miniconjou, Rides Swift and Seven Ponies,
who were already mounted, waiting for the
women to bring Hannah outside. But he
said nothing more to Abby.

She forced herself to duck back in
through the low door-opening, to run to
Hannah and wrap her even more tightly
against the chill morning, the heavy dew.
The women nodded and signed to her in
the faint light from the fire. Hannah was
ready.

And Abby might as well be. There was
no turning back.

Outside, she ran straight to Ohapia,
leaned on her for a moment, trying to soak
up the mare's warmth to stop her insides
from shivering. She was doing what had to
be done. Hannah's life was more important
than the agony ripping at her heart.

But, oh, dear God, how could she leave
Nokona? She was *leaving* him.

With the smell of him still on her body
and the taste of him on her lips.

Wild despair grabbed at her, tried to
drag her down.

"Mount up," he said.

Abby jumped, whirled around to find

him right behind her. She dug her fingers into the blanket and bit her lips against a cry.

"The men will take turns carrying Hannah. In danger they'll need their hands free for weapons or if one rides ahead to scout, you'll have to take her."

His tone was dispassionate as it had been all morning.

Anger, savage anger, boiled up to engulf her despair. She wasn't leaving Nokona.

No, Nokona was leaving her. And only because of his stubborn, foolish pride.

"I can carry Hannah every step of the way if I have to," she snapped, and turned back to the mare.

She stuck her toe into her stirrup and swung up into the saddle, clucked to Ohapia to move up beside the two warriors' horses. The one called Rides Swift held Hannah's blanket-wrapped form cradled in his arms.

The women who had been taking care of her were making sad, moaning sounds.

Nokona took a long step and caught Ohapia's bridle.

"Let go," Abby growled, and took a deep breath to try to stop her trembling. "You won't go with me, so step back and let me get on the trail."

The Miniconjous' horses had started to move.

"Take this," Nokona said, and kept holding her mount.

She snatched the small bundle he thrust at her and set her head not to look back. Ohapia broke into a lope to keep up with the others.

Abby rode over the hill and down toward Fort Lincoln, holding her face straight ahead in that very same way. This time, she couldn't bear to look back at Seven Ponies and Rides Swift.

She would not look back. She would not.

They had been kind to her and marvelously kind to Hannah. They were hardly more than boys and they had been her true companions, even if they hadn't shared a language.

And they were her last link to Nokona. Nokona.

He was the one she needed by her side to really feel that she had a family again.

Guilt struck her like lightning, made her tighten her arms around poor, darling Hannah.

"I'm sorry, sweetheart," she whispered. "I need you, too. Truly I do. You're my family now."

She forced her eyes and her thoughts onto her destination, clucked to Ohapia. They must hurry—Hannah was weaker than ever.

The fever was coming back, too. She'd

known it since the instant Seven Ponies had laid the child in her arms. Thank God in heaven that the doctor was near.

The bay mare carried them at a brisk trot toward the garrison stretched out along the river. The doctor *was* near because the soldiers were still here—even from this distance she could tell there were so many people around that surely none had yet ridden out to fight the Indians.

Maybe they wouldn't. Maybe there would be no battle for Nokona to fight!

Barracks and houses stood in rows facing each other, the houses with a long string of high bluffs at their backs. They looked strange to her, so strange that she had to blink and look at them again.

She hadn't seen wooden frame buildings since—another lifetime.

Blue-clad soldiers, carts, wagons, and mules crossed and crisscrossed the wide parade ground in the middle. Outside the main compound, down near the river, were stables and pens with what looked hundreds of horses and, farther on, small houses with laundry swinging in the wind.

A shout and the sound of pounding hooves drew her eyes back to the winding dirt road that led down into the fort.

Three soldiers were galloping out to meet her.

Their faces looked strange to her, too, strange and pale and bearded beneath their blue caps. Time collapsed as she watched them come, clutching Hannah closer in her arms.

Then they were there, one with his horse nose to nose with hers, the others riding to each side of her.

"She's a white woman!"

"Never mind them buckskins, she shore as hell is!"

"Watch yore language, Murphy! This here's a white woman, I said!"

"Where in the world did you come from, ma'am? Are you Sioux captives?"

"Want me to he'p you, ma'am?"

That one was reaching to take Hannah from her.

His hands were pale as his face, covered with curling, reddish hairs. Not smooth and brown like Nokona's hands.

"No," she said, her throat gone suddenly dry with loss. "She . . . she's all I have left. I'll carry her myself."

Her arms clutched tighter.

"What happened to you, ma'am?" the one on her right asked. "Where'd you come from?"

From the arms of Nokona. Whom I'll never see again.

The thought drained her heart's blood away.

"The doctor," she muttered, "I've got to get this child to a doctor."

They turned and started their horses back toward the fort.

"Go on ahead, Kinnick," one of them said. "See what shape Doc Matthews's in."

Kinnick loped off ahead of them.

Abby cradled Hannah's head closer to her shoulder and turned back the blanket to see her face. Nothing about it had changed for days. Her eyes were still closed, her lips parted slightly to help with her shallow breaths.

"She's a good-sized young'un for you to be carryin', ma'am," the first helpful voice said. "Why don't you let me have her?"

"No!" Abby said, and set her jaw. "I've brought her this far, I'll take her on in."

"It'll be all right," the man said, kindly. "Don't worry 'bout nothin'. We'll have yore little girl to a doctor now, quicker than three shakes of a lamb's tail."

Abby rode with them through the blazing sun of the spring morning. All that mattered now was Hannah.

The words beat a path down the middle of her brain.

All that mattered now was Hannah.

She and Nokona could never have made a life together, anyway, no matter how much they loved each other.

Her heavy heart sank.

Nokona didn't love her. If he did, he would have come with her.

Then they were inside the garrison,

crossing the parade ground, and people were coming from all directions to stand and stare at her and Hannah. Several women, in skirts and petticoats and starched white aprons, appeared on the stoops of the small houses set in a row facing the barracks.

The soldiers led her up to the front of one long building with a saddled horse tied to a railing outside. The whole world started swirling around Abby the minute her mount stopped moving.

But she could see Kinnick, coming out a door, clattering across the porch and down the rough, wooden steps, accompanied more slowly by another man.

"I'm Doctor Matthews, ma'am," he said, and came to Abby's stirrup, touching his hand to his forehead as if to say he'd tip his hat if he had one. "Bring your little girl right in here."

Abby sat still, fighting the dizziness, clasping Hannah closer so they wouldn't both fall off the horse.

"Come on in and let me do something for her," the doctor said.

Abby looked down at him. They were here. They truly were here. She'd brought Hannah to the doctor, the white doctor at the fort and here he was.

He would heal her, bring her back to herself, make her well at last.

Abby leaned over and let Hannah down into his arms.

"She was captured by Indians," she said. "She had a fever and it's coming back up again, but she can swallow broth. She won't open her eyes."

"You're in bad shape yourself," he said, and looked at her sharply as he took Hannah. "How'd you get away from them?"

"Low-down savages," one of the soldiers muttered. "Look what they've done. How'd you get away from them, ma'am?"

Abby ignored the question, let go of the reins, and got down.

Ahead of her, Kinnick reached out and took Hannah when the doctor wobbled a bit on the steps.

Worry gave Abby the strength to walk up them, with a soldier supporting her elbow. And to hover over Hannah, whom the doctor placed on the bed.

Two women came bustling into the room as if they were accustomed to being there and they helped turn the child's small, bony form as he listened to her lungs and her heart, looked into her eyes, and pried and poked her all over.

Finally, he announced that she did have a bad case of pneumonia and that she was in a coma caused by her terrible experiences. Abby sat limp in a chair as he pulled up a stool and talked to her. She was trying to take in the words he was saying.

And trying to identify the smell on his breath.

"Some of my medicines are in my packs," he said, as he finished reciting the diagnosis. "I'll get them while these ladies bathe your little girl and then I'll start her treatment."

As he turned away, she recognized that odor. Dr. Matthews smelled like Cousin Josh, the family black sheep. He smelled like liquor.

Stunned, she watched him go out, then turned to the women.

"Is he *drinking*?" she cried. "I smelled liquor on his breath! How can he take care of Hannah . . . ?"

"Jeremiah Matthews doesn't let that get in the way of his doctoring," the shorter, round-faced woman said, not pausing in her preparations for Hannah's bath. "And he mostly indulges only when his memories of the War come back to haunt him."

"He's dreading the summer campaign," the tall, rawboned woman said, and strode to a corner cabinet to take out a clean gown. "That's got him started again."

Abby's blood roared in her ears.

She had lost Nokona and dragged poor, weak Hannah all of these miles—to a *drunk* doctor?

What little power she had left drained out through her fingers and toes.

"It'll be all right," the little, round

woman said. "I'm Mrs. O'Roarke, darlin', and this here's Mrs. Nash. We think you're a brave, clever woman to escape from them godless Indians the way you did."

Her voice trembled with curiosity, and she left an expectant silence hanging, but Abby didn't oblige her with the story she was hinting to hear.

"I'm Abigail Briscoe."

"We'll do all we can for your little girl," Mrs. Nash assured her. "And we won't ask what happened to your husband. We know it's likely something you don't want to speak of."

"Thank you."

Abby didn't care if they had everything all wrong, she didn't have the energy to say Hannah was her sister. She didn't have the strength to take a deep breath.

She had lost Nokona to bring Hannah to a drunk doctor.

Mrs. O'Roarke glanced up from sponging Hannah's skin.

"I know people say that we army people are overly loyal to our own," she said. "But truly, my dear, Doctor Matthews is never incapacitated. He'll do everything that can be done for your little girl."

"Hannah."

"Your little Hannah," the sweet voice said.

Abby sat like stone, watching with half-blind eyes, while the two capable women bathed Hannah and pulled the clean, white gown down over her head.

Then she stared at the pathetic picture she made, lying there on the narrow bed.

She bore no resemblance at all to the plump little girl dressed in white who had come West such a few months before. Mama and Papa would not have recognized her.

Thank God they weren't here to see this.

Doctor Matthews returned, went to a pile of packed bags near the fireplace, lifted one to a rickety table. He opened it and mixed some medicines with water, went to Hannah, and started dribbling the concoction from a spoon into her mouth with Mrs. Nash's help. Mrs. O'Roarke came to Abby and touched her shoulder.

"My dear, why don't you come with me? My husband is an officer and we have one of th' private houses. You could bathe there and put on some of my clothes, get out of those heathen buckskins."

"I can't leave Hannah!" Abby cried, fighting down the hysteria she could feel rising inside. "She's all I have left and I love her so."

"Of course you do. Well, then, why don't you come out here on th' porch for some fresh air while I run across to my house and get some broth for Hannah and some coffee for you?"

Abby barely heard her.

She had to do *something*. Something. But what? Was this drunk better than no doctor at all?

If she snatched Hannah away from him, there was no place else to take her.

Numbly, Abby got up and allowed Mrs. O'Roarke to lead her to the door and out onto the porch, but she refused to sit down in one of the cane-bottomed chairs. Mrs. O'Roarke left her, ran nimbly across the parade grounds toward the tiny houses, holding her skirts away from the dust, dodging the mule teams and wagons, horses and soldiers that seemed to be swarming in every direction at once. The wagons were all heavily loaded.

The summer campaign. Dr. Matthews was dreading the summer campaign.

These soldiers were preparing to ride out and fight the great battle. One of those guns or one of those swords glinting in the sunlight right in front of her eyes might be the weapon that would wound—or even kill—Nokona!

The panic building in her blood set her pulse racing. There were hundreds of soldiers, thousands of weapons!

She needed to warn him! She needed to jump right back onto Ohapia, standing there at the foot of the steps, and ride west again to warn Nokona!

Then she whirled and looked through the

open door at Hannah. She couldn't leave Hannah. What should she do?

She couldn't leave Hannah and she couldn't stop the soldiers from riding out to the battle.

If only she could bring Nokona to her! If only she could find the Grandfather Bear and send him to lay tracks for Nokona to follow.

The thought transfixed her.

The bear truly *was* Nokona's medicine spirit or they'd have never found Hannah.

She ran across the porch and down, her moccasins silent on the steps and on the ground. The soldiers who had escorted her in were gone, but two others loading a cart nearby kept casting curious glances at her.

Ignoring them, she untied the parfleche behind her saddle and thrust her hand inside for the small bundle Nokona had pressed on her as she rode out of the Sioux camp. Bearroot.

He *did* care for her.

She pulled out the beaded bag, opened its drawstring, slipped the root into her hand. Then she leaned her forehead against Ohapia's hip and closed both palms around the bearroot's smooth warmth.

Come to me, Nokona. Look for the Grandfather Bear to lead you to me.

She kept her eyes closed and let the shouts of the men and the rattle of wagons, the creaks of the wheels and the clinking of trace chains, the thud of horses' hooves and the mutter of voices close to her all fade away. All her senses, all her waning strength, all the desires of her heart poured themselves into sending that message to Nokona.

Dear God, Great Spirit, send the bear to Nokona.

Then she walked through the whole remembrance of the morning she and Grandfather had arrived at the same time in Nokona's camp. In her memory, the shaggy brown body rose up again, higher and higher, looming in the mist.

The One Who Owns the Den! Find Nokona and bring him to me!

At last, she replaced the piece of root in its case, tucked it into the waist of her skirt, and, with a pat on the neck and a hug for Ohapia, started back up the steps to her sister.

God was bigger than she had ever thought. He was the Great Spirit, too. Her message could send Nokona a vision.

"Oh, Mrs. Bris-coe!"

Abby turned, her hand on the doorframe of Hannah's sickroom.

"Would you please hold this tea tray for me?"

Mrs. O'Roarke came puffing up the steps and thrust a small, silver tray into Abby's hands, continued to juggle a cloth-covered basket and a glass jar full of broth.

"Let me give Hannah's broth to Mrs. Nash and you and I will have something in th' doctor's other room."

"I should feed Hannah. I know the best way to get her to swallow."

"Mrs. Nash is an experienced nurse. You'll come sit with me and rest, Abigail."

Abby followed her into the sickroom, where the doctor was squatting down by the fireplace, again digging into his packs. Mrs. Nash was bent over Hannah, stroking her forehead.

"Hannah swallowed all of her medicine," she said, happily, as if announcing that the child was now well.

Abby could see no change whatsoever.

Then she couldn't see anything.

The scents of the coffee and the custard on the tray she held were growing stronger by the second, filling her nostrils, and then her lungs.

A strange blackness fell across her eyes.

"I . . . Mrs. O'Roarke . . ."

She leaned forward, over the tray, as a giant hand slapped at the back of her head. Her stomach turned.

"Oh! Here . . . here, I have it! You can let go, Mrs. Briscoe . . ."

The next thing Abby knew, she was sitting down, in an inner room, looking at Hannah through the doorway.

"That's exactly how coffee affected me when I was with child," Mrs. O'Roarke said, as she patted Abby's shoulder. "I could not bear that smell!"

She took a wet towel from Abby's forehead and, with another comforting pat, went to wring out the cloth again.

Abby stared at her plump back, at the perky bow in the middle of it that tied her starched apron.

. . . when I was with child . . .

Could that possibly be?

Frantically, she racked her brain for the last time she had had her monthly visitation.

When she'd still been with Mama and Papa.

The Apache attack had come in the last week of February.

"What . . . day is it?" she croaked.

"Today? Why, it's May fifteenth, my dear."

Abby had never thought of such a thing.

And she'd never noticed her body, she'd been so caught up in journeying on the trail.

But it was true.

Somehow, she had known that it was true the instant those words had come from Mrs. O'Roarke's mouth.

Instinctively, she locked her hands across her still-flat belly.

She was with child!

Nokona's child.

Through the numbing shock, a great joy welled up.

She and Nokona had made a child of their love that day he'd pulled her out of the river! Both of them, *both* had always wanted children, and now they would have this one.

Now . . . now there was even more reason that he must come to her. Oh, dear God, he must come to her!

She reached beneath her loose blouse, clasped the bearroot, beaded bag and all, in her hand.

"You've gone pale, Mrs. Briscoe—pale as milk," Mrs. O'Roarke said, coming back to her with the cool cloth. "I'll call the doctor in a minute, but right now he's busy with your . . ."

Mrs. Nash's sharp summons cut her off. "Maureen, get in here, this child is convulsing!"

Mrs. O'Roarke dropped the wet rag into Abby's lap, whirled on her heel, and ran through the doorway.

For a long, numbing instant, Abby clutched the seat of her chair and stared after her.

No! Hannah couldn't be getting worse, she could not! Not after all Abby had put her through to bring her to someone who could make her well.

"Help me hold her!" Mrs. Nash cried.

"We have to hold her down so the doctor can bleed her."

"It's the fever! It's coming up so high, so fast."

Bleed her?

Hannah flailed her stiffened arms like blades on a windmill.

Abby pushed up from the chair and ran without taking one step at a walk.

"Boiling water!" she shouted.

She grabbed Maureen O'Roarke and shook her, waving the bag of bearroot in her face.

"Get me some boiling water and I'll bring that fever down. Nobody's going to bleed this child—she's already too weak to breathe!"

"Mrs. Briscoe," the doctor boomed, from his position on the other side of the bed. "If you disturb my helpers, I can't take care of your child. Please go into the other room and take your chair."

"You can't bleed her, nobody bleeds people anymore! It's *insane!*" Abby screamed. "I have bear medicine here, a root. It's brought down her fever before."

"You've been with the Indians so long you don't know if you're white or red," the doctor roared. "There'll be no filthy, heathen medicines dispensed out of a beaded bag used in my establishment!"

"There'll be no barbaric, useless bleeding

341

treatments used on Hannah! That'll kill her for sure!"

She turned to Mrs. O'Roarke, dug her fingers into her plump shoulder.

"Boiling water," she ordered, and glanced at the doctor again.

He held a knife, a shining scalpel that caught the sunlight pouring in through the doorway.

He poised it above Hannah's stick of an arm, which Mrs. Nash held over a bowl set on the bed.

"God help me, I'll kill you!"

Abby shrieked the words in a voice she'd never heard before and threw herself across Hannah, straining to knock the scalpel from his hand.

He jabbed it down, stuck the point into the tender inside of Hannah's elbow. Blood, red as the feather that had lured Hannah to this desolate pass, showed against the white of her skin.

Abby tried again. The knife clattered onto the floor.

"I'll kill you," her new voice screamed again. "Because I've put this child through hell to bring her to you—so you could save her—and now you'll be the cause of her dying!"

Mrs. O'Roarke grabbed Abby's sleeve as she rushed past her, but Abby jerked away. She was around the end of the bed and at the doctor before she'd even known she was going to move.

"You stay away from her!" she screamed, hitting at him with the beaded bag and her empty fist, gasping to bring air into her tightening chest. "You'll not kill Hannah as long as I'm alive!"

The doctor staggered backward before the onslaught of her fury, slipped, and went down, flat on his back on the floor. Abby threw herself on top of him, slid the rawhide loops of the bag over her wrist to free both her hands.

His throat lay bare above the open collar of his dirty shirt. The scalpel lay on the floor directly above his head.

She grabbed it, swept it high, started it slicing downward through the air. Just as he had done to Hannah.

"I'll kill you for cutting her!" that strange voice screamed.

She brought the knife flashing down in front of her eyes.

But a stronger arm caught hers.

An arm encased in blue.

"Let me go!"

She fought like a wild woman, but the soldier only grabbed her other arm, too, dragged her off the doctor and up to her feet.

"She's crazy!" Mrs. Nash cried.

Another soldier stood behind the one who held her.

"Lock her up," he said.

Abby twisted in the hard grip to look down at the doctor.

"Nokona will come," she said, "to force you to do as I say."

"She's crazy."

"Poor thing has lost her mind."

"It's all been too much for her," Mrs. O'Roarke said.

"Take her to the guardhouse," another man's voice ordered. "She's dangerous."

"No!"

That was Mrs. O'Roarke.

"Take her to my house and I'll see after her. She's become overwrought in trying to protect her little girl. Any mother might behave so."

It was the last thing Abby heard.

"Bind Hannah's arm, please, Mrs. O'Roarke," she said, pushing the words out one at a time as the darkness came to take her.

But it didn't get her spirit. She sent it away from that time and place, back to the west of there. To find Nokona.

She would have killed the doctor, she knew, as she felt her body sag into the soldier's arms. Now she knew how Nokona had killed that other one.

There was no difference between them after all.

19

Tall Bull's words went on and on, full and fast as the river ran.

"The battle is sure this time," he said, over and over again. "No more running and dodging and hiding from the soldiers. This time we ride out to meet them. This time will be the great reckoning."

Nokona nodded and handed over the pipe, fighting the restlessness raging in his limbs.

Then he gave in to it.

"You speak the truth, my Uncle," he said. "Now I will ride up the river to repay your hospitality by hunting for meat—the journey to the Little Bighorn is long."

"Ha!" Tall Bull snorted. "The *Crow* gave the prophecy that the great battle will be on the Little Bighorn. The Crow don't know a battle from a powwow."

Tall Bull wasn't going to give up his audience easily.

But Nokona got to his feet anyway. This was enough sacrifice for the sake of being a good guest and honoring Tall Bull's friendship with Windrider.

"That's true," he agreed. "The soldiers might even meet up with us right here. In either case, your women need more meat to prepare."

He strode away, fast, to his lodge to get his weapons. He hated going in there. The tipi reminded him too much of Abby.

He snatched the bow and quiver, then his bridle from their pegs on the lodgepoles, picked up the rifle from the folded pile of robes, and ducked outside again.

Tonight he'd sleep in the open once more. Her scent lingered in the tipi, it made tears lurk like wolves behind his eyes.

He slipped the bow onto his shoulder and began to trot through the noisy camp toward the horse herd. Surely, Rides Swift and Seven Ponies would return at top speed to their band. The little sister probably would not live, but surely they would say that Abby had reached her people and was safe.

Would she turn around and return with the Miniconjou if Hannah died on the way?

He slammed his mind shut against that thought, which had visited him before. No, she would not. And if she did, he would not take her back.

He would not.

Maanu whickered to him and separated himself from the herd, Nokona waved to the boys on ponies circling the horses as a signal they should let him come.

Nokona slipped the bridle on and leapt onto him bareback, gripping the warm sides against the skin of his legs.

"Find a deer, my old friend," he said. "Or an antelope or even a rabbit. Anything to take me away from here."

He maneuvered the stallion back toward the river, sending him through the village at the point where two crescents of tipis touched tips. All these lodges choked him now, all these people smothered him. He ought to ride away now and head west for the battle alone.

But only staying with the Miniconjou would bring him the last news of Abby.

Abby.

By the Sun Father, he would stop thinking of her!

The earth was warm beneath him, sunshine bathed his body. The grass leapt from the ground with the eagerness of spring, lushly tall and a bright, bright green. Along the river, trees grew thick.

They moved in the wind, limbs heavy with leaves brushing together like clapping hands.

They threw shade along the bank of the

river. In places, they touched arms over-head. They beckoned to him.

And the stinging muscles in his legs and arms pulled him that way. Maybe there, in the quiet, the heated knot in the center of his belly would go away.

He kneed his mount toward the sanctuary. The hunt could wait.

The river ran high with spring runoff from the snow high in the mountains but it didn't roar and crash like the one he'd jumped into to save Abby. It was a different river.

This was a different world. She was gone now, back to her people, where he would never follow, even if he could.

He slowed the buckskin when the trees closed behind them. The children from the camp played in the water, but their cries and splashings floated up to him from far downstream. Within the arch of cotton-woods, the roving breeze made the only sound.

Nokona had ridden the length of an arrow shot when his instincts for danger finally roused.

Hackberry trees mixed with the cotton-woods all the way up the river. There were no birds in them after the berries.

He pulled Maanu to a halt and slipped the bow from his shoulder. There might not be time to get the rifle out of its case.

As soon as his own movement stopped,

he heard someone else's. Ahead. On the other side of a huge cottonwood that grew in the shape of a vee.

He kicked the dun, walked him closer.

Something or someone with much *puha* shook the tree.

Its leaves whispered and screamed.

Then something moved out from behind the trunk, something huge, that filled the open space.

Nokona's thighs froze to his horse's hide.

The One Who Owns the Chin.

It loomed higher, then settled, lurched closer.

Maanu stood. Trembling.

But this was not Grandfather. Grandmother or Cousin this time, for a frantic cub clung to her leg.

She watched him, her amber eyes burning with fear and rage.

Nokona waited, not drawing a full breath.

She jerked her head and then he saw the loop around her neck.

Instantly, he looked for the heavy log on his side of the tree that a hunter building a snare would've tied to the other end of the rawhide rope.

But a second glance showed this was not rawhide. It was vine, growing all along the tree, naturally twisted and strong.

Somehow the Grandmother had trapped herself.

She had pulled at the loop until it cut into the flaps of skin around her neck where the winter fat had been. She'd tried to get her claws under it, too, but had only scratched long gashes into herself.

She would die.

Unless he cut her loose, she would die.

He touched the medicine bag at his belt. Then the sheathed knife he wore beside it.

Slowly, carefully, he lifted his leg over Maanu's withers and got down.

Cousin did not move.

But when he got close enough to slash the vine she could raise her claws and kill him with one swipe of her paw.

Her eyes never left him as he moved through the sun-dappled shade. Amber eyes. She was hurting, they said.

"I will help you, Cousin," he murmured. "Stand still, I will help you."

The musty scent of burrows in the earth and the long cold winter, the smell of ancient days, rose from her as he got closer.

He could cut the vine between her and the tree, but that would do no good. He would have to walk into her arms, he would have to touch her.

She tilted her head and it came out of the shadows, looked at him with her sun-lit eyes.

She would not attack him. He had been sent here for her. She had been sent here for him.

That knowledge dropped into his mind, sudden and sure.

He took one long, slow step closer, raised his hand, and slipped his finger in and twisted it between the vine and the rough hair of her neck. Rough hair coarsened with blood. She'd torn her flesh open everywhere in her fierce efforts to break loose.

With his other hand, he brought the knife up and, using only its tip, cut her free.

She turned away, dropped to her all fours, and glanced back at him with a look of gratitude that was almost human. Then she ran toward the river, the cub scampering beneath her, within the haven of her legs.

Nokona's fist closed hard around the bone handle of his knife, let the vine keep holding his other hand in its sticky grip.

She was gone. The Great Spirit had meant for him to loose her.

The wounded Cousin with eyes the same color as the Daughter of the Sun.

Abby stood beside the bed and stared through the doorway on the other side of the doctor's room, at the morning sunlight falling across the chair where she'd been sitting when she'd first known she would have a child. A baby.

But that news couldn't touch her, couldn't bring her comfort today.

Hannah was dead.

"I'm not afraid of Mrs. Briscoe. Leave us, Sergeant," Mrs. O'Roarke said.

But he didn't. He walked a few feet away from them and paced up and down along the porch.

Abby didn't care. The soldier could do anything he wanted to, even come into the room and drag her off and lock her into Mrs. O'Roarke's spare bedroom again. She didn't care.

Hannah was gone.

Nokona was gone and now Hannah was gone.

"I dragged that poor darling over miles and miles of wilderness on horseback only to deliver her to a butcher."

She made the confession to the doorway, to the chair, to the wall, to the very air.

"The pneumonia was too far gone when you got her here—I nursed enough during the War to know that when I first saw little Hannah."

Mrs. O'Roarke's voice was calm and very sure. She gave Abby's shoulder a pat, which Abby saw from the corner of her eye, but couldn't feel.

She had gone numb and she would be numb forever.

"A drunken butcher who calls himself a doctor," she said.

But that didn't make her feel anything, either. She couldn't even work up any more anger against the doctor.

"The doctor didn't bleed her," Mrs. O'Roarke said. "He didn't kill her, Abby."

Abby didn't answer.

"And he didn't desert her. Now he's gone off to the camp downriver to prepare for the campaign with the troops, but he stayed right here last night until Hannah passed on."

Abby stood silent.

"Doesn't Hannah look beautiful? Mrs. Watts, one of our laundresses, brought an outgrown dress of her daughter's when she came up from Suds Row to lay out your little girl," Mrs. O'Roarke said, in a tone desperate to rouse Abby and bring a response.

"I thank her."

Whatever happened, happened. She, Abigail Briscoe, as a weak, puny human being could do nothing about any of it.

Things are in the saddle and ride mankind.

By now, even Nokona knew that was true.

She looked down at Hannah. They had washed her and combed her hair and arranged it with a blue ribbon. They had dressed her in a white dress, as she had been when the Apaches attacked.

That was the last time she'd really seen her, Abby thought. That was the last time Hannah had truly been herself.

She leaned over and took the frail body into her arms. But that gave her no comfort, either. Hannah was gone. Her spirit had left her.

And Abby's had left her, too.

On that awful, false-spring day late in February, she had been in the bosom of her family where she'd always been. Now, in the middle of May of that same spring season, she was alone.

Nokana had not come.

She straightened and simply stood by the bed, looking down.

" 'Tisn't seemly to rush the burial," Mrs. O'Roarke said, in her lilting drawl. "But the weather is warming. And the itinerant clergyman who has spent the winter here will be leaving tomorrow morning to go on the summer campaign with the troops."

She took hold of Abby's elbow, turned her to face her.

"I've taken the liberty of sending someone down to the camp to fetch the reverend for a service this afternoon."

That information only brushed Abby's brain.

"So," she said. "We will bury Hannah today?"

"We have no choice."

"Where?"

"In the post cemetery—a short way from the garrison up on the side of the hill."

Abby looked at her.

Mrs. O'Roarke's kind blue eyes were so sad that her own filled with tears. But all she could feel inside was a great emptiness. She couldn't even feel sorrow.

Her heart was frozen. It always would be.

She walked through the funeral like a puppet and lay stiff as a stick in Mrs. O'Roarke's spare bed through the night that followed. Sleep didn't come, not real rest, but she did close her eyes and drift off into a strange, empty blankness.

A clattering of dishes and the smell of something baking brought her out of it.

Mama? Was she home, home at last?

No. She opened her eyes to the gray dawn as everything came rushing back to her.

She would never be home again.

Reaching for the wrapper Mrs. O'Roarke had loaned her last evening, she got up. She glanced at the black dress flung across the chair that some other army wife had provided for her to wear to the funeral. The buckskins lay in a heap on the floor.

They belonged to Sky.

Home, she thought wryly. She didn't even have clothes of her own, much less a home.

Thank God, the numbness had not left her.

Flinging the wrapper on over her borrowed nightgown, she tied it and walked through the tiny parlor into Mrs. O'Roarke's kitchen.

The short, rotund woman looked up from her work without stopping the motion of the wooden spoon in her mixing bowl.

"Good morning, Mrs. Briscoe," she said, with a tremulous smile. Tears glittered in her blue eyes.

"Good morning."

Abby hardly recognized her own voice.

"Sit down and I'll bring you some tea. I'm making scones to give to my Sean when the troops ride up from camp for the good-bye parade."

She wiped her eyes with one chubby hand wrapped in a corner of her apron.

"I can't wait to see my husband, but I dread that infernal parade. It's torture for th' families, that's what 'tis, and the Crow scouts play their drums so sad, like a dirge."

Her voice caught.

"I can hardly bear to let Sean go this time. He's a-gettin' too old for Indian campaigns."

She sniffed back her tears, tried to brighten.

"But you'll get to see General Custer and Mrs. Custer. She and her sister will ride out the first day with the troops and then come back to wait with us."

"I can make my own tea."

It was the old Abby who said that. The old Abby who did what needed to be done no matter what she was feeling.

This Abby couldn't think how to begin, so she walked to the table and sat down.

Mrs. O'Roarke brought a shawl to wrap around her shoulders and a steaming china cup of tea.

"The tea's made, dearie. My, I hope it don't affect you the way that the smellin' of th' coffee did," she said. "My own children are grown and gone now, but I still recall how sick that sick can be when a woman's expectin'."

Abby stared at her, clasped both hands to her abdomen. She had forgotten about the baby!

"I'm gettin' you a warm scone to go with that," the kind woman said, as she bustled back to her wood-burning stove. "You must eat for that baby's sake."

A stab of pain shot through Abby. This baby! This baby would never know its father. He would be in that coming battle, too.

"I know one child can never replace another, but it can help," the soft, sweet voice went on. "You must think now about the baby you're carrying and not so much about the one who is gone."

Abby looked at her in the gray light from the window.

Nokona hadn't come. Had he had time to get here?

"I don't have the strength to love anybody else," she said. "I never will."

"Ah, now, and you'll surprise yourself someday soon, you will!"

Mrs. O'Roarke made sympathetic sounds while she dropped another batch of scones onto the griddle. Then she slipped a cooked one onto a plate and came to set it in front of Abby.

Abby pushed it away. She took a sip of tea.

"That baby's trapped inside you with no way to get nourishment but from you," her hostess said. "I always thought about that when I was expectin'."

The baby! Nokona's baby was inside her, right now!

Abby picked up the scone and took a bite. Then another.

Mrs. O'Roarke encouraged her with little clucking noises. Suddenly, the food and drink warmed her stomach, began to send comfort all through her rigid body. She was famished.

The baby was famished. Its mother had a duty to feed it. Feeding the baby was what needed to be done.

Abby began to eat with more interest and Mrs. O'Roarke brought her another scone. She talked about her husband and the Indian campaign, she brushed away tears the whole time she kept up her cooking, walking back and forth between the stove and the table. Abby tried not to listen, not to think about the fighting to come, but she did hear "twelve hundred men and seventeen hundred animals" and, later, "artillery."

She tried not to let that information catch in her brain. She couldn't think about the battle now, she simply could not.

And she certainly couldn't talk about it.

"I have to get out of here . . . I mean, I'd like to get out and take a walk," she said, and stood up.

"Good! That'll get your blood moving for the baby."

Mrs. O'Roarke put down her spoon.

"I'll get you some decent clothes . . . Mrs. Thomason sent more than just the black dress for the funeral . . ."

"Never mind," Abby said, turning toward the little bedroom. "I'll wear the buckskins. You need to finish the sconce for Sean."

Mrs. O'Roarke called after her, "You make yourself to home here, Mrs. Briscoe. Stay as long as you like. The steamboats run both ways on the river all the time—when you're ready to go back East, you can send word to some of your people."

Go back East! Her people!

Nokona was her people now. She wanted Nokona.

Abby dropped to her knees on the misty hillside to lay her hands on the earth of Hannah's grave. It was still cold, cold as the pain flooding through her, because the sun drifting in and out among the clouds hadn't grown strong enough yet. It was fresh-turned and damp from the foggy mist and it clung to her fingers.

"I'm sorry I couldn't tell you good-bye, darling Hannah," she said. "And that I couldn't save your life. I tried, honey. I tried."

She stopped, choking on a knot of tears.

"Please know that I did the best I could and that I love you."

The gravels and dirt clods bit into her palms and the tips of her fingers. All her blessed numbness was gone—from the outside *and* inside of her, it had disappeared the moment Mrs. O'Roarke had made her think about the baby.

The real baby who needed her.

The baby who would never see its father.

Nokona had wanted a child all his life.

The pain was almost more than she could bear.

But she had to bear it. For the baby.

She had to think what to do, she had to go back to her old way of putting her duty ahead of her feelings.

She had to try to forget about Nokona.

For the baby's sake.

"I want you to know that I'm going to have a baby and I have a feeling it's a girl," she said, hoarsely. "If it is, one of her names will be Hannah."

A cloud of mist, thick and heavy as smoke, swirled in around her, blotted out the raw dirt of the grave. The wind that brought it up from the valley carried the sounds of voices and horses' hooves and rolling wagons.

And the drums.

Mrs. O'Roarke's parade had begun.

Twelve hundred men and seventeen hundred animals marching out today to look for the big Sioux encampment. Which, when they got close enough, would send out its warriors.

Nokona would ride with them.

Squeezing a handful of dirt, she scrambled to her feet and looked down toward the garrison.

Twelve hundred men?

They looked like thousands.

The procession was moving slowly, crawling like a gigantic blue snake with yellow spots and stripes, slithering up the valley and into the post so people could say their good-byes. Sunlight here and there glinted off the burnished metal of guns and swords, flashed them at Abby in taunting winks of light.

The men rode into the garrison, around and around the parade grounds. Women and children ran out to them, reaching up to touch their loved ones, waving and waving after they'd passed. Abby caught the wrenching sounds of sad, sobbing wails over the laments of the drums.

First came the cavalry, then the infantry marching in rows, then a group of Indians that must be their scouts. After that, a long line of white-covered wagons, hundreds and hundreds of pack mules and horses, and huge guns on wheels. They must have stretched for two miles.

Or more.

Her heart left her body. The Sioux had no artillery. Did most of them even have rifles?

But their warriors were relentless and brave. They were like Nokona, who, on foot, had chased down a mounted soldier and killed him with his hands.

The battle would be brutally fierce.

She laid her palm flat over her baby.

The leaders circled the parade ground for the last time and rode out of the post, pulling all the others, mounted, on foot, or on wheels, out behind them. They headed into the low hills on the faint, curving road.

The wailing and weeping grew louder, lifting and falling on the misty air already full of the thunder of hooves and the rattle of wheels. Poor Mrs. O'Roarke.

The sun broke through the mist completely as the last of them left Fort Lincoln and moved slowly toward the west. Abby stared, astounded.

Above the winding column, in the sky, the same procession marched.

Just as clear, just as plain, as the caravan of soldiers and horses and wagons that wound around the low hills on the earth, another train of them moved across the sky.

The white covers of the wagons shone against the opaque gray mist left behind by the early dawn, the yellow trimmings of the cavalry glittered as they did on the ground.

Her blood stopped still.

What did it mean, this sign in the sky?

That the majestic army moving slowly west both in the heavens and on the earth would win the victory?

The damp, cold earth dropped from her hand, forgotten, as her feet began to move.

She could not just stand here and watch this and hope. She had to *do* something.

She had to warn Nokona.

Even if he was not on his way to her, even if he had not received her vision, even if he was too proud to come to her because she had chosen the white doctor over his medicine, she was going to warn him.

The thought beat at her brain, over and over again, as she flew down the hillside that rose behind the garrison, heading for the long rows of stables that stretched along the river. Nobody in all of that huge Indian encampment knew what a menace was marching their way.

When her breath grew short and her side began to hurt, she pressed one hand to her abdomen to cradle her baby.

20

Between the corner of the garrison and the end of the stables, she forced herself to slow to a walk. Not one of the sad inhabitants of the fort paid her any mind, but they wouldn't have noticed her if she had still been running full out. They were too far gone in their grief.

The wives of the Indian scouts crouched on the ground outside their log cabins, built in a row between the stables and the river, their heads covered and bowed down, wailing. Their old people moaned and called to their restless children, some of whom were trudging down the dusty road, apparently trying to follow their fathers.

Abby tried not to think about them or about all the more sorrow to come. She had to think about Nokona and herself and the baby now; she had to hope he'd received her vision and was coming to her.

If he wasn't, she had to find her own

food for several days. She slipped into the open south side of the first, long stable. It was empty.

So was the next one.

But, to the side of it was a circular pen, where ten or so horses stood idly watching her. One of them, miracle of miracles, was Ohapia.

Thank God! She breathed a little prayer. Now, let Nokona be on his way to her.

She had a feeling that, maybe, he was.

In the middle of the stable row was a half-closed shed that looked to be for feed and tack. She took time to run and look in it, and then went weak with thankfulness that she did. Someone had piled her saddle, bridle, and bags all together, had just thrown them carelessly in at the door when they'd untied her mare and taken her from the doctor's door.

Even her rifle was there!

She thought about that while she took her bridle and caught Ohapia. There was little chance she could shoot well enough to kill game, and she didn't really know how to clean it; she certainly wouldn't have time to cook it.

She would be traveling through miles of wild country with only what few supplies were left in her bags. But it was spring. She had learned in those long days with No-kona which berries and plants to eat. She could survive until she found the big encampment.

Until she found Nokona.

She threw herself onto the mare and left the stables at a walk, just in case anyone was watching.

The effort was wasted. Only the Crow were here, outside the walls and only a few of their tear-stained faces turned toward the sound of her horse's hooves. The few pitiful children who ran that way as she crossed toward the river dropped their heads when they saw that she wasn't their fathers returning.

She rode fast, away from them, along the river and then west, into the rolling, low hills. Somewhere, back toward the west and the south of the garrison, would be the place where she and Rides Swift and Seven Ponies had parted. From there she could probably find her way back to their trail.

After all, it had only been . . . how long? A day or two that she'd been here! It seemed like a year, but it hadn't been long.

The realization filled her with a great jubilation.

Nokona hadn't had time yet to come to her. Maybe he did get the vision she sent him after all!

She crossed the path of the army, which was barely out of sight over the next hill. Then she recognized the knoll where she'd left the Miniconjou and rode around the

end of it to avoid being seen on the crest.
The army was going in the same direction
she was. She must make sure that she
wasn't heard or seen by the soldiers.

What would they do to her? Hang her as
a spy?

The thought made her blood roar like
thunder. She must be careful, very careful—her fate now would be the baby's, too.

Ohapia carried her around the next rise
and deeper and deeper into the rolling
hills. The huge, rolling caravan of the army
was to the north of her, angling more to
the north-northwest. She knew, because she
could hear them clearly.

She couldn't resist picking up her speed.
The thin layer of tiny blue-gray flowers that
blanketed the ground blurred before her
eyes.

Surely Nokona had received her vision
and was riding toward her at this very minute! Surely he was!

Her heartbeat quieted, slowed down, as
she let her mind roam to him, let herself
truly believe it for a moment that she
would see him soon.

The next instant, her breath stopped.
Hoofbeats were pounding toward her.

Frantically, she started sawing at Ohapia's head, looking in every direction for
cover. If she could hear the army, maybe
they could hear her, maybe one of the out-
riders was coming to challenge her!

A horse whinnied, loud. From somewhere very near.

The mare answered, circled one way and then the other, tried to run toward the sound.

A horse came around the side of the hill, galloping relentlessly toward them. A spirit horse, running at her through the mist which was still heavy as fog in the low places. She couldn't even see the rider.

But she made herself keep trying to see him, looking back over her shoulder while she fought Ohapia for control, expecting to see the shining blue coat of a soldier and feel her heart break.

Instead, it flew out of her breast and began to sing.

The spirit horse wore the flesh of a tall buckskin with black legs, tail, and mane. Maanu.

Nokona had found her.

Abby had only a glimpse of his eyes, flashing with joy, and then he was upon her, a spirit rider rushing through the misty morning, reaching for her. He plucked her from her saddle and swept her into his arms.

She clung to him, wrapped her arms around him, buried her face in his chest.

"Hold me, hold me!" she said, against his skin, over and over again.

He folded her to him so hard, so tight, that she couldn't breathe. Then he loosened his hold and began kissing her forehead, her cheekbone, the edge of her hair as he loved to do.

The horses circled, snorting, slowed, and then stopped.

Abby looked up, starving for the sight of him.

He gazed down at her, his muscled chest rising and falling against her breasts. She threw her arms around his neck and pressed against him to keep his very breath from pushing them apart.

"You don't look hurt," he said, and ran his hands over her body. "Thank the Great Spirit, Abby, you're not hurt!"

She shivered from the pleasure of his touch.

""No! No, I'm not. Why did you think I was?"

"A Cousin, a mother with a cub who is One Who Owns the Den, was sent to me. I found her bleeding in a snare."

Abby tilted her head to see into his eyes. She gave him a slow, knowing smile.

"Perhaps it is something else about her that is like me."

He ran his finger down the side of her neck. A delicious thrill darted through her.

"I feel no vine trapping you to a tree."

"Something else," she said.

His dark gaze roamed over her, raised a wild wanting deep in the core of her.

"What?"

"The other thing you said about her."

A flame sprang to life in his face.

"*A mother with a cub*? Abby, is it true?"

"It is true, my love," she said. "In the winter we will have a little one to hold."

His eyes blazed with happiness.

His horse moved beneath them, stepped back and then sideways to nip playfully at hers.

"Then we'd better hit the trail for New Mexico," he said. "We go south from here, not west. We will raise this little one with his own family, with his own band, on his Aunt Sky's *rancho*."

Abby burst into laughter.

"That sounds like me instead of you! When did you become so practical and full of common sense?"

He raised one black brow and lanced her gaze with his slanting glance.

"When you let your feelings run free and you followed them."

Abby stopped laughing.

"Following my feelings at the fort nearly made me kill the doctor," she said. "Now I know how you killed that soldier, Nokona. I truly would've killed the man if a trooper hadn't pulled me off him."

Sympathy flashed across his face.

"Because of his treatment of Hannah?"

"Yes. He wanted to bleed her and I wanted to use the bearroot. She died. Nokona, she died."

"I knew it would happen. I share your sorrow."

He bent to place a kiss on her cheek.

She leaned into the warmth of his lips.

The sun came out full and strong, burnishing his face through the mist.

Abby let herself go into the haven of his arms; he held her close for comfort and leaned out to reach for Ohapia's rein.

"The army's still too close and so is the fort," he said. "We need to be riding south."

Abby sat up straight.

"But what about your fighting in the battle? Your dream of living in the old ways? I would give my life to keep you safe, Nokona, but I don't want you to have any regrets."

"I won't."

She searched his eyes to make sure he was telling the truth.

"The army is huge—I guess you saw it," she said. "I'm afraid after the battle the old ways will be gone."

"I know the Sioux will win this time," he said. "The soldiers will die. But soon more will come, more than all the Lakota Nation."

He gave her a straight, sharp look.

"No matter," he said. "Old ways or new ways I could not live without you. Abby, you are a constant murmur in my blood."

She turned within his arms to sit astride and face him, to hold his beloved face in both her hands and kiss him with all her heart.

Avon Romantic Treasures

Unforgettable, enthralling love stories, sparkling with passion and adventure from Romance's bestselling authors

CAPTIVES OF THE NIGHT *by Loretta Chase*
76648-5/$4.99 US/$5.99 Can

CHEYENNE'S SHADOW *by Deborah Camp*
76739-2/$4.99 US/$5.99 Can

FORTUNE'S BRIDE *by Judith E. French*
76866-6/$4.99 US/$5.99 Can

GABRIEL'S BRIDE *by Samantha James*
77547-6/$4.99 US/$5.99 Can

COMANCHE FLAME *by Genell Dellin*
77524-7/ $4.99 US/ $5.99 Can

WITH ONE LOOK *by Jennifer Horsman*
77596-4/ $4.99 US/ $5.99 Can

LORD OF THUNDER *by Emma Merritt*
77290-6/ $4.99 US/ $5.99 Can

RUNAWAY BRIDE *by Deborah Gordon*
77758-4/$4.99 US/$5.99 Can

Avon Romances—
the best in exceptional authors and unforgettable novels!

MONTANA ANGEL   **Kathleen Harrington**
77059-8/ $4.50 US/ $5.50 Can

EMBRACE THE WILD DAWN   **Selina MacPherson**
77251-5/ $4.50 US/ $5.50 Can

MIDNIGHT RAIN   **Elizabeth Turner**
77371-6/ $4.50 US/ $5.50 Can

SWEET SPANISH BRIDE   **Donna Whitfield**
77626-X/ $4.50 US/ $5.50 Can

THE SAVAGE   **Nicole Jordan**
77280-9/ $4.50 US/ $5.50 Can

NIGHT SONG   **Beverly Jenkins**
77658-8/ $4.50 US/ $5.50 Can

MY LADY PIRATE   **Danelle Harmon**
77228-0/ $4.50 US/ $5.50 Can

THE HEART AND THE HEATHER **Nancy Richards-Akers**
77519-0/ $4.50 US/ $5.50 Can

DEVIL'S ANGEL   **Marlene Suson**
77613-8/ $4.50 US/ $5.50 Can

WILD FLOWER   **Donna Stephens**
77577-8/ $4.50 US/ $5.50 Can